CW00586823

THE LAMB

THE LAMB

Lucy Rose

WEIDENFELD & NICOLSON

First published in Great Britain in 2025 by Weidenfeld & Nicolson,
an imprint of The Orion Publishing Group Ltd
Carmelite House, 50 Victoria Embankment
London EC4Y 0DZ

An Hachette UK Company

1 3 5 7 9 10 8 6 4 2

A CIP catalogue record for this book is
available from the British Library.

ISBN (Hardback) 978 1 3996 1971 4
ISBN (Export Trade Paperback) 978 1 3996 1972 1
ISBN (eBook) 978 1 3996 1973 8
ISBN (Audio) 978 1 3996 1974 5

Typeset by Input Data Services Ltd, Bridgwater, Somerset

Printed in Great Britain by Clays Ltd, Elcograf S.p.A.

www.weidenfeldandnicolson.co.uk
www.orionbooks.co.uk

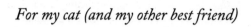

For my cat (and my other best friend)

One

On my fourth birthday, I plucked six severed fingers from the shower drain.

The tub yellowed near the plughole and there was a peachy hue up the curve of the bath. It was the same colour as my skin. Milky and a little buttery, like the outer edges of a bruise. Mildew and dried-up water peppered the glass screen. Black mould had crawled up the plaster and between the grout. The bathroom was small and the dark corners harboured cobwebs, rings of damp and hairline cracks.

I wanted to lick the black speckles of mould littered along the wall. I hoped it would taste as it smelt. Like musty brambles or rain splashing in a muddy puddle.

The first finger I picked up had purple polish flaking away from its nail. The second was clean of cosmetics, but it was short, bitten at, and uneven along its ridge. My fingertip followed the edge of the nail. When I looked down at the plughole, I realised the rest of the fingers were too far gone to tell anything about who they'd once been attached to.

All I knew is that, at some point along the way, strangers had come to our homestead and Mama had gladly taken them in. There had been at least one girl, wearing purple nail polish, and a clean-cut boy who nibbled at his fingernails when he was nervous.

The boy was especially nervous around Mama, wide-eyed and alert. They had strayed too far from the main road and ended up here, tangled up among the knotted hair gathered in our shower drain.

The girl liked Mama very much. Before she was reduced to just a couple of fingers at my feet, Mama plied her with wine and they danced to old cassettes in the living room until it was dark.

We'd mixed the wine with mashed-up hemlock. Just enough to make a stray woozy, but not enough to harm us when we later consumed them. Mama told me it was a hex – one that took them to slumber, calm and quiet. It made their lungs slow to a pulse.

The boy sat, taking up very little space. He watched as Mama slowly took the girl's clothes off. It started with one of Mama's bony fingers sliding beneath a spaghetti strap and plucking it from the girl's shoulder. Then she left a trail of messy lipstick kisses across the girl's collarbone, probably imagining just how she would taste after being seared. Mama told me she loved the strays she took, and this is how she showed them.

The girl danced as Mama stripped her down one piece of clothing at a time. Their eyes were locked. That was when I knew Mama was hungry. She told me a good meal had to feel happy and whole before it was consumed, otherwise the meat would taste bad.

We are what we eat, Mama always said. I wondered if it was worth the fuss of making them feel loved if we were only going to pull them apart in the end.

I put the severed finger with the purple nail polish back down onto the drain. Following the freckles of black mould along the wall, I traced my fingers. It was dark like charcoal. In my wake I left the outline of a Ferris wheel and a pirate ship on the wall. As I looked at my blackened hands again, I *had* to know how the mould tasted. When I put my fingers in my mouth and sucked, the dusty blackness I'd dreamt of had the same earthy must as dried-up summertime brambles. The black mould was probably crawling down my throat, leaving little black pinpricks across my lungs.

I wish Papa could have been here to see the mess, but he'd left a long time ago and I didn't know if he was going to come back.

I spent the night helping Mama make stock out of the bones.

Two

Mama had roasted the nervous boy's rump slowly, toasting it off with a few drops of vegetable oil. Peeling away his skin and plucking out her favourite organs, she'd stripped him head to toe and frozen the rest of his body in pieces. Only minutes after serving him up, her plate was licked clean. Mama ate quick and messy before going to the hearth. Sleeping by the fire and breathing in the embers, Mama dreamt. A big meal always made her tired. Even though her hair was matting in the soot and ash, in slumber she was beautiful.

In this little pebble-dashed cottage, we packed everything we could into one room. There was a battered old couch before the fire, kept company by an old telly that dithered on static every time we changed the channel. The antenna was duct-taped to the top, leaning towards the window. The kitchen counters were on the far side of the room near a small dining table, big enough to seat three. Maybe four at a squeeze. Photographs and memories were rare here, with blank spaces grieving picture frames that had once lived upon the wall. There was a mirror, which Mama had hung from a small hook. How Mama loved to watch herself.

'Four whole years since you came out of here,' Mama whispered, rolling her fingers over her belly and taking a deep breath of the red wine in her glass. 'It doesn't feel like four years at all.' She put the glass to her lips and tipped it back. Down it went. Every last drop swallowed into the deep black of her gullet. 'Happy birthday,' she whispered to herself.

I hadn't quite finished my dinner. There were still bits of the nervous boy left at the edge of my plate. Cabbage and carrots nestled by the stray, keeping him warm. Mama had even roasted potatoes and made Yorkshire puddings to soak up the gravy. The nervous boy was the best I'd ever eaten, the best birthday present I'd ever been gifted, but he didn't taste nervous at all. After I'd chewed for too long, he tasted contrary and difficult, like he didn't want to settle in my mouth. He wanted me to spit him back out onto the plate.

I used a small bone to pluck a tuft of meat from between my two front teeth. As it dropped onto my tongue, I realised the meat had lost its taste. Now, it was just tough.

Three

Nestled between the groves, we spent our days waiting for strangers to find us. Some nights, the rare sound of cars sang me to sleep as they raced up and down the distant roads. I liked it when dim headlights cut between the curtains. Those nights were easy. I'd fall into a slumber fast and happen upon dreams of rabbits and their kits. One dream, with Mama's blade in my hand, had led me to a burrow keeping newborn kits. It was always the quiet and dark nights that kept me awake. The ones vacant of far-off engines, stormy weather and headlights. Keeping to ourselves, we shared a provincial homestead just off a quiet road. One rarely used. It was half hidden among the trees, littered with potholes and puddles.

When Mama felt kind, she told me bedtime stories. She sometimes spoke of the trees.

The giants sprinkled the trees here to guard us from the outside world, Little One.

The day before my eleventh birthday, there was

a knock at the front door. Mama had already made dinner. The plate harboured something modest but meaty. Impatient for a bite, Mama had made sure the food was still a little undercooked by the time it reached the plate. The meat, a small ruby kidney, tasted rotten next to a side of beans and a crusty potato waffle fished from deep within the freezer. I took my plate to the rug and sat in front of the telly, picking at the waffle and separating the baked beans into their little tribes.

That's when the knocks came. Smiling for the first time in weeks, Mama basked in the echo they left behind. Her yellowed teeth ground together. She wouldn't have to be hungry anymore. And neither would I.

'Little One, a couple of strays have come to our door. Would you put on the hot water and heating? We want them to be toasty warm.' She always spoke softly when strays were near, as though the small offering of our homestead was a safe one, but leaks came from the ceiling and rusted pots caught almost every drop of water that fell. Light bulbs flickered, unburdened by shades. Beds were free of the fine linens and sheets people used to make their resting place soft and safe. A plain blanket and pillow would do us just fine.

I dropped my fork on my plate and went to the boiler, which was hidden in the kitchen cupboard close by. When I turned it on, it roared to life, pipes clanking from within the wall as Mama cleared her throat and put on a disarming smile. She answered the door to the new strays, who had wandered too far from the woodland paths. I watched them both. Two young men,

7

one with rounded glasses and the other with chapped lips, soaked through as they stumbled to the mouth of our homestead. Exhausted, they dropped to their knees as they stepped over the threshold, leaving behind a trail of shallow puddles. They looked hungry and cold as Mama coaxed them inside. She smiled as she settled them on the couch.

Mama touched their knees with her fingers. But when the men saw me closing in from behind Mama, they looked right through me. They wanted Mama's fingers on their skin. That's when I realised that, as adults look at children, they don't really see them. They see a body without a mind. Something that does what it's told. Something that will only understand when it's older.

Mama sent me to our bedroom and shut the door. We'd shared a room since Papa disappeared. Two cast-iron single beds sat across from one another on either side of the window.

Mama and Papa's old double mattress had been fly-tipped at the side of the road somewhere far away. After that, their bedroom had been locked, with only the bare frame left inside. Their bedroom was desperate for human touch now, and it only received it when strays ventured into our home. It stank of rot and the floorboards were stained auburn from the cut of a sharp knife and the spill of blood.

I'd heard Mama tell many folk tales. I heard her whispers through the door, now. Mama told stories to the strays to make them settle. It was a way of pulling them in. Making them trust us. All strays loved stories.

We'd had all sorts of strays here. Some of them had come away from car crashes, but what they didn't know was that Mama had a little habit of leaving nails and glass on the back roads when she left the house. Some of the strays were lost, trying to hike across the fells without knowing that this gloom was where they'd spend the rest of their short lives. Mama could tell a stray just by looking at them – it was something in their soul.

The thing that bound them together was the flood of relief they felt when they found our little house tucked away between the trees. When they saw our modest pebble-dashed homestead, they saw sanctuary. They felt lost, and that is what beckoned them to us.

I heard the cassette player switch on and the popping cork from an old wine bottle. She'd had trouble with the men before, but she knew how to handle them now. She'd learnt to make them feel invincible. She made them feel in control. *Men are stupid when they feel powerful, Little One. They become complacent.*

That night, they didn't scream much. It must have been quick.

Four

Mama was once in love with the local gamekeeper. He always wore green. He kept a blade strapped to his thigh and his combat boots were always laced in a firm knot. He visited Mama after his daughter got home from school – something he knew would occupy his wife's attention. He came to us, always the same, with dirt speckled across his cheeks from riding his quad bike across the fells. I used to think the dirt was freckles until I wiped his cheek and they brushed away. I counted each speck. Dirt crumbled on my palm like grains of sand.

The gamekeeper's palms were large and coarse, and he used his stubby fingers to push the dirt I'd collected into the creases of my palm. He liked holding my hand in his. A warm smile emerged when our fingers found themselves entwined. He used to measure the size of his fingers and palms outstretched next to mine. *I forget I am a giant*, he once said. *Did you know giants sleep under the crust of the fells? If you look carefully, you'll see them breathing in and out as they slumber.*

The gamekeeper's daughter was called Abbie. We sat near each other at school, but she didn't know her papa was visiting Mama and retreating to the shadowy corners of our homestead. Neither did his wife. They were blissfully unaware of the new memories Mama and he made together, both in shadows and sunspots. Wherever they pleased.

In the spring, I heard him and Mama talking in the kitchen. I was watching a bluebottle bump its soft head against the window over and over again. It was woozy from a long day. Mama's words were lost in the air, but I could still hear the sounds their mouths made. Euphoric, languid echoes. When I looked through the slip of the door, they were moaning, bundled together on the surface of our kitchen table. The table legs scraped over the floor. Back and forth. Mama's head draped off the back edge as her neck craned. The buttons on her church dress were loose and her breasts hung free. Papa wouldn't have been happy, but Papa was gone. Keeping himself hidden somewhere we couldn't reach.

In our homestead, it was easy to pass through unseen. I wandered between our bedroom and living room, following the wall towards the kitchen in the back corner. Their bodies twisted together over the table.

Mama slipped her hand over his, twining their fingers. A wicked smile captured the gamekeeper's lips. Eyes wide, he was red in the face. Mama was breathless but in control. She cried out one last time and so did he. As he pulled away from her, she buttoned up her church dress and bit her lip. The gamekeeper went to the window and gathered his breath. The sunlight touched his skin. Sweat dripped down from his forehead to his thighs. Mama came to her feet and wrapped her arms around him, brushing her fingers over his hip bones.

'I've felt nothing like this before,' she said, but I knew she didn't love him the way she thought she did. She'd *loved* others before. Not quite strays. Not quite passers-through. People who would satisfy Mama while she waited for the next infatuation. But the hole in her chest was never filled. And, with every passing day, it grew.

The gamekeeper turned and pressed her palm against his cheek. 'I want you,' he whispered, but there was something in his words that felt hollow. The words were spoken like a half-truth. I wondered if he was as fickle as she was. His breath brushed lone strands of her hair back onto her cheeks.

Mama caught his eyes in hers and led him away from the kitchen table. She passed by, brushing me to the side as though I were not there. Together, they wandered into our bedroom. And he closed the door behind them.

I tried to remember the gamekeeper's name, but I couldn't quite form it in my mouth.

Mama's hoarse cries echoed like songs through our homestead. The floorboards groaned, toadlike.

I glanced in the mirror that hung on the living-room wall. It was old and dirty with speckles across it. When my reflection stared back, I saw the nuisance everyone thought I was. Always in the way. Bright-green eyes that did a bad job of hiding my feelings. My teeth were gappy, crooked and overlapping. I was an ugly child on the outside, but even more ugly on the inside. Maybe a changeling. Or something worse.

When Mama was finished with the gamekeeper, he cleaned himself up, buttoned his camouflage trousers, splashed water on his bashful face and left with a smug grin across his mouth. He went back to his family, and kissed his wife and child with the same mouth that kissed Mama.

Mama lay naked in her bed and daydreamed of things she liked about him. The gamekeeper didn't mind that Mama was a lonely woman. That's why she let herself enjoy him. He wasn't observant like others were. He was someone who only saw what he wanted and nothing else. But Mama was fickle. More fickle than most. Her wants faltered on a whim.

Later, when we cuddled by the ashen fire and cinders, Mama told me I was to forget the gamekeeper and all the times he'd made her scream. She told me he'd scampered back to his obedient wife and child. *Coward*.

'The people out there, Little One, they will never understand us.' Her words were gospel. 'We aren't like them. We're woven from different cloth.'

Mama paused, taking my hands in hers. They were warm and I let my fingers explore the creases near her thumb.

'They will never accept us.'

So, we both forgot about the gamekeeper and loneliness found us once again.

Five

The bedding tickled my calves with its fibres. I scratched my skin with the ridge of my fingernail, but, finding my thigh, the sensation climbed my leg. Red bites and stings paved their way up and down my calves, followed by a trail of clumsy white scrapes. The bedding wasn't cleaned often. Sometimes a little woodlouse would scale the high peaks of the blankets, twisting through the curves of the fabric.

Mama slept with her mouth open. Beneath her blanket she sounded like an old vacuum. Her breaths, in and out, were coarse like whispers. Though I couldn't see her mouth, I knew a string of drool would slip between her lips. Come morning, her pillow would be damp.

The trees sometimes kept the light from us. Mama liked to sleep with the window open, no matter what time of year. Silver showers or snow, Mama wanted nature's touch, which usually came with a red nose in the morning after a long night in the cold.

Just like Mama, I buried myself. My spine curved

and my knees met my chin. She once told me I was her sweet ammonite fossil and I was only hers to unearth. Since then, I'd grown fond of the idea of becoming lost under layers of muck and rock and sand. I coiled up in my blanket, squeezing my eyes shut. I pretended to be a well-slept ammonite fossil just like Mama wanted.

Though it was dark out, I thought of sunrise. When the sun would surface, Mama would wake me, tapping my forehead with her dirty fingernail. She sometimes liked to leave a groove on the crest of my brow, before pressing a kiss on top of it to make it all better.

The distant road was silent. Mama slept through the quiet. Always. She fell quick and deep, grasping onto dreams. Sometimes she murmured and trembled, entwined in her linens. It made me wonder what she was dreaming of. I hoped she dreamt of love. Of me and her and sunsets and tree bark binding us all together.

Deep in slumber, Mama unbundled herself from her blankets. Her flesh looked blue in the dark. Or grey. Her teeth ground together. Such crooked teeth. Never cleaned properly, they had a thick layer of plaque near her gums. Mama rarely brushed her teeth. She washed her mouth out with water from the beck and gargled it in her throat. Sometimes she wore red lipstick to try and make her teeth look pretty.

Mama told me her teeth were the only thing she wanted to change about herself. *Even though I am beautiful, Little One, people don't trust women who have bad teeth. I've met men who called me a savage because of these things*, she once said, pulling up her lip with her finger to show me her canines.

Mama wore lipstick if she brought men home with her. I watched her drag the deep red paint across the plump of her bottom lip before I hid beneath the bed and counted her heavy breaths, springs tensing and relaxing. When she was done with the men, they'd leave our homestead and head out into the night. The lipstick would be smeared across Mama's cheek like a bruise. Strays were not the same as the men she wanted to keep.

But tonight, we were alone together. Mama's lips were free from lipstick, and she slept soundly as the quiet wind shushed the trees outside. She was dreaming again. I knew she was because her mouth mumbled a string of words I couldn't understand.

'I hope we are in a deep forest together, Mama. I hope it is deep and dark, and a place that no one will ever find us.'

Six

'I can't sleep,' I whispered into Mama's ear. Her breathing slowed and her eyes stilled beneath their lids.

'What time is it?' she asked, keeping her eyes closed.

'I don't know,' I said.

Mama opened her eyes and sat up. 'I was deep in my sleep,' she whispered. Mama shuffled out from beneath her blankets and took me by the hand. 'Come, then.' When I couldn't sleep and her heart was warm and full, her stories were abundant.

I followed Mama to the living room. She led me to the ashes of the fire and left me at the foot of the hearth. The cinders brushed my legs.

'Are you listening?' she asked, lighting a match and putting it to the coals and wooden splints broken up in the fire.

I nodded, watching the flame take light.

'The first time I found a stray, I was eleven years old. I had my father's green eyes and my mother's fair hair. But I wasn't like them in my heart. They always felt different.

Cut from the wrong cloth. They were so mundane it verged on strange.' Mama let the match's flame run to her fingertips. She liked the sensation of burning and ground her teeth together when the fire singed her skin.

I blew out the match before the spark touched her fingertips. Mama smiled.

'I liked mud. I liked scrapes on my knees. I liked the taste of my own blood when I pulled my baby teeth from their sockets. I did that when I was at school, Little One. I locked myself in the bathroom and pulled out every single one of my baby teeth. It's hard to explain it. Every intrusive thought felt like a desire unfulfilled. I rattled my teeth around in my palm like an instrument. It made me wonder a lot about humans – if the body would still sing if it wasn't mine. If other teeth sounded the same as mine did.' Mama closed her eyes, falling deep into the memory. Her brow softened as she explored the lost folds of her past. 'I was born this way, Little One.'

I waited for her to speak again.

'The first time I found a stray, I was walking home from school. There was this woman hanging around the back roads. Her tights were littered with rips and tears. She wore a short dress. Tight. Even at eleven, I knew she was a stray. That's what I'd decided to call them: *strays*. She was untethered. Unbound. A bit of a lost soul. Strays are the ones without houses.' Then, coming out from the memory, Mama explained to me that a house didn't mean bricks, four walls and a roof. A house meant something in our hearts and people without them were called strays. They were the lost ones.

Mama's face was softer than I'd ever seen it. Her jaw relaxed and her mouth settled into a soft line. This is what it looked like to dream when awake.

'She was a stray alright. And she was beautiful too. Her brown hair clumped together with at least a week's worth of grease. Her lips were chapped. Her skin was blemished, covered in spots, and her eyes were weary. She looked so *human*. As I got closer, I smelt her. She left this thick tobacco smell in her wake. I watched her for weeks. After school I would walk the same route. I wanted to know her inside out. Her story had to be mine. I wanted to plant those eyes of hers like the pit of a fruit tree in my stomach. From across the street, I pulled at the edges of my mouth until a smile came. And, just as I had planned, she smiled back. Of course, I was certain she'd smile back. I'd watched her for weeks. I knew what she liked and what she didn't like. I knew she smiled at children and old people. But she didn't much like people her own age. And they didn't much like her either.'

I settled in the ash and warmed by the fire, taking in the words of Mama's story. I imagined I was there, on those back lanes with the thick smell of smoke.

'The first time I spoke to her I was a week shy of turning twelve, just a couple of years older than you. The closer I got, the more the tobacco subsided. Underneath the must she smelt like almonds. I took a heaving breath of the smell. It was unexpected. I wondered if she was more complicated than I'd first imagined. One day later I came to the street corner, panting and crying, and I told her that someone had fallen into the rubble a few streets away. I told her someone was trapped inside an abandoned fridge. A little boy with blond hair. A child. I fumbled my words and worked her like clay. She was putty between my fingers. She followed me down back streets until we found the rubble and, once we were there, I took a brick to the back of her skull.'

Mama stopped, holding her breath.

'And she sang. She sang just as I had planned. Her cry was quick, but it was beautiful. It took her longer than I thought to die. She couldn't speak, but I could see everything she was thinking as I rolled her over. Her mouth shuddered as she tried to get words out. Her eyes were wide and bloodshot. Teary even. I smiled to her, just as I had done before, sweet and tame. But she didn't smile back. Reaching into my school bag, I took out my protractor and cut the gash open even wider. All the way to her forehead. It was surgical. Precise. While she still lived, I dipped my fingers inside her skull and I tasted her brain. That was my first stray. She tasted delicious – she would have tasted better if she'd been more content. Less stressed. Less afraid. I ate as much of her as I could manage, feeding on all those things she felt as she drifted in and out. Little One, she was like a river, but not powerful like the Gelt or the Eden. She was slow and languid. My fingernails were brown once the blood had dried. I sometimes think it was the first time I properly ate. I was *full*.'

Mama heaved a breath as I squeezed her hand tight.

'But I felt something new too. This sense that nothing

would ever be enough. I'd always hunger for the promise of the next meal – whoever they were. When I was finished, I took her to the river and let her drift towards the sea. She was lost in the Eden. No one noticed that the shy woman who hung around street corners had disappeared. I heard my father tell my mother she was a whore. It was then that I knew my next stray would be a boy or a man; a perfectly ordinary one who sat inside a suit and tie because we all taste the same.'

I'd never had my own stray before. I ate the food Mama gave me, but I had never taken a stray the way she had. If I did, I wouldn't hesitate or play. I wouldn't fool around, luring them from street corners. I would take them with me into the night. It would be quick. They would rest inside my stomach and I would digest them quietly.

Seven

Three days had passed without food.

The morning was brisk as I leant my head against the window of the school minibus. The window shuddered against my skull. Vibrations travelled down my spine like whispers. We sat warm inside, settled into the seats. They reeked of PE kit and game. The school sent the bus into the wilds every morning and then beckoned it back to the edges of the playground so the rural kids could escape their quiet homes. They were changelings. Just like me. We were caught in the in-between, no longer children but not yet grown enough to be big.

I'd got into the habit of sitting with the driver in the front seat. Before, when I'd burrowed into a seat near the back of the bus, Patrick and his friends had thrown cowpat at my jumper and pulled on my seatbelt to strangle me. When they were angry they'd show me their papas' bloody penknives, or they'd press their fingernails into the crease of skin around my neck. *This is where my blade will cut you up, Little Margot.*

The bus driver used to watch us in his rear-view mirror. After one too many red marks around my neck, he let me sit with him in the front. What he didn't understand was that blood and bruises were normal where I came from.

Mama didn't feed me from breast or bottle. She gave me blood.

Something else he didn't know was that Mama called her violence by a different name. Only when she was really angry, the sort of rare anger that burns out of control, would she give me bruises or marks. She told me these marks were called *special kisses*. Special kisses on my cheek. Special kisses on my neck. Special kisses on my arms, ankles and wrists. So, those little boys on the minibus with their silly knives – they did not frighten me. They were no match for me or Mama.

But it didn't matter. The front seat was where I belonged.

The bus driver didn't say much. He drove, intent on watching roads he'd driven twice a day for at least ten years. His skin was coarse and he had wrinkles rippling out from his eyes to his cheeks. For someone who looked so ungentle, he was a calm soul. Not monstrous, but curious and kind. He still drove along these roads as though he'd never seen them before. Old skin. Young eyes.

'Do you like music, Youngen?' he asked out of the blue.

I nodded. At first I was quiet. I knew most adults were up to no good. I didn't trust a single one. But this one was different from the others. He wasn't a stray. There was something of a house about him – something all strays were without.

'Go int' glovebox and pull out the cassette,' he said. The bus driver's voice was heavy and he smelt of cigarette smoke.

I pulled open the glovebox and took the cassette out of its case. When I passed him the tape, he smiled, and I saw his teeth for the first time. They weren't nice, but he had the kindest smile I'd ever seen. Mama's smile was the opposite. There was something about it to be frightened of.

That smile helped Mama take men and turn them into lovers. They all smelt like mud and beer and smoke. Mama's smile always got what it wanted from people. Especially when she wore lipstick.

'My daughter loves this song,' the bus driver said. The tape rattled in the player and the hum of a guitar overcame the vibrations in my skull. I didn't know the name of the song, but I remembered every word and recited it like a hymn at night. I whispered the words until I fell asleep.

*

When we got to school, we didn't go to the playground like we normally did. It was too cold. Our breath formed frosty clouds as we breathed out. The cold blistered our skin and turned our fingers grey.

Inside, the classroom was warm and our cheeks soon

turned red, blood rushing to the surface. It was a crowd-
ed room, and children had etched their names into
the tables over the years. The walls were mostly bare.
Colourless. And out the window, I saw the fells.

I looked over the worksheet Mr Hill had slid in front
of me and watched him crouch over his laptop. He was
tall and gangly but with a thin nose that ran down his
face and pointed at the end.

This teacher was an absent-minded man but when it
came to me, he was impatient, somehow always waiting
for me to slip up. Observant. I was his failure. The child
that couldn't learn. I never picked up long or short
division. I couldn't spell, even if the word was sitting
right in front of me. Times tables were too hard, even
when he gave me the song to remember them with.

Just this morning I'd heard him talking about anime
and art films to the Year Three teacher, Miss Quinn.
She was infatuated by how worldly he seemed and how
clever he thought he was. But he wasn't otherworldly at
all. He was mundane.

The worksheet was filled with fractions, something
else I couldn't wrap my head around. Still warm from
the printer, my sheet of paper was clean. Though the
room was quiet, the sound of children picking up their
pens and pencils murmured and the echo of pages folding and flapping filled the quiet. The overlapping sounds
made my insides itch. I bit down hard on my tongue.

I looked at my sheet, trying to untangle all the
numbers and symbols, afraid to wander beyond the easy
problems like *write one half as a percentage*. I wondered

what all these numbers really meant and if I would ever understand them. Or use them.

I felt my hand sliding out from beneath the desk and snaking up into the air. Mama would punish me for that. She'd warned me not to draw attention. *Don't put up your hand to answer questions, and if you are called upon, say you don't know the answer. Always hand in your homework on time. Draw. No. Attention.*

'I can help.' Abbie's voice came in a whisper. She was a tall blonde girl with bright-brown eyes, freckles all over her face and gaps between her teeth just like me. But Abbie was cleaner than I was. Her mama always brushed her hair at the school gate, kissing her cheek and letting her free into the playground.

I wasn't supposed to speak to Abbie.

Mama told me Abbie liked the attention, which is why she worked so hard to get all her answers right. But Abbie was pretty. And she was nice to me. I liked the way she looked. I liked her eyes and her freckles, and sometimes, when I found myself drifting away from fractions, I imagined putting my fingers through her hair to untangle all the knots and pull at her green ribbon.

I daydreamed of smelling her scalp.

Abbie sat at the table in front of mine. She leant back on her chair to speak.

'You look lost,' she said.

I pointed at one of the questions on my sheet. *Add twenty per cent to forty pounds.*

'It's simple division and multiplication, really,' she said, certain of herself.

I stared blankly, hoping she'd just tell me the answer so I could write it down and be done with it, but her mouth stayed closed. I looked back at my sheet.

'Well, forty divided by ten is ten per cent, which is four,' she whispered, leaning over and pressing her fingertip on the paper in front of me.

'Times that by two?' I asked, but maths felt like an unknown language to me. Something I couldn't understand.

'So the answer is eight pounds added to forty. Forty-eight.' A smug smile came to her face, but it softened. I scratched the answer down onto the page. 'It's all much easier than it sounds,' she said.

'It feels complicated.'

'It doesn't have to be. The way *they* explain it to us is what makes it complicated.' Abbie looked to the front of the classroom where Mr Hill still sat hunched over his laptop. The way she said *they* with such contempt sent a chill down my vertebrae. Maybe she was like me.

'I don't like him,' I said. 'In fact, I don't like most of the people here.' I wanted to call most of the children here *strays* but that word felt forbidden in this room. So many of them felt untethered, drifting without direction. I wondered if Mama would let me bring them back to the homestead, one by one. She would know if they were strays or not. Proper strays.

'Me neither.' Abbie chewed on the end of her pen. 'I especially hate Patrick. He's a brute.' She affixed the word to the end of her sentence as though it was one recently learnt. New and exciting and clever.

'I could tackle him if I wanted to,' I said beneath my breath. 'But I don't want to get into trouble.'

'You're not supposed to say things like that,' Abbie whispered, but there was a hidden smile on her face.

'He deserves it,' I said, thinking of the penknife shimmering and the cowpat smeared down my jumper.

Abbie smiled at that, too. 'You're weird,' she said, raising her eyebrows at me. 'But I like that. I like that you're weird.' Abbie smiled at me again before hunching back over her workbook.

I watched her through the day, glancing over the backs of heads to see if her cheeks were still rosy. To see if she'd fixed the green ribbon sitting lopsided in her hair. To see if she'd straightened her collar. But all was left unfixed.

A little bit wild even.

Eight

As I hopped off the school bus and walked home, I looked over my shoulder. For a moment, the bus hesitated by the verge. The bus driver watched me over his steering wheel. Putting a smile on his mouth, he waved. He couldn't see what sort of beastie I really was.

It made me wonder what sort of beastie Mama was. My mind swam, thinking of all the creatures I'd seen in the wood and read about in books, but there was nothing quite so fitting as what she already was. A human. Cunning, beautiful, brilliant, and all without drawing suspicion.

Mama had once taught me the different hexes I could make by stealing pieces of fauna and growing flora. Some of them were potions to make people *behave*, like the hemlock hexes. Mama made others too, but those were the sort you could hold. Wishes. On my way home, I collected ingredients. I could usually find most things in the grass verges of the track that led back to our homestead. The other, more finite ingredients I kept in a shoebox beneath my bed.

Little One, you will need chicken bones, mandrake, hemlock root and cockleshells. Though powerless apart, when brought together you can hold the power of the cosmos in your palm.

Mama had taken me to the beach the day she told me that. I collected as many cockleshells as I could carry. That day was warm, but the breeze whipped sand into my eyes. Mama held my hand as we got to the edge of the water. She pulled me down onto the sand and we sat together as the white waves brushed up against our thighs.

'Lots of people died here,' Mama said, drifting her fingers through the sand. 'They got stuck in the quicksands and drowned as the tide pulled them in.' It was the first thing she told me before she let me run about the shore and tide pools. 'I want you to imagine them with me,' she said. 'Think of their legs stuck in the sand as the breaking waves hit them. Think of the rain. Think of their screams turning into bubbles.'

It was a strange afternoon, but I got my cockleshells. I ran the length of the sands, hoping to return one day and imagine the drowned once again, but we'd never been back. Their ghosts were lonely as they watched children play by the water.

I kept all the ingredients in the shoebox beneath my bed, but the hexes craved sunlight. Even though I'd collected my ingredients and practised weaving my hexes exactly as Mama had taught me to, I'd never given one to anyone before. I buried them in our home, hoped no one would find all the bodies we kept, and promised to give a hex to someone one day.

Nine

With our home unburdened by the meat of a stray, Mama sobbed at the kitchen table. Her cheeks were red and her eyes puffy. We'd journeyed to the back of the freezer for remnants of food. Mama's fingernails scraped against the wooden tabletop as her gaze darted around the almost-empty plate. I think she hoped a slice of meat would appear on the side, but the meal stayed as it was. Runner beans and plain pasta, still with a soup of starchy water from a clogged-up colander.

When Mama wept, she looked like a painting. She was something otherworldly. Blotchy but beautiful. I watched her from my seat, sucking on the soggy pasta shells floating around my plate. They broke softly between my canines.

I'd learnt not to speak while Mama was sad or angry. Or happy. It was only safe when she seemed like she was floating. When she was like that, I used to imagine parts of her would disperse like dandelions in a gentle breeze. Mama was most loving when she was somewhere else. I loved her the most when she was on the verge of falling asleep. Mama was softer then, like a real human.

'I'm hungry for fingers,' she said, rapping her knuckles on the table. A strand of hair fell loose from her scrunchie. It was overstretched, oily and incapable of keeping Mama's hair bound up tightly. Mama watched me closely. She wanted me to speak, to break the silence, but my lips stayed closed. They were chapped, and stray webs of skin scraped against one another as I rolled my lips.

I thought of the advert I'd seen on telly. The one with fish fingers, flaky on the inside but crispy on the outside. Fresh catch. Fresh *kill*. But fish fingers didn't taste like cooked lips.

'The crunch of a small bone and the chip of a nail,' Mama whispered. She closed her eyes and took a breath in, as though she imagined the tender meat of a finger slipping right off the bone. I saw her disappear into a memory. A warm one. It was a memory that held her and made her feel safe.

I'd drifted into memories like that before, but they'd been more like dreams. Glancing at Mama, I wondered if she was thinking of the first finger she'd ever eaten. In my dreams, Mama had taken Papa's wedding finger and snapped it clean off with the ring still coiled around his bone, nibbling away, sucking at the veins and tearing at tendons. There was only a little meat on a finger, but they went crispy when we roasted them. My favourite.

It'd been years since I'd seen Papa. All I could hold on to was the sad smile he always wore and the oversized, smelly jumpers with wool fumbling into little balls. They always carried the scent of smoke with them wherever they went. When Mama was tired, she let me visit them in the loft. I'd pull away at the sticky tape holding the cardboard flaps on the boxes. Once I was inside, I'd unfold the jumpers and wrap the sleeves around my shoulders.

Mama hated Papa, though, because he hadn't given her what she wanted: a love that burnt like fire and left the world around them charred. So, she left the smelly jumpers and the cardboard boxes for me. It was all that remained of Papa. It was all he'd left the day he ran away from us.

I prodded a piece of pasta onto my fork and took a bite. It was so soft it fell apart on my tongue, but I liked pasta hard, with a bit of crunch. Sometimes, if Mama wouldn't cook, I'd eat the shells raw, wondering if they would chip away at my teeth.

'I miss Papa,' I said.

Mama was still, eyes following the grooves on the table until they found me. Her eyes were always wide like spotlights, but especially so if the words I'd spoken were ones she didn't want to hear. 'Papa is a selfish man,' she whispered. 'Selfish.'

Her fingers gripped the side of the table until her knuckles turned white. Her jaw tensed and her eyes dropped back down to the unsatisfying meal before her.

'He didn't care about me. He cared even less about you.' She took her fork between her fingers and prodded the pasta shells. She put them in her mouth and swallowed. 'I want to hear you say it. Say that he is selfish and he doesn't love you.' Mama bit her lip so hard I thought it might burst. She glanced at me, waiting for me to speak.

'Papa is selfish,' I said, hoping she'd relax, but she didn't.

She swiped her hand across the table. Watery plates of pasta hit the floorboards and rug in one sweep.

'Papa is selfish and he doesn't love me.' The words sank through me, embedding themselves in my skin, drifting through my arteries like blood cells. The words were a part of me. *Papa is selfish and he doesn't love me.*

'Go to bed.' The words were spat out into the room.

I stared at my feet. My toes poked out the end of my socks. I wiggled them about, pretending Mama wasn't mad at me.

'Now,' she said, her voice low.

I stood from my chair, collecting rogue pasta shells from the floorboards and fumbled them into my pocket. I felt dust balls and clumps of old hair stick to the starch. As I closed the bedroom door, I sucked on the now-fuzzy shells. As hungry as I was, they did not fill me.

*

My bed was cold. Even though it was spring, outside it had begun to snow. It should have been a pitch-black sky, but it was mild, with soft snow clouds stretching out above.

It was rare that strays found us in the colder months.

Each year, it made Mama more impatient than the last. More hungry than the last. Less human than the last.

She needed my help to lure the strays because, in her words, *there is no one more vulnerable than a lone mother and her child.* And that is who we were to these people. We were stories and preconceptions and prejudgements. She let them believe we were weak, but we would be their end. Behind the thick snow piling down, a set of car lights passed through the trees and went low in the mist. The car slowed as it came past our homestead, hesitating, but hurried on into the countryside before long. Mama would find me if she needed me. I shimmied deeper into my blanket, coiling up and hoping for cars to pass over the distant road. The sound of engines always got me to sleep.

Ten

The bath was yellowing at the curves again. Mama didn't like cleaning. I dipped my head below the water and tried to picture the outside world. I'd spent years waiting for a trail of petals to lead me away from this place. I hoped they'd be carried by the breeze and lead me northward. Away, somewhere Mama and I could go. Somewhere we'd never be hungry or cold.

I surfaced for a breath. Outside the window, winter was weeks gone, but the snow was thick. Roads got lost in the blizzard.

I stood, pressing my nose up against the window, and tried to picture petals sprouting from beneath the snow. My favourite day of the year was when the first snow-drops bloomed by the beck. I'd sit by the window and count baubles of rain left behind from the showers until I noticed white petals flowering from the dew-coated grass. They grew in clusters, like pocket-sized groves hiding among the weeds.

My skin prickled as the water cooled around my

ankles. Mama opened the door and watched me. 'Get that bum in the water,' she said. 'You need to be nice and clean for the strays. Nobody feels drawn to an ugly child.'

I nodded and sat back down in the water. The nip of cold bit at the water until it was tepid. Mama came and sat by the tub. She was wearing her dressing gown and her just-washed hair was scraped back in the twist of her towel.

I realised I was bathing in her filth.

'Settle,' she said as her fingers brushed through my hair. 'I'll wash you.'

I pulled my knees close and stilled.

Mama took a sponge and covered it in washing-up liquid. It smelt like plastic as she smothered suds across my back and rubbed. My skin turned pink. It stung. She lifted my arm and scrubbed my armpit. Mama paused, holding my arm up high and looking beneath. She squeezed out the sponge and dried her hands on a nearby towel. Using the pinch of her fingernails, she plucked a lone hair from my armpit and studied it. Her eyes narrowed.

'Face me,' she said, nipping at my arm and pulling me close. Taking the sponge from the water, she scrubbed my chest and my belly and my legs and my groin. Mama grabbed the shampoo and poured it onto my crown. She rubbed it into my scalp and then used the jug to wash away the suds until I was clean. She put a little kiss on my lips. 'Get dry,' she said, leaving me behind in the bathroom.

I wanted to stay in the bath and get clean all over again. When I looked out the window, the blizzard was thicker than before.

The road was gone. We were cut off from the world.

Eleven

The stray that changed everything was called Eden. She found us in the heart of a snowstorm. When I first saw her, I was peering through the bedroom window at night. She was a shape in the mist and snow, something fluid and inhuman. At first I thought she was a ghost.

I wondered if I should warn my slumbering mama about the stray approaching our door, but I didn't move. My eyes were fixed on the figure outside.

From the corner of my eye I saw the bundled-up blankets hiding Mama from me. When I couldn't see Mama, I couldn't remember her face properly. I could picture her mouth, her eyes, her nose and chin, but never together and all at once. It was only when I saw her that she fell into focus.

The figure in the snow became clearer. She had eyes like puddles and her hair looked like straw, blonde, and pulled back into a ponytail, but it escaped out from a black woollen hat, unruly and wild. She walked with a slight hunch and when she got closer I saw the faint wrinkles on her hands as she reached to knock on our door. But something made her hesitate.

The figure paused, lost in thought. I wondered what her fingers would taste of. They hovered in the air. Finally, she knocked. Her knuckles made a firm sound as they rapped on the door.

Looking out into the snow reminded me of something Mama told me once. *The snow is beautiful and glittering, especially if it goes untouched. It is magic in some ways. It gives hope. But it is easily spoilt by selfish footsteps that crunch into it. Those who relish putting their footprint down into fresh snow are the worst of us. Then, when the snow freezes over, everything beneath it dies. It either ices over or turns to sludge. That is what motherhood is like. Treacherous and disappointing.*

Mama woke at the knocks and bounced out of bed, pulling her dressing gown over her bare shoulders. She went to the living room in search of her lipstick. The stray waited outside for one of us to answer. Mama fussed in the living room, fumbling to remove the cap from her lipstick.

The stray knocked again.

I craned my head to see her face through the window once more.

When Mama answered the door, the stray smiled. It was strange – like something from a glossy magazine. Her teeth were white and straight. I wondered if she'd ventured from the city. I wondered if Mama would pluck out her beautiful teeth one by one and shake them in her hands to make music. Or maybe she'd find a way to make the stray's teeth her own.

'Little One,' Mama shouted, 'come through. We have a visitor.'

I heard the low hum of her voice as she spoke with the stray, but her words were lost. I tumbled from my bed and came to Mama in the living room. When I stopped by her side, I noticed her toes were turning blue at the threshold of the door as the frost crept inside.

'Come in from the cold,' Mama said to the stray.

'I'm not sure I should,' the stray said, looking back towards the road. 'They say lost souls go astray in these parts.'

'It's safe here,' Mama said.

The stray watched Mama, eyes moving over her shoulder so she could see the inner coves of our homestead.

'This is my Little One, Margot.' This is how she spoke to strays, like a housewife from an old black-and-white show on the telly. 'When the storm passes over, we can come help you with your car.' The memory of strays before was left unspoken, but we thought of them and how so many, lost in a storm or hurt from the trail, had left their cars miles away in search of refuge.

Children at school made up stories of wailing roadside ghosts without fingers or lungs or bones, wandering, dragging themselves up the tarmac, hoping to be seen or saved. But they were never seen, and the stories were just that. Stories.

I did as I always did. I reached out my hand to her in the hope that she'd take it, but the stray looked at my hand with a knot in her brow. She was the first stray I'd found difficult to read. She was the first stray to hesitate.

In her heart, perhaps, she was a wolf, or something older and more watchful, like an oak. Her fingers were cold when they finally coiled around my palm. These were hands that didn't trust mine.

'I can take you to the shower,' I said, going towards the bathroom. 'It's plenty warm.'

'I think I'd just like a warm drink, if that's alright,' she said. Her voice was calm.

I looked at Mama, who watched the stray while she shut the front door. For the first time, she was uncertain, too.

'But the shower is warm,' I said, rubbing her fingers between my palms to heat them. 'You need to warm up.'

The stray knelt on the floor, her fingers slithering across my cheek. 'I'm quite alright, *Little One*.' She echoed Mama's words as though they were her own. They sounded at home in her mouth. 'I'll just have that warm drink.' Her smile dropped and her jaw relaxed. Her eyes moved over my face, taking in details I didn't know I possessed. Freckles I'd never spotted before. Scars I'd yet to catch in the mirror.

Mama went to the kitchen and hit the kettle. My attention found the stray again. Her smile reappeared. She stood tall, moving towards the couch. I'd never met someone who felt quite so safe here. Comfortable. Even Mama felt like she'd disappear sometimes, not wholly wanting to exist in this space.

I felt this woman take root in our homestead.

'My name is Eden,' she said.

'Eden,' I said, tasting the word. 'Like the river?'

'Exactly like the river,' she whispered.

Twelve

'What's your name?' Eden asked Mama.

Mama was silent. Her eyes scattered across Eden's face. I'd never seen her look at a stray this way before. She moved for the cassette player and pressed play. Music crackled.

'Tell me your name,' Eden said again. Looking at the walls of our modest home, she took in each hairline crack and every cobweb.

'My name doesn't matter,' Mama said.

'I want to see what you do when you put the word in your mouth and speak it.'

'My name is Ruth.' The words slipped out of her mouth. Obedient.

I passed a cup of tea into Eden's hands. It was made with an old teabag from earlier that day, and the hemlock hex Mama had crushed up to make our strays feel woozy and warm.

Eden looked at Mama. 'Ruth,' she whispered.

Mama stared, almost shivering at the call of someone

using her name for the first time in so long. She'd not even told the gamekeeper her real name. As the lip of the cup touched Eden's lips, Mama reached out her fingertips and pulled it down. 'Don't drink that,' she said. Her words were soft. 'I'll make you something nicer,' she said, prying the cup from Eden's fingers. 'Margot is terrible at making tea, aren't you?'

Eden smiled and Mama watched those lovely teeth spread. Mama wanted her, but not like other strays. She wanted her like she'd wanted the gamekeeper.

'Has anyone told you that you have a beautiful smile?'

Eden laughed, gently throwing her head back. She would have looked bashful had the cold not washed the colour from her cheeks.

Mama put her hand on Eden's knee. Mama's want was stronger than her hunger sometimes. I hoped she'd have her fun and then maybe we could make a stray of Eden yet.

'You really do have a beautiful smile.'

I knew the silent end to that sentence. *You really do have a beautiful smile, but can I have it for myself?*

Thirteen

Mama invited Eden to sleep on the couch for the night. Eden wasn't like the others. She was calm and in control as she sank into our couch, which secreted a sickly smell. I was used to collecting strays' knots of hair from beneath the cushions. I'd made a game of trying to figure out which lost soul they belonged to, but this time it would be easy. Eden's hair was blonde and curly, with strands of silver. It was perfect hair.

Mama sat on the couch, keeping her distance from this strange new woman. Eden rubbed her hands and fingers, warming herself up. She blew warm air out onto her palms. Eden's eyes were open, watching over Mama. Together, they were silent between sputters of the crackling fire.

I watched through the crack in the bedroom door. A daub of yellow light from the overhanging bulb caught my face and cast a spotlight over them. Dust feathered down to the floor. I slipped out through the door and sat back against the wall.

It was like the two were not strangers. In a way, they were kindred. Like they knew each other from another life and now they were simply reacquainting. Mama stood, smiling, but she hid her crooked teeth behind her lips. 'I'll come to find you in the morning,' she whispered. Her fingers hovered by Eden's face, but they didn't linger. And they didn't trespass on her skin the way they wanted to. She restrained herself.

'Thank you for this,' Eden whispered. 'Your hospitality.'

Mama gazed, watching the curve of her chin as Eden bit her lip.

Eden's fingers followed the seam of the couch cushion, brushing gently back and forth.

Mama went to the bathroom, turning off the light behind her, leaving Eden and me in the dark together.

My eyes adjusted. Eden's form became more prominent. Less of a shadow and more of a shape, with lines and features and colour. Her eyes were bright in the dark, fiery and hungry. She was even more beautiful in the dark than she was in the light. As she settled into the cushions and pulled the blanket over her skin, she turned to watch Mama's silhouette move beneath the bathroom door.

Eventually, Eden closed her eyes, but she looked dead when she slept.

Fourteen

Mama was restless in the night. She murmured in her sheets, waking every few hours to peek through the door and make sure Eden was still asleep on the couch. She was worried our stray might've escaped us, but Eden was exactly where we'd left her, sleeping soundly, breathing softly. Dreaming. Her features moved every so often. Her lips twitched and her brows knotted.

We were both quiet, guessing what was crossing her mind every time she whispered in her slumber.

Taking it in turns, Mama and I kept watch over Eden, sometimes peering from the door and sometimes getting closer, sitting on the floor next to her. It was Mama's turn again and her bedding crinkled as she sat up and pressed her feet onto the rug. She crept to the door and slid through the gap. I stayed put in the bedroom, watching her from the dark.

Mama stood over Eden. She studied her features, memorising every single detail. Mama's eyebrows relaxed and her mouth was slightly open – this was the look of a woman who was ready to follow a stranger into the dark.

I slipped through the door and came close.

'Shhh,' Mama whispered, but she didn't look at me.

My footsteps were light as I moved to sit on the floor by her side.

'I've never understood why mamas are expected to be perfect,' she said. 'Men are forever thought of as boys. But girls? Once we're mamas or once we're ripe, we can never be girls again. Not in their eyes. But we are always girls and daughters, underneath. Always.'

She watched over Eden's sleeping body. For the first time, Mama looked like a daughter. She might have even looked hopeful were it not for her wrinkles carving a sadness over her lips.

Standing in the moonlight, listening to the howl of the storm, Mama reached out her fingers, brushed Eden's hair aside and felt the warmth of her cheek. I stood and nestled close to Mama's side. When I looked down at Eden, she was sound asleep and lost somewhere wonderful. I reached my fingertip to her cheek but before I could touch the blushing crest, Mama pulled my hand away.

'Don't touch her,' she whispered. 'Go back to bed.'

I looked at Mama, hoping she would look back and find me, but her eyes stayed set on our sleeping guest. The stray who wasn't a stray.

Fifteen

I don't know if Mama ever came back to bed. When the first morning light touched the homestead, she was in the kitchen fussing over breakfast, pulling together a meal with what little we had left in the cupboards. Stale bread popped out of the toaster and cooled while Mama cut the mould away from the butter. Mama's quiet feet pottered on the tiles and the kettle whistled as she got to work.

While I stood in the kitchen, twisted between the linens I'd dragged from my bed, I listened to Eden singing in the shower. The soft echo of her voice found its way to me and settled in my ears. I heard the water topple over her shoulders and splash at her feet while she moaned the lyrics of something old.

I wandered to the couch and sank into the cushions. They were still warm, and the blanket smelt like Eden. It was a musky smell, like gunpowder or smoke from fireworks in the cold. I held the cushion she'd laid her head upon and searched for the smell of Eden's hair.

The fibres scratched against my nose but the scent was beautiful.

Mama came with a tray of breakfast for two.

'What will Eden eat?' I asked Mama, putting the cushion back down.

She placed the tea tray on the floor by the sofa and sipped from the cup of tea she'd made herself. 'This is for me and her,' Mama said. 'You can forage something from outside.' When Mama spoke, her words came out in a lazy breath.

There was nothing to forage this early in the year, especially not with the snow. I might have found a rotten bramble hanging from a branch somewhere.

I noticed she'd pulled back her hair and put on some lipstick. Smudging in all the wrong places, it was strewn across her mouth like thick paint in an uneven line. I wasn't sure how old the lipstick was, but it looked crusty on the edge of her lips. Mama practised her smile, pulling at the corners of her mouth with her fingers over and over until she found one that was soft enough to make Eden comfortable, wild enough to keep her interested, but vulnerable enough to make her stay as long as Mama wanted her.

'She's different from the others,' Mama said, mouth falling back into a straight line. 'She's not untethered. Or lost.'

Mama knew the difference better than anyone, but I was still learning. I thought of the lonely woman on the street corner with the ladders in her tights. At a glance, she'd probably been no different. Not really. She'd just been a mind woven in skin. Our tendons all tore the same way.

There'd been the nervous boy who bit his nails and the girl with the purple nail polish too. There'd been dozens of them. Maybe even hundreds. Mama herself had said, *We are all the same.* But the others had all kissed her, given themselves to her so freely. They'd been greedy for her with want. Eden differed from them in that way.

The shower switched off and Eden's singing ceased. Mama turned, peeking over the sofa cushions as Eden emerged from the bathroom. She'd tied a towel around her body and her hair was draped over one shoulder.

Over the top of the couch cushions, in the light, I saw her clearly for the first time. Her skin prickled in the cold air. Goosebumps formed, shivering down her arms and calves. She had freckles sprinkled across her cheeks and nose, but her features were sharper than I had thought. There were purple stretch marks up her belly where the towel parted, and it made me wonder if she'd ever had a baby or if her belly was just a little bit round. When I looked at her bare face and body, I saw a woman. She looked the way I imagined women had looked thousands of years ago, without airs and graces and preconceptions. She was just a person, held up by bone.

'The storm hasn't cleared yet,' Mama said to Eden. 'Not properly.' She came to her feet with the tray in her hands.

'It sounds terrible out there,' Eden said, stretching

out her neck. It looked like an old branch dithering in a gale. Her veins looked like tree roots.

'You can stay as long as you need,' Mama whispered, taking the tray over. She stopped a short distance away from Eden and held out the tray.

Eden kept her towel up with one hand. With the other, she took the mug of tea, tracing Mama's fingers as she went. 'Have you heard the stories of those who go missing?' she asked.

Mama was silent.

'Hikers,' she whispered. 'Those passing through.'

Perhaps Mama was playing a game. Maybe the way we hunted was changing. Or perhaps the prey was.

Eden took a sip and smiled. 'I'd very much like to know where they go.'

Soon, she would. Mama and I would see to that.

'It's sweet,' Eden said. 'I've always loved indulging in sugar.' She put her mug down on the tray again. She pressed her thumb inside her mouth and sucked, licking the length of it before pressing it on Mama's mouth.

Mama was still.

Eden's wet thumb travelled over the crest of Mama's top lip. She wiped away the lipstick smudges. 'Beautiful,' she said.

Sixteen

The windows of the school bus rattled. They always rattled, vibrating as we followed the bends of the road.

The wilds weren't quiet here. The wind outside whistled and the roads twisted, cutting through the pastures. Snow turned into mud rivers as cars and tractors and vans trudged through the newly fallen, pristine snow. Nature was beautiful. But we did such a good job of making it ugly.

The usual bus driver was sick, so I sat with the other children. The journey seemed longer without him.

The boys on the bus were laughing at something on one of their phones. They laughed so loud I thought it might overcome the sound of the engine. Boys were always shrill and intrusive. Patrick got up from his seat, thrusting his phone in everybody's face so they could see the video too. But when the phone got to me, it was nothing I hadn't seen before. Bodies entwined. Nothing would subdue them. Nothing would sate them. They were hungry for each other.

'Laugh,' Patrick said, glaring at me. He never blinked. His eyes were dark and old, trapped inside the body of someone young. A changeling. 'Why aren't you laughing?'

I stayed quiet, staring at my feet and imagining my toes wiggling beneath the tip of my shoe.

'Oi,' he said, grabbing my face with his podgy little fingers. 'Laugh.'

I bit my tongue. In my head, I thought of the strays and how one day he might make a nice one. I wondered how he would taste if I just took a little piece of his skin, chewed for a while and swallowed. I wondered if his teeth would click and clack together after being pulled out from his gums. And then I wondered, if this boy screamed, would he sound like a man?

Patrick leant close, breath touching my cheek. 'Uptight freak,' he said, hovering closer until his mouth grazed my chin. The bus jostled again as one of the wheels hit a ditch. Patrick steadied himself, leaning down towards me. His teeth bared, sliding across my bottom lip. This boy was hungry just like me. He was too beastly to be a stray. He bit down and tasted blood.

Closing my eyes, I imagined Mama telling me to be still.

Then, to sate the hunger within, I pictured how pretty Patrick would look on a plate as Mama took a carving knife to cut away at his thigh. 'You're an uptight freak,' he said again, but this time he grinned before meandering back to his seat. He made sure I saw the sharp edges of his teeth.

*

I wandered into the playground. Children scampered to their corners. Some to the climbing frame, some to the bark pit and some to the hopscotch chalk. I went to the wall where stones were haphazardly piled on top of one another. Moss spread across the stones. Out from the gaps crawled woodlice and worms. I'd had daydreams of smashing boys' heads against this wall, especially when they were cruel to me.

When the school bell called, the children swarmed to the front door. The problem with other children was they never knew how to shut up. Not unless someone made them. The shouting and laughing came to a stiff silence at the coat hooks.

The room, which usually was filled with jeering and shouting, had never been so silent. Some cocked their heads with intrigue. Some paled white with fear. But the boys from the bus smiled. Their hands coiled around the hilts of their penknives, items they kept well away from the prying eyes of nosy teachers.

I looked at the coat hooks and the things hanging from them.

Dead rabbits, with their throats slit, were draped from each child's coat hook. Blood trickled down the walls. It glimmered beneath the light. Fresh. It was the first time I had ever felt at home away from Mama. An iron smell filled the air. Fruit flies gathered in clusters to feast upon the animals' limp bodies. The silence broke. Weeping began. I closed my eyes and thought of home.

Mama came up with a rhyme after that day at school. She sang it to me when I was naughty, poking my arms and thighs with her fingernails. I was her little kit, and she loved to keep me hanging.

Hopscotch, a grazed knee, and rabbits hung on hooks. Kits' blood bleeding out and staining school books.

Seventeen

After the rabbits, there was an unsettling hum throughout the lessons. Quiet whispers were passed from child
to child like precious secrets.

'I heard Marcus did it,' Abbie said. 'He snuck into the
school at night and hung them all up on the coat hooks
after he trapped and killed them in his garden.'

I stared at Marcus's empty seat, trying to picture
the tufts of black hair sprouting out from his hunched
back. A whistle always came through his buck teeth.
I wondered where he'd been taken and if he was
scared.

'He put blood on the walls in the nursery too,' Abbie
whispered to me, her voice trembling. Abbie looked like
a perfect child, with that shining green ribbon in her
hair, and her buttons done all the way up to meet her
collar, but there was something else just beneath the
surface. Something I wanted to uncover.

'Margot,' Mr Hill growled, 'stop distracting Abbie.
You'll sit outside if you carry on like this.'

I'd broken Mama's rule. I'd brought attention to myself.

Abbie hunched over her workbook and carried on. I was invisible to her again. I wished we could graze our knees together on the gravel in the playground and be messy, but she would always follow butterflies and good behaviour. Maybe one day, with me, Abbie could un-ravel. She would leave the safe nook she lived in and become forgotten, unnoticed by the outside world.

'I don't understand the work,' I said, pointing at the maths problem on the page. 'Can you help me? I don't—' Before my words were fully formed, Mr Hill knelt down, sighing and brushing his hand through his thick black hair. It smelt of apples. I peered at him, following the dark bags beneath his eyes to the wrinkles forming on his forehead. He was a very tired man.

'What's confusing you?' he asked, leaning over the desk. His shirt was just a little too tight and the split ends of his hair brushed my forehead. It wasn't long, but when he leant in close to see my worksheet it tickled my brow.

I pointed to the paper, leaving graphite fingerprints smeared in patterns along the edges. We were doing ratios.

'We've been working on this for a week. You should understand this by now. You have to get to grips with this before we move on.' Mr Hill sighed and rubbed his temple with his fingers.

'I don't understand,' I said again, grabbing my hair in my fists and pulling tight. Mama would've scolded me. This wasn't staying quiet or out of the way. This was demanding attention.

Mr Hill furrowed his brow and widened his eyes. I wondered what he wished he could really say to me. Or do to me.

'I don't know how you don't understand.' There was a long pause before he spoke again. He searched within for a measured tone and some words to pair up with it. 'Let's try something else,' he said. 'Do you like animals?'

Thinking of the rabbits on the hooks, I nodded.

'Mammy badger shares her food with her little kit. She gets three paws of earthworms, and the kit gets one because Mammy is bigger and needs more food than the little kit.'

I nodded.

'She always gets the same relative amount. So, if she gets six paws of earthworms, how many paws of earthworms will the kit get?'

'One paw,' I said.

Mr Hill sighed. 'The answer is two. I don't understand how I can make this any simpler for you. How are you not getting this?' He wanted me to disappear.

But the problem was that I *did* understand. It was just that my answer was different from his. Mama badgers didn't care much about their kits. The answer was that the kit got what Mama badger couldn't be bothered to eat, or sometimes nothing at all. In fact, the kit had once been scared that Mama badger would gobble her up.

'I think we should get you to do some lunchtime classes if you're *really* struggling,' he said.

It felt like a punishment or a test. His face shifted. His eyes dropped to my neck. The pen between his fingers twitched as he raised it to my collar and pulled back my shirt a centimetre or two. 'How long has that been there?' he asked.

'How long has *what* been there?'

Out of the corner of my eye, Abbie stared at my neck. I prodded my skin with the end of my thumb. A dull pain ebbed. I recognised that feeling. A bruise had formed. It was probably purple and blotchy with clouds of brown and green.

'I don't know,' I said. It could have been the boys at the back of the bus or it could have been from Mama.

'Right, well.' He coughed. 'Perhaps stop messing around so much and be more sensible, and you won't be so blotchy.' He stood up and brushed himself down, shrugging off the concern. He was back to normal in a breath. And I had been forgotten entirely.

Eighteen

When I looked out into the world, I could no longer see the quiet road in the distance or the cars that drove there. No passing headlights. Only darkness and falling flakes of snow burying us all in this house together.

The whistle and bubble of pots on the stove pulled me away from the window. The heavy scent of a hearty meal overwhelmed us. My stomach rattled. I'd not had the taste of good food in an awfully long time. I'd settled for scraps for too long. In the corner of the kitchen, Mama bounced between stirring the stew and peeling tateys. Eden shaped dumplings from dough. It was stray-free, of course.

Just for now.

There was flour all over Eden's hands. They'd brushed up against Mama's dress. Ghostly handprints disrupted the floral pattern on the cotton.

'Mama?' I asked, but she didn't look up from the potatoes. 'Can I help you with them?' I reached for her carving hand and pulled down the knife. 'I can do this,'

I said. It was always my job to do potatoes. 'I want to help,' I said, but she snatched her hand away.

'Don't touch,' she said, putting the blade back on the potato and shedding it of its skin. She did a wonderful job. The way she carved skin was a craft. She always angled the knife to form a perfect ringlet. 'The cleaner the slice, the crispier it cooks.'

Mama dropped a handful of potatoes and carrots into the stock and put the potato skins aside for later.

When I looked up, Eden was mixing dough in a bowl. Flour was strewn across the countertops and caked her skin. It softened the colour of her lips to a petal shade of pink. This was the first time she'd looked gentle. When she saw me staring, she smiled and put down the bowl.

'Come to me, Little One,' she said. Her voice sounded old, crisp like a cassette.

I shuffled out from behind Mama and wandered towards Eden. She pressed her nose to my head and took a deep inhale.

'I've missed the scent of a bairn's head,' she whispered to me, a precious secret for just her and me – one that Mama did not hear. 'Have you heard the story of how flour was made when humans still worshipped the land?' Eden dabbed a spot of flour on the tip of my nose.

I shook my head and she knelt before me.

'Let me tell you,' she said, brushing flour across my mouth with her fingers. 'Once, there was an old beggar woman who lived in a hole in the hills,' she began, sitting down on the floor in front of me and holding my hands. Mama looked over her shoulder and smiled.

'Like a rabbit?' I asked, sitting next to her.

'Exactly like a rabbit.' Eden smiled. I wanted to make her smile again because her teeth were beautiful and straight. 'She lived in a hole in the ground and she ate mushrooms she foraged from the land. And worms that trespassed into her burrow. But one day she returned from her foraging. Down deep in her burrow, a hunter had come to steal her coat of fur.'

'Women don't have fur,' I said, tugging at Eden's hair. It was soft and bouncy.

'They did once upon a time. We all had coats of fur and whiskers near our noses,' she said. 'All women used to have fur until the hunters decided it wasn't what they wanted anymore. And having her thick coat stolen from her – that changed her. Her spine straightened and she stood on her hind legs, not like the hunched creature she'd once been. She looked like a hunter. The woman she used to be was gone forever.'

'Why did the rabbit woman change? Why couldn't she find a new coat to wear on her back?'

'The things that happen to us change us, Little One,' she said. She sounded like Mama when she said those words. 'The rabbit woman asked herself, over and over again, *Why did the hunter have to find me? Could it not have been my mama, my sister, or the other wise women of the burrows?* Because that was true, it could have been anyone, anyone whose coat was shiny enough to tear from flesh, anyone who caught the human hunter's fancy. She was just in the wrong place at the wrong time, with the wrong person.' I watched Eden fall deep into her own mind, wavering on a thought that made her puddle-grey eyes go black. 'Maybe that's why we are the way we are.'

She disappeared into her thoughts but returned after a deep breath from her lungs.

'One day, when the sun was at its highest point in the sky and the heat was beating down onto the currents of the beck, she lured her mama, her sister and the other women of the burrows out into the pastures. And then she skinned them alive, pulling out their muscles and leaving their skins to rot in the hot sun. She didn't want to be the only one changed. She took their bones and left the rest to ferment. Crushing down the bones, she formed flour, hoping that the femur's dust would let little rabbit hairs sprout from her back once again.'

'But it wasn't their fault,' I said, thinking of hot meat rotting beneath the sun and larvae hatching into maggots close by.

'We can't save each other. Not really,' Eden said, pinching my shoulder with her fingers. 'What people don't know, Little One, is that the most dreadful things happen out in the open while the sun shines bright up in the sky and no one can do a thing about it. Those who watch don't care and pretend they don't see. They burrow and forget.'

If Mama's fur was stolen, or Abbie's, I would find the hunter that stole it and I'd make him my stray. He would be the one to rot beneath a burning sun.

Eden got up from the floor and lingered close to Mama. Her eyes danced on Mama's mouth, but settled on her cheek. I think she wanted to place a kiss there.

Nineteen

The dumplings were soft. The meat fell away from the bone, melting in my mouth as I chewed. The stew was perfect. It wasn't a stray's meat, but it was delicious. I'd take it any day over freezer food or soupy pasta.

Eden was a calm eater, taking bites as though she had the rest of time to finish what was on her plate. There was no food smeared around her mouth because she used a piece of tissue to wipe away dribbles of gravy as she went.

Mama was the opposite. She feasted, pecking and slurping and guzzling at the meat and stock. Gravy oozed from her chin and soaked into the fabric of her dress. Eden didn't seem to mind. She watched Mama, content, as though it was somehow charming that Mama ate like an animal.

'Eat up,' Eden said, staring at me. 'It will go cold if you eat too slow.'

'It's divine,' Mama said, lamb catching between her teeth. She used her fingernails to pry the meaty bits loose from her gums.

64

'The best stew I've ever made has a very special ingredient. I'll have to make it for you sometime,' Eden said, gazing at Mama.

'What's the special ingredient?' I asked, wanting her to look at me.

We exchanged silence around the table, but three knocks cut through the quiet. They came from the front door.

Mama wiped her mouth and glared at me. 'Answer it, then,' she said, brushing herself down and throwing on a cardigan to hide the patch of gravy that bonded to her dress. From her pocket she pulled out her lipstick and applied it in a thick coat across her mouth. Eden watched her, hungry to reach out and smear it across her cheeks and chin.

I shuffled out from my seat and went for the door. When I opened it, I found the face of the gamekeeper. He looked more tired than usual. His face was red and his eyes were bloodshot. He looked down at me before drifting past to find Mama.

'I've missed you,' he said, words slurring. I recognised the smell he carried about with him. It was a stark mix of his wife's perfume, fresh game and the twang of whisky. Mama loved that smell.

'Shut the door, Little One,' Mama said, standing from the table. 'We'll all catch a death.'

I closed the door and returned to my seat. Eden stayed sitting, watching the gamekeeper with a close eye. Her hackles were up. Mama folded her arms, though it didn't stop his fingers trailing up her dress between her thighs. Eden's eyes followed his fingers.

65

'We have company,' Mama said, not that company had ever stopped her before. 'It's not a good time.'

The gamekeeper looked Eden up and down. 'Who's this, then?' he asked.

'Her name is Eden. She's a guest.' Mama pushed him away.

The gamekeeper glanced at Eden, but drew his attention back to Mama.

Eden's eyes washed over the gamekeeper. She was trying to do what I had done so many times: figure out what he wanted from this home and why he couldn't get it elsewhere.

'Can we take this somewhere else?' the gamekeeper asked Mama. He leant in close, hands travelling the lengths of her thighs, then hooked his fingers beneath one of her knees and pulled her leg up to his waist. He whispered something in her ear. Mama would usually go red and bashful but this time she stayed still and pale. Her expression didn't waver.

'You left me,' she whispered, 'for *her*. That silly wife of yours.' Her eyes were like stones. Unfeeling and unflinching.

Eden watched Mama as she stood from the table.

'And now I'm back.' The gamekeeper smiled, but Mama shuffled out of his arms.

Mama watched him, her eyes turning a deep black, pupils growing as she took in his boyish smile. 'Can I get you a drink first?' Mama asked, touching his arm and pulling away.

The gamekeeper smiled and nodded.

'Why don't you fetch this stray a drink, Little One,' Mama said to me. I recognised the look upon her face. She was hungry. Lost in the stare of the gamekeeper, Mama smiled. She was lucky we were his dirty secret. No one would know he'd come here.

'I think I should go,' Eden said, voice breaking. She pushed her chair beneath the table.

'No,' Mama said. 'Stay.'

Eden froze behind her seat as I went to the kitchen, rummaging through the cupboards for the hemlock tin. *The bigger the stray, the bigger the dose.* I strained leaves into a glass of ale, something the gamekeeper drank by the gallon when he visited us. I passed him the glass, but he didn't look away from Mama. When he pressed the glass to his lips, Mama gently grazed the end of it with her finger, tipping it back.

Eden was silent but she was curious, tilting her head to one side. As the gamekeeper swallowed the last of the ale, his cheeks blushed.

'Take me to the couch,' he said. 'I won't leave again. This is where I belong. With you.'

Mama held his hand and took him to the fireside. She helped him lie down on the couch and brushed his forehead with her fingertips. A soft smile came to his mouth. 'Close your eyes,' she whispered to the game-keeper.

He did as he was told. Slow and steady, his head tipped back as the hemlock did its work. The gamekeeper was on the edge of sleep.

'Eden,' Mama whispered, 'come close.' Mama pressed

her hand against the gamekeeper's chest. 'Come feel his heartbeat slow,' she whispered in Eden's ear. She was quiet and careful with her words. Eden leant close, pupils dilated, as she watched the gamekeeper's cheeks grow rosy and red.

The gamekeeper would soon lose his breath. His face would turn bright, burning as his lungs reached for air they couldn't steal. In his slumber his pulse would slow and his lungs would choke out. And Mama would smile. Wide.

Eden's parted lips formed a smile as she brushed his forehead and felt his pulse.

She would be a natural. I just knew it.

Twenty

Loud music was rare, but today the cassette played from Mama's stereo. An orchestra crackled and a singer fumbled over her words where the tape had become worn and scratched. It was an old tape. One from Papa's collection of blues and love ballads. I tried to imagine this was Mama and Papa's wedding song and that they'd danced to it on their quiet wedding day.

'*Love, after all these years, has finally found us. No more lonely days for you and I. Amour. Amour. Amour,*' Mama sang, coming out from her and Papa's old bedroom. The place she took the strays. Eden peered inside, stepping over the threshold. Her toes sank into a puddle of blood.

Mama brushed herself down. She was on edge, like electricity was murmuring on the surface of her skin. This was how she always was after a fresh kill. Careful in her carving but not as meticulous as she could be. Her lipstick smudged over the edges of her mouth, colouring outside the lines. Her dress had small specks of blood near the collar. Mama hadn't noticed them. 'I've always loved this song,' she said, gazing at Eden and smiling, but Eden was still. Her fingers stayed firm at her side. A stray hair escaped out from Mama's up-do and her brow was coated in a light gleam of sweat. 'Always. Since I was a girl. It's just so . . . serene.'

Eyes wide, Eden came to Mama's side and reached out as if to pet an animal from the wild wood. Her fingers brushed the specks of blood away from Mama's cheek but smeared them along with her lipstick. She held Mama's face between her palms. Eden's lips trembled. She was on the edge of speaking, but the words wouldn't come.

Mama pulled Eden to her knees. 'It's okay if you can't find the words,' Mama whispered, her hand resting on Eden's cheek. 'It's okay. There really aren't words to describe what it feels like, are there?'

Eden's eyes watered. 'I—' she began, but then she stopped, looking at the fresh blood on her hands. I knew her palms would be sticky. They always got sticky if a thin layer of fresh blood dried fast. I hated that feeling. 'There was no screaming,' Eden said. 'He was so quiet. It was like he was sleeping.' Eden didn't try to wipe away the blood; she watched it dry, crusting from red to orange between the creases of her palms and knuckles.

'Now he can dream forever,' Mama said, taking Eden's hand and steadying it in her own. Mama had never said that to me before. 'Can you imagine what his dreams will taste of?'

'What would he have dreamt about?' Eden asked.

'I once watched him sleep.' Mama recalled a hot summer's day, post-euphoria. 'He twitched a lot while he dreamt. When he was awake, he was impulsive. Wolfish. Animal. When we taste his dreams, they'll taste of fell mud and rainwater on our hot cheeks, and long grass tickling our fingers as we move through darkened woods. Forever. We will taste the wind on our knees and the babbling river on our toes.'

'Tell me more,' Eden said, leaning closer to Mama, lips almost touching.

'He had a child and a wife, but I think he was falling in love with me before *she* made him leave. He will taste adulterous.'

'They will be better off without a wolf,' Eden said.

'He smelt like cigarettes, but there was always a hint of his wife's desperate perfume and shampoo. I hated it. I hated that he brought that little piece of her here to be with us. He promised himself to her a long time ago, but he was always mine.'

Eden brushed Mama's hair behind her ear.

'She must have known he went somewhere to get his fill because each time he visited me the scent was stronger. Every day she was trying harder to hold on to him.'

'Mama?' I asked, looking at them on the floor together. 'The smell.' Iron. It was stronger than it had ever been. Metal and musty now, but come tomorrow it would smell of rotten eggs. Mama had started to pull him apart. The blood smelt fresh, but the stray had been dead for four hours and twelve minutes.

'This moment is important, Little One,' Mama said. 'Eden needs this. Let her take it in.'

The smell was like a ripple. It kept hitting me. The first ring was metallic. The second was worse. Bile moved in my throat.

'Come to us,' Eden said, her gentle gaze fixing on me as she reached out her hand.

Mama smiled with her teeth as I crawled over and sat by them.

A smile crept in by the edges of Eden's mouth. Her fingers rose, reaching out towards me. They were bloody, shining beneath the flickering yellow light above. No, it didn't shine, it *glistened*; the same as the kits' blood on the school coat pegs, orange and red. The smell was stronger now as her fingertips loomed closer and pressed the soft part of my lips. Eden pulled them along the curve of my bottom lip and smudged the rest in a line across my cheek. 'Like lipstick,' she said in a haze. 'All grown-up.'

I'd never tasted raw blood. I thought of Mama's first stray, the woman from the corner, and how Mama had cracked open her skull and dipped her fingers inside. I wondered if this was the same. My tongue lapped up the blood on my bottom lip. My stomach didn't lurch. The taste stayed in my mouth, heavy and metallic as I washed it over my teeth.

Mama's arms reached around us both, pulling us in. Locked in this embrace, I thought of Abbie, and wondered if she would smell her papa's blood on me come Monday.

'This is what family is supposed to be,' Mama said. 'Togetherness.'

Eden smiled, closing her eyes and leaning her head against Mama's shoulder. She took my hand in hers and held it tight.

'I want you to stay here,' Mama whispered in Eden's ear. 'With us.'

Eden glanced at me, pausing as she held Mama's words. She took a deep breath.

'Please, Eden,' Mama whispered. 'Let me keep you.'

Twenty-One

When I looked at Eden, I felt like she was from another world. She reminded me of black-and-white starlets from sleepy Sunday-afternoon movies.

Mama and Eden were cooking together. They acted as though they'd known each other forever, but it had only been days. Eden brushed a hair from Mama's face while Mama used a mallet to crush the meat and pack it in Tupperware.

There were specks of blood on Eden's dress, but she wore it like it was her Sunday finest. She'd borrowed it from Mama. It was a cotton floral church dress that had been stuffed at the back of Mama's wardrobe for too long, sun-bleached and riddled with moth-made holes. It was a little big on Eden. She had a small frame and the dress hung from her shoulders, coat-hanger-like and wiry.

Mama nibbled on one of the gamekeeper's fingers that Eden had cooked up.

'Can I have one?' I asked as Eden fried them one by one in the pan. 'I'm hungry.'

She sprinkled the pan with salt and added more butter to keep them crispy. At her side, Mama diced up rosemary she'd plucked from the plant pots on the windowsill and tossed it into the searing butter. Eden fried one more finger before nipping it out of the pan with her fingertips. The butter turned her fingers red as it spat out from the pan.

'Here, Little One,' Eden said. 'Only one finger for tonight. A grown-up tummy is much bigger. When you're grown, you can have as many fingers as Mama and me.' She dropped the finger on the table before me. It landed with a soft bounce and the wood slurped up the butter, absorbing it into the fine grain.

'It was Eden's idea to breadcrumb it,' Mama said, fussing over a bowl of flour. 'And she's used salt and rosemary. It's about time we started eating as we deserve.'

'And tomorrow we can go and find some more wild herbs. Some more rosemary and some garlic. Who knows what we'll find out by the woods. Imagine the flavours,' Eden said. But she didn't know the land like we did – herbs would not bloom in this frost. We'd have to make do with the potted plants by the window.

I picked up the finger and nibbled away where I imagined the fingernail used to be. Eden had plucked it from its nail bed. Pulling away at the thin layer of meat wrapped around the bone, I chewed. It didn't taste like dreams, as Mama had said it would. It didn't taste like the other strays either. Promises of taste and flavour, of wind on my face and the patter of mud as it splashed up from the earth, faded.

It only tasted human.

I thought of the gamekeeper. His red cheeks and his muddy boots. He had not been a stray like the others. He was the man that compared our hand sizes, realising his were much bigger than he'd ever thought they could be. He was a man with a wandering eye and a wife who kept herself busy at home. He was a man with a daughter I would see at school on Monday. This was no stray or stranger.

Mama was getting reckless.

Twenty-Two

I stayed alone at the dinner table while Mama and Eden sat cross-legged by the fire. The music was low. Mama sang along. Every time the song ended, she rewound the tape and started it from scratch. *Love, after all these years, has finally found us. No more lonely days for you and I. Amour. Amour. Amour.* I hadn't realised Mama was lonely, because she had me. I hadn't realised something was missing until the missing piece came along in the snow.

My toes brushed the floor, catching splinters as they moved. I wanted Mama and Eden to take their seats so we could eat as a family, but they stayed far from me, entwining their fingers and catching each other's eyes by the cinders. Together, they laughed and sang, feeding on finger food and lifting their dresses so their knees could graze one another.

Mama had said the pan-fried fingers in breadcrumbs were *beautiful. Real food. Cooked to perfection.* The thin layer of skin and meat slipped straight off the bone as they placed the fingers in their mouths. They broke up mouthfuls with quiet kisses, tasting the tenderness on one another.

I looked at the lone finger on the table, but I couldn't bring myself to eat it.

The smell of blood was getting more rotten with each minute that passed. There were small dried-up splashes of it scattered about the floorboards. Mama and Eden hadn't cleaned well enough. They were too hungry. Desperate.

A strand of Mama's hair came loose from her knotted bun. When Eden looked at Mama, her eyes stayed wide open. Her cheeks were red. I imagined they would be hot to touch. No, *searing*. She pushed the rogue strand of hair back behind Mama's ear and brushed Mama's cheek with her fingers. No one had ever looked at her so earnestly before. The gamekeeper had looked at her like he was hungry. I can't remember how Papa looked at her, but it was not with as much love as this. I took a deep breath and closed my eyes. I tried to forget Eden's face, the curve of her hot cheeks, her hair.

I thought of Papa. He wouldn't have liked Eden. He liked quiet and unambitious women. Women you could look at but not hear. I knew that because Mama had been quiet around him. Only giving small pieces of herself if he was in a good mood, she hadn't shared herself with him wholly.

Papa left us long before he had the chance of becoming a stray. Wherever he was in the world, whatever he was doing, he probably wouldn't remember my name or face.

I slipped off my chair and moved to the couch. The last of the gamekeeper's clothes were strewn over the side, bloodied up. I held his jeans between my fingers. They were heavier than I thought they'd be. His wallet was packed into his back pocket along with his wedding ring and his dog tags. The plastic bag the clothes were supposed to be packed inside was abandoned on the armchair, carrying dried-up beads of blood in the creases. His big boots were neatly pressed with their heels to the wall. Big, old, empty boots, leather-worn and mud-sprayed. Used. Lived in. These were boots bought to last.

'Little One,' Eden said, pulling away from Mama and dropping the last finger into her palm. She eased Mama's fingers around it and kissed them. 'Why don't you take those outside? Clean up the clothes for Mama and me?' she asked.

'You know where to put them,' Mama said, catching me over Eden's shoulder. She smiled to me. Even with her yellow teeth, slightly crooked, I knew it was a warm smile. I pulled the gamekeeper's jumper into my arms and bundled it up with his jeans. Peeking out from the neck, I found a label. Something was scrawled on it in faded blue biro. *Mark Greene.* His wife's tired handwriting. I held the label before putting the jeans and jumper in the plastic bag. I picked up his boxers and socks from their heap on the floor. Into the bag they went. Twining my fingers through his shoelaces, I heaved up his steel toecap boots.

Leaving Mama and Eden behind, I slipped out the

back door. The snow was starting to clear. Mud squelched between my toes as I fumbled over the ground. Flushing my skin pink, the cold bit at my goosebumps. I followed the garden path to the bottom of the plot, where a heap of shrubs and sticks covered our burial ditch. It was near the back hedge.

I brushed the shrubs and sticks aside and, left atop the soil, I found the hex I'd made to keep our secrets hidden. It was a cockleshell wrapped in twine. There were dead herbs and plants coiled within. Mama had been proud of me for making the hex. She'd even kissed me for it in earnest.

I took a nearby trowel and dug up the shallow earth for the gamekeeper's clothes. Pulling back the crumbling mud with my fingernails, the strays' belongings surfaced.

A pair of red trainers. A purple hoodie. A lacy pair of knickers. Countless socks of all different colours, sizes, patterns and states. A vest top with spaghetti straps. A pair of jeans. A tight dress Mama was too big to fit inside.

I added the gamekeeper's clothes to the pile. The plastic bag rustled as I settled it in the earth. Holding the boots over the ditch, I hesitated.

I thought of Abbie. I couldn't bring myself to part with the boots.

Putting the boots aside, I pulled the earth back over the ditch. Back over all the clothes. The socks and the T-shirts. The remnants of the strays we'd long since buried. Placing the hex back into a little nook of soil to keep our secret safe, I closed my eyes and stroked the grooves in the shell. Mama loved it when I made her hexes. She loved collecting my strange little trinkets and admiring them. She loved it even more when I made them to protect us from the outside world.

I pulled the sticks and shrubs back over the ditch and held the boots. They smeared mud across my skin.

'I know you weren't a good man,' I said to the boots, 'but I don't think you were a bad man either.'

Putting them in a small clearing beneath the hedge, I sheltered them from the rain. Keeping them safe from the elements, they would rest some place safe. Somewhere they wouldn't rot.

Twenty-Three

There were rain clouds nearing, but I waited by Eden's car where it nestled in a lay-by at the end of the track. The homestead was in sight, but I was well hidden from Mama and Eden. While I watched the clouds, I pressed gravel into my thighs. The clouds had been lingering on the edge of our lands all morning. I'd woken to them, all grey and rumbly, coasting by. Mama said she was keeping the storms away. They were not brave enough to venture close to her temper.

My fingers fussed with the gravel stones. When I looked at my palms, the creases were filled with dust. There were imprints left deep in my skin from the tiny stones I'd embedded there. I plucked a few out and dropped them on the ground, building a small cairn.

No cars passed today, but for the first time in a long time I didn't worry that we'd go hungry. We had all the stray we needed in sandwich bags packed up in the freezer. The gamekeeper would last us a few weeks. He was a big man, with big muscles and lots of fat. He wasn't like the weedy strays Mama was used to pulling in on her line. The gamekeeper was a feast.

At the edge of the gravel lay-by, Eden's car still waited to be pushed closer to the house. She'd been here almost a week now.

I crossed the road, dragging my feet and kicking up the dust. The car was beaten up and rusty around the wheel rims. Eden had told Mama it was a death-trap. I wondered if she'd ever fix it. I pulled on the handle, but it was still all locked up. A newspaper lay on the front seat. Looking at it, I realised it must have been old or, at the very least, mistreated. The edges of the pages were torn and browned, and the paper was crumpled.

I read the passage on the front page. *The search for missing teenagers Alison Blacklock (15) and Kayley Radcliffe (18) continues. The two went missing in early October after they went hiking across the Pennines in the Cumbrian regions.*

'Alison. Kayley.' I whispered their names, hoping to remember the faces of two hopeless strays bundling into our living room. Whoever they were, they were gone now. Lost to nature, a few mossy skulls half buried in the ground, ants crawling out from where eyes had once watched. Bones scattered around them. Lifeless. If they had ended up strays, their bones would have been left to the mouth of the burial ditch nearby after being basted, stewed and stocked. Only once we'd farmed strays for *everything* did we put them in the ground.

There was little else in the car. Eden had packed light. She wore all Mama's clothes and she slept in my bed.

She ate the food from our freezer and cupboards. Even though she'd only been with us a short time, Eden was part of our home, like an old piece of furniture worn in and used. Loved to death.

Twenty-Four

Abbie was quiet. The green ribbon was slightly lopsided in her hair again, loosely tied, holding blonde strands away from her face. It was one light tug from being pulled free altogether. I watched her mouth as it chewed the end of a pen. Her fingers fiddled with the nib, each fingertip now covered in black ink. Her workbook had a trail of black daubs left in a messy pattern up the margin, each fingerprint a forest.

The details of her face shifted. Thoughts were moving through her head faster than she could understand them. Worry. Then sadness. Confusion. And then anger. Her cheeks and nose went red as she took a deep sniff. Dropping her pen, she bit her lip. It looked like she was caught adrift somewhere I couldn't reach.

'Abbie?' I asked, tapping her on the shoulder, but she didn't move. 'Abbie?' I asked again, prodding her arm with my finger.

Her eyes stayed closed and her mouth shut. I pulled on the end of her ribbon and it came free in my hand.

'Why are you being so quiet?' I asked.

Abbie reached out and pulled the ribbon from me. It slid away from my fingers. 'My da hasn't come home yet,' she said. 'Mam hasn't stopped crying.' Abbie opened her eyes and looked at me. 'When she cries, she screams. She's louder than a baby and she holds me too tight.' Abbie paused before speaking again, as though the words were clutching onto the back of her throat. 'But I don't feel anything like she does. She feels big and she puts her feelings everywhere. I feel small and I keep them inside.'

I tried to imagine Abbie and her mam snuggling into the couch, Abbie silent and her mama wailing, echoing, over the morning cartoons.

'I went to *our* place. He takes me up the fells on his quad bike and we eat dinner at the big rock on weekends. I went there to look for him. But there was nothing. I think he's gone.'

I thought about the gamekeeper's hands and how he'd measured them against mine. His fingers had tasted beautiful, after all. I didn't want them to, but they did. They weren't filling, but the skin and the thin layer of meat was enough to satisfy my hunger.

'Has anyone seen him since he left?' I asked.

Abbie shook her head. 'I'm scared the ground has eaten him up. He once told me the fells are alive, hungry and watchful. I keep thinking about the earth opening up into a big hole and him falling down deep. Until he's gone. That's what happens to wanderers around here.' Abbie closed her eyes again, banishing the image of her slowly disappearing papa. 'I don't think he's coming back. Mam says he will come home to us. But the ground has already eaten him up.'

I reached for her hand. Her skin was soft. 'You and your mama will be okay,' I said. The weight of her palm in mine was like a heavy stone. I wanted to stay this way forever.

'Margot,' Mr Hill whispered from across the classroom. His beady eyes watched me over his glasses. His lips moved, mouthing a single word. *Focus*. But I couldn't focus. Even if I only stood at the edges of it, it felt like our world was unravelling and fraying into pieces. Mine and Abbie's.

I squeezed Abbie's hand. She chewed on her pen. There was a new feeling growing inside, like tree roots taking their place in the soil. It sent a sharp pang through my sternum. I wanted to tell her I was sorry.

Twenty-Five

When I looked in the mirror, among all the features bundled up on my face I could see Mama, but not where it mattered. My eyes were absent of her. My mouth was smaller. My cheeks were fuller. I think those bits belonged to Papa. Or I hadn't yet grown out of my baby fat.

My memories of Papa were fragments, but still, I caught slips of him in my reflection. The puppy fat around my neck covered it, but his chin would someday emerge around my jaw. And his eyes; I hoped I had his eyes. They were round and green, rare like stones earth-plucked and muddy.

The bathroom mirror was foggy. I wiped away the cloud and tried to find Papa's features hiding behind my chubby cheeks. I wondered if the chub would fade, making way for Mama's sharper bone structure. I hoped, years from now, that Papa would recognise himself in a girl lost among a crowd. He'd see me and know we shared blood. I narrowed my eyes and wriggled my nose.

In every corner of the room, mould was closing in. Its darkness speckled the walls. The beige paint was rotting and peeling. This is what Papa had run from.

The soap tray was empty, but caught in the dip was Mama's lipstick. It was a gold tube, scuffed and dented from being dropped and scraped. We didn't look after our things in this home. Mama rarely ventured to the shops. She hated it. The busyness. The sounds. The strays all bunched in together like sardines, acting like people and not food.

Mama had kept the same tube of lipstick for years and years. I think she'd stolen it from a stray. I took the tube between my fingers, pulled off its lid and took a deep breath. The smell of cheap lipstick overcame my senses. It smelt of wax. Mama was always in a good mood when she wore lipstick. The scent made me calm.

I funnelled the lipstick and daubed my finger on the end. The colour was a stroke of plum on my fingertip. Pressing the lipstick over the curve of my bottom lip, I slid it over my mouth. I couldn't keep the colour inside the lines. Deep plum brushed my chin.

When I was done, I forced a smile. Looking at my reflection in the mirror, it looked as if two fish hooks had caught either side of my mouth and pulled wide. Wider.

I'd wanted to look exactly like Mama and now I did, but all I saw was ugliness.

Twenty-Six

The night I wore Mama's lipstick, I had a dream that I pulled out her teeth so she couldn't smile anymore. I didn't want to see those teeth.

She was still as I held open her jaw and pulled them out one by one.

'I love you, Mama,' I said. 'You don't have to be hungry anymore.'

I left her teeth in a pile and kissed her cheek. I expected her to be warm, but she was cold. Inside her eyes I sought love, but there was nothing there. They were empty.

Eden's hand fell on my shoulder. She knelt before me, taking my chin between her fingers. Our eyes met, and then she spoke. 'Listen, Little One,' she said. 'Know that you can't ever curb someone's true nature. It can be wrapped up warm by skin and clothes, but it can't be curbed forever.'

Mama started to fidget in her chair. She was restless. Impatient. Eden brushed me aside and kissed Mama on the lips. When Eden pulled away, Mama was wearing lipstick and a toothless smile overcame her.

Taking the first tooth, Eden opened Mama's mouth with her fingers and placed it back into the first socket.

*

Twisted in an old blanket, I woke alone on the couch. From the quiet, Mama snored and Eden whistled through her nose. The door had been left open. Peering over the top of the couch, I found them fast asleep. Dreaming.

I wondered if we shared our dreams.

Twenty-Seven

The gamekeeper's boots looked like they were becoming part of nature. The bush they were nestled beneath was unruly. Stems and thorns made their way inside, past the leather. Little leaves sprouted from within. The boots sagged beneath the weight of the rainwater they'd collected since I'd hidden them.

'I think Abbie misses you,' I told them, thinking of her little green ribbon. 'She hasn't said it but I can tell. She's quieter at school and she told me she went to your place – the big rock on top of the fell.'

The boots stayed still, dripping water into weeds.

I cocked my head. Thoughts of Abbie dissipated. 'Something is different,' I said. 'I don't think Mama loves me anymore.'

If Papa was here, he would have said, *Don't be silly. Of course Mama loves you.* Then he would have tickled my nose with his finger.

'She loves Eden more than she loves me. She *really* loves her.' The love she had for me was like embers, burning in and out with her whims, but the love she had for Eden was a bonfire.

I picked up one of the boots and emptied it of water. A small puddle in the soil had formed by my knees. My kneecaps sank into the ground. Beneath me, there were hundreds of trinkets hidden among plastic bags and mud. But not the gamekeeper's boots. I let his boots breathe.

'Do you miss Abbie?' I said, holding the boot in my hand. Mud from the sole smeared my fingers and palms. 'Did you miss her while you spent hot summer afternoons in Mama's bed, away from your wife?'

The boots were quiet.

'I ate three of your fingers,' I blurted out. 'They were tasty. Tastier than any of the others. Eden cooked you with butter and breadcrumbs and rosemary.' I paused, putting down the now-empty boot and picking up the waterlogged one. 'When we run out of stray, I eat cold beans and tateys. It's horrible. It makes me feel sick.' I emptied the boot and the puddle grew bigger. My knees sank further into the mud. 'Do you think Mama would be angry with me if I took something of you to keep for myself?' I whispered, looking at the shoelace as it threaded through the eyelets. 'Eden has Mama wrapped around her finger. She'd be angry if I took these laces from this burial place,' I said, but I plucked the lace from the eyelets and wound it round my knuckles. I took the other boot too and pulled out its laces. Like twine, I plaited them and bound my wrist with the new bracelet.

Putting my nose to the laces, I took a deep inhale. Though the scent of the gamekeeper was not lost, it was slipping. There would come a day when my bracelet would only smell of earth and rain.

Mama told me once that what we do when we take a stray into our body is put it back into nature so it can be forever. But the gamekeeper was not forever. And neither were the other strays. All that was left of him were these boots and these laces. Everything else would soon disappear.

'What are you doing?' Eden's voice called from the house. 'Who are you talking to?'

I shoved the boots beneath the hedge and stood. Eden came down the garden path. She wore Mama's dressing gown and her milky thighs slipped between the gap as she came closer. Her feet were bare, pressing into the muddy path that led down to the strays' ditch.

'Little One,' she said, coming to my side. Her fingers drifted into mine. 'You shouldn't be here. We buried these keepsakes for a reason. They aren't supposed to be unearthed.' Her fingers clutched a little too tight. 'They should be in the ground or hidden well at the back of the bush.'

I looked up at her. Jaw locked, her eyes were dead set on the boots shoved beneath the hedge. 'I was just talking to them,' I said. 'I'll bury them. Once I'm done speaking to them.'

Eden planted a knot in her brow. 'Are you going mad?' she asked. 'Don't let this unravel you. Stay sharp, Little One.'

'I'm not mad,' I said. 'He was different from the other strays. We knew him.'

Eden knelt, her pale knees becoming soiled in the mud. Her hair curled from her shower and her face was damp and dewy. She pressed her hand to my face and set her eyes on mine. 'They are all strays,' she said, using our words and tasting them. 'How they speak. How they look. Who they are. Those things don't matter. They are *all* strays.'

But Eden was wrong. They weren't all strays. Mama taught me that young. She knew the difference just by looking at them. It was gospel that everyone had their different uses. Some of us were strays, some of us were just here for pleasure. And the rest of us were here to fill our stomachs. To *taste*. There was no in-between. Strays, even if they had a place to sleep and eat, were bodies without homes, listless and lost.

'I think you should come back inside. The stray who walked in those shoes is gone now.'

'He was Abbie's papa,' I said.

'Abbie?'

'A girl from school.'

Eden's brow knotted again. 'You're not to speak to her. Not anymore. If her papa was a stray, then so is she. Do you want to be a stray too? Is that what you want?' Eden's grip on my hand tightened. I thought all the bones in my fingers would break at once but they were steadfast.

'I don't want to be a stray,' I said. I'd never considered I could be a stray.

'Good,' Eden said. 'I think you should go inside and help Mama clean up. You've left your bedding out in the living room.'

Pulling my hand free, I kept my eyes on my toes and nodded. When I looked at Eden, there were only a few things I knew for certain. She was beautiful. Her face was forgiving and warm, trusting even, but for some reason, even when she called me *Little One* the way Mama did, there was this space between us. She kept me at arm's length.

'I'm only looking after you, Little One. I hope you know that.' She pushed me away, up the garden. I followed the twists in the foot-fallen path until I reached the door.

When I looked back at Eden and the boots, she was still on her knees. She dug a small ditch with the trowel and buried the boots in a shallow grave.

At least I had the laces to keep close.

Twenty-Eight

Mama curled up on the armchair, watching the telly get lost in static, but she looked monstrous. Hunching, her bones nestled beneath sheetlike skin. Mama reached to the side table and pulled a toothpick from its surface. She smiled at it and kept her mouth open before keying it between the two front teeth of her bottom jaw. She picked food out from between her teeth and gums, fiddling until the toothpick snapped in her mouth.

The telly flickered on static. Mama didn't want digital. She loved the spontaneity of analogue television. In her armchair, she watched. Between flashes of light, I saw the monster. Mama was gaunt and her eyes were sunken. When the light flashed back and the picture settled on the screen, she was herself again. A full set of teeth sat in her jaw, lipsticked lips and rosy cheeks held her face still. In the light, Mama's hair was full and her complexion was clear. She looked beautiful when she was well fed, and she was kind when she was sated. I pictured myself in the future, sitting in the same chair, picking skin and bone and fingernails from between my teeth.

When I moulded my cheeks in the mirror and looked at my reflection, I wondered if I'd be the spitting image of her, inside and out. I was made from Mama's womb and skin and bone, so I knew, in the deepest pit of my stomach, that I would grow to be just like her. Beautiful in my own way, but hungry. Insatiable.

In the thickest tissue of my brain, dark thoughts and impulses formed. I didn't feel the *hunger* in the same way Mama did. When it was quiet, a voice that said terrible things goaded me. It told me I could get away with murder if I wanted, but I would never be as clever as Mama or as cunning. The voice sounded like Mama's, but it was the sweet voice she used when she wanted something from me. The voice that made me throw reason out the window.

'What will I do if I run out of toothpicks?' Mama asked me. She smiled, dropping pieces of the bloody, snapped toothpick onto the floor.

'I don't know,' I said, keeping my eyes fixed on the telly, which was still flickering on static.

'I'll have to use bones, won't I?' she laughed. 'Clean that up,' she said, relaxing her wrist on the arm of the chair and pointing her fingernail to the floor. I looked at the toothpick before shuffling over to it on my knees. Mama watched me. Her features softened.

I picked up a piece of the toothpick and studied where the pale beige turned to pink. The place she'd shuffled the point just a little too hard into her gums. She loved the taste of blood. But so did I now. I knew it tasted like metal and that it would make me big and strong.

Once I was out from under her watch, hidden behind the door of a kitchen cupboard, I looked again at the toothpick, marvelling at the rosy-red point.

I opened my mouth and I sucked.

Twenty-Nine

Though I couldn't see the clock, I knew midnight was near. Mama was listening to music again. The cassette bundled over itself, skipping and larking about. It was louder than it should have been. So loud that the words became a distorted hum.

Mama liked being cut off from the world, somewhere so remote she could get lost in vibrations. The room trembled and I felt each tiny movement.

I sat on the floor by the window. My fingertips grazed the glass. Even though the dark outside called to me, I stayed on my perch. I ignored the beckoning coax of the wilds calling me to go and play in the beck. I tucked away my impulses to climb the highest point on the fell in hopes of catching city lights on the distant horizon.

Mama loved to dance. When she drank too much wine, she floated. Her smile was soft and relaxed, and her eyes closed as she lingered. Eden held her hips and nibbled on the skin of her neck. When she did that,

Mama's smile turned hard. Her teeth appeared slowly until her mouth was fully agape.

She liked that. The nibbling.

They swayed together while I sat by the window. Over Mama's shoulder, Eden glanced at me as she touched Mama's skin and smelt her hair.

Remnants of our dinner floundered about Mama's feet. Her bare and wrinkled soles brushed by plates almost licked clean as she danced.

I wanted to hold on to the seams of her dress and move with her. But I couldn't. Not unless I was invited.

Mama looked at Eden, her eyes resting, proud and soft. Eden's breathing stirred as she burrowed into Mama's collarbones. Mama shifted her gaze. Her eyes sparkled when they settled on me but there was something distant about her expression. Still swaying, she reached out her hands. I slumped down from my shelf and walked to her.

The world melted away. Her hands were moments from mine and I wanted to hold them so badly. She was a magnet. I was pulled into her arms. Her body was warm and soft, and as her lips pressed against my cheek they left a trail of kisses over my face. Each of them perfect. Her black jumper scratched my skin. I felt every thread against my cheek. The wool was greasy from dinner.

I knew blemishes would come to my face by morning, but I didn't care. I would take a thousand blemishes and look like a monster. Mama's fingers clutched my head. I caught a glimpse of us in the small mirror hanging on the wall. We looked like a beautiful painting, even with Eden standing so close, drifting by us.

I wondered how Eden's fingers looked so relaxed and yet, when they touched me, felt so sharp. They held the small of my back as she lifted me away and fell into Mama's arms.

Eden picked up her wine and nursed it as she danced, grazing the lip of the glass with her mouth. Her eyes fixed on Mama. I realised that perhaps there was some-one else who wanted her more than I did. I don't know how long we all danced for, but splitting aches cut through the arches of my feet.

Mama pulled her hands away and let me go. I grazed my knees on the rug as I fell, but falling felt like floating around her and pain was overwhelmed by the feeling of being held. I sat on my knees, staring up at her while she swayed her hips and pulled her arms through the air. She should have been a terrible dancer because her movement was loose, unfocused and gale-like, but she looked perfect when she was this lost.

If I wanted Mama to hold me again like that, even if just for a moment, I had to make Eden love me.

Thirty

I looked out from the window as we descended further
into the wilds. It was a quiet day on the school bus and we
only had minutes left until we'd reach the school gates.
We drove past an eternity of fields, each one the same as
the last. Neat squares kept lush and green by grey stone
walls, each flecked with scales of lichen and moss. We
flocked deeper and deeper into the countryside, roads
like arteries, all hidden among fells.

I sat in the front seat, legs dangling in the footwell.
The stagnant air was filled with a faint petrol smell and
I took a deep breath of it.

'This place doesn't have eyes, but I know it feels each
of us moving like tiny ants on its skin,' the bus driver
said.

'I read in a book that giants sleep under the fells,' I
said, and the bus driver smiled as his eyes wandered
across the road. 'When they take deep breaths, the
wind rushes through the valleys and tears trees from the
ground and roofs from the tops of houses.'

'The Helm Wind,' the bus driver said. 'That's what they call it, but adults like to make things so simple and boring, don't they? It's giants sleeping under the fells. Not wind. My da called it giants' breath when I was a bairn.'

When I looked through the window, I glared at the fells' ridges as we passed, as if all the big feelings I kept inside could somehow move mountains.

'How are things at home?' the bus driver asked, dropping his smile and replacing it with a firm, straight line.

I looked down. My lunchbox was covered in my greasy fingerprints. I studied each of the mosaic patterns. I didn't want to answer the question. The world felt like there was nothing outside of it again. Just the rolling hills for miles and miles, until there was nothing.

'It's okay to tell someone,' the bus driver whispered. 'Sometimes, when things aren't okay, I don't want to tell people either, but you have to be braver than this old man.' Then came the soft tick of the indicators as the bus coiled round towards school. It sounded like a metronome bouncing back and forth.

At the end of the road, the bus rolled to a stop and the engine silenced as the bus driver pulled the keys from the ignition. Children swarmed off the bus.

'Mama has a new friend,' I said, sitting still in my seat.

The bus driver kept his eyes forward. They were glassy and tired. He did what most adults do in front of children: pretend he was not afraid. I wondered if he was as scared as I was of the things in this world.

'You know, it's my job to look after you all,' he said.

'I thought you were just supposed to drive the bus,' I said.

'Being a bus driver is much more than just driving,' he said, forming a quiet smile. I waited for him to tell me I could go, holding on to my lunchbox, keeping it tight on my lap, but I didn't want to leave. I wanted to stay here in the bus and see where it would take us next if we just kept driving. 'You tell someone at school if something is wrong.' He looked at me for the first time that morning. 'Promise?'

'I promise,' I said, but I couldn't form the words I needed to tell him about Mama and the strays.

Thirty-One

Mama sat by the window while Eden cooked dinner. As the last of the day's light came down upon Mama's face, she closed her eyes and took a deep breath of the herbs Eden ground up with our pestle and mortar: rosemary and garlic paste to slather over the gamekeeper's thighs before he was roasted in the oven. He was going to taste delicious again.

Mama's skin was pink from the heat of the warming spring. Little brown freckles sprouted on her skin. Condensation crawled down the window and her brow formed new beads of sweat. She looked like a beating heart, fleshy with a blue vein prominent on her forehead. I'd never seen her like this. Eden had given her a taste of wonder.

Eden slathered the thighs with her paste. Her palms worked the meat, massaging the tendons. When she was satisfied, she wiped down her hands. Once the meat was in the oven to roast, she smiled to herself. Soon there would be nothing left of the gamekeeper, save for his boots and buried clothes. Quietly moving across the kitchen towards us, Eden placed her hands on Mama's shoulders and rubbed. Mama closed her eyes and took a deep breath. Her shoulders dropped as she relaxed back into Eden.

'You're not as tense as you usually are,' Eden said, grazing kisses up Mama's neck and leaving one on her cheek. Eden's fingers toyed with the buttons on the back of Mama's dress. Once she'd fiddled them free, she touched Mama's spine with her fingertips, sliding over the bumps of her vertebrae.

'It's you,' Mama said, eyes opening, pupils dilating. 'I know you're right here with me, but I'm trying to hold on to every detail because I'm scared you might disappear. So, I hold on. To the lines by your eyes. The corners of your mouth. Your eyelashes. Your freckles. I want to remember everything.' Mama took another deep breath. 'Just in case you disappear down the long road and never come back to me.'

'I'll never leave you,' Eden said, putting her hand on Mama's cheek.

Mama turned, sitting on the windowsill, knees parted. Eden slipped between, pressing her torso against Mama's breast. Their hands found each other and held on tight.

'Now that I've found you, I'm never going to leave. I will stay with you here in this little house forever. And we will pick up strays. And we will eat. And we will never tire of each other. We will always be full.'

They gazed into one another's eyes, flitting across

one another's features, taking in every detail. I held my breath. And did not trespass. I stayed on the couch, looking over my shoulder and holding on to the cushions.

'Do you understand?' Eden asked, pressing her forehead on Mama's. 'I'll never leave you.'

'I'll never leave you,' Mama whispered back. 'Something is alight in me. Something I've only felt once before. My first stray. This woman from my childhood who wandered the corners of a back street.'

'You've loved another woman before?' Eden asked, pulling away. She wanted to be Mama's first.

'No,' Mama said, her chest rising and falling as she clutched on tight to Eden's hands. 'This love feels the same way,' she continued, gathering her breath. She took her two fingers and held them together, brushing them over Eden's chin. The fingers fiddled with the knotted ribbons on Eden's dress. 'I dipped these fingers inside her skull, and for the first time something filled the emptiness inside me. I had never felt full until then. That *something* that I felt as I watched her eyes go out like a light. I thought that was love, but now I realise I didn't know what love truly was until you found me here. You make me feel full. *Real* full. You make me feel so full I could be sick, like I've eaten all day since waking. I never want that feeling to go away.'

Eden's face softened. A smile emerged, tight and measured, but holding something back. 'Hopefully not too full,' she smiled, pressing her palm on Mama's cheek. 'You have a whole roast thigh for dinner, with potatoes.' She held Mama in an embrace, whispering in her ear.

I saw it then, more clearly than I ever had done.

The absence of love had spoilt something in their souls and mine. Our love was rotten, but still looking for the burning it craved; for anything to revive the embers that had gone out long ago.

*

Eden placed a meal before Mama. The plates were clean for the first time in a while because Eden liked things just so. There was a juicy cut of leg on the side, but Eden had also made a sweet gravy with shallots and garlic from our newly formed vegetable patch.

'This looks beautiful,' Mama said, but she wasn't looking at her food.

'The trick is to baste it with red wine every few hours,' Eden said, putting my plate down before me and then sitting at the table. 'I've always loved cooking. It's nice to have good produce to work with.'

My portion was smaller. But the slice of meat was fattier. I knew it would have a bit of chew to it. It would be gamier than the other slices. I wondered which part of the gamekeeper's leg it belonged to. I imagined it was somewhere near his front pocket.

'I think this will be the nicest meat from our stray, so enjoy every bite,' Eden said, looking at Mama. 'We may not have anything like this for a long while.'

Mama smiled. There would be another stray soon. There always was. The last time we'd gone without, soggy pasta shells had driven her to the edge.

'To new family!' Eden said, raising her glass of red wine and gently touching the rim of Mama's glass. I held up my glass of water. Eden gave me a passing smile from across the table, then her eyes glanced down at my plate. 'Go on, then,' she said, brushing her wine glass against her lips. 'You'll love it. It's the sort of food that makes me insatiable.'

I took my knife and fork and pulled the meat apart. It was tender. So tender. I'd thought Eden had given me a gamey piece, but I'd been wrong. She had given me something beautiful. When I put it on my tongue, it fell apart at first bite. It was the most delicious thing I had ever tasted in my short life. I wondered if this was what Mama had felt when she'd dipped her fingers into the brain of her first stray.

It made me think of Abbie. Poor Abbie being held too tightly by her mama, the wailing woman, on their tatty couch, in their little cottage. Her papa was never going to come home to her. He would never hold her or read to her. I made a quiet wish that she'd forget about her papa, that he would evaporate, along with his memories, but somewhere inside I knew she would always remember him and wonder where he was.

And I would always remember how delicious he'd tasted.

Thirty-Two

I put sticks together to form a square, then twined fishing wire around its edges. The growing pile of sticks and twigs at my side had all fallen from trees in the forest. Each one, once a little bit damp and covered in moss, we'd stripped down with a small Swiss Army knife found among Papa's old tools. I'd never built a trap before, not like this. Eden helped me unspool the twine as I sat in her lap.

'Feed the fishing wire around and through,' Eden said, guiding my hand with hers. Her fingers were cold and light, and her nails tickled my knuckles. 'Around and through,' she whispered in my ear. Her words sounded like brushes of wind. Eden's hands took hold of mine, weaving the twine around and between the sticks. They were relaxed and light, ghostlike. 'Then the trap will be nice and sturdy when it's finished.'

'What will we catch in the trap?' I asked her, looking up. I cosied between her legs and leant against her tummy. She'd borrowed one of Papa's old T-shirts and shimmied into some of Mama's old jeans. There was a laundry-faded band logo on the front of the T-shirt. It was tucked in and her hair was down, teasing the passing breeze. She looked more relaxed than I'd ever seen her. She even looked a little bit sun-kissed where freckles sprouted near her nose.

'A rabbit,' Eden said, licking her lips and smiling. 'A tasty rabbit we can bake in a pie, with a nice crust of golden pastry.' She closed her eyes and imagined the taste.

My mouth watered.

'We'll eat it for dinner while we wait for more strays to come find us.' Eden's finger tapped my nose. I felt warm inside. 'A rabbit is no stray, but it will make a nice meal.'

'This looks too big for a rabbit,' I said, holding out the frame we'd half built and imagining the size of it once it was finished. 'And what if its teeth manage to nibble all the way through?'

Her hands snaked around my waist and pulled me closer, up onto her knee. Then I saw her as closely as I ever would.

I saw what Mama saw.

Her eyes were somehow fiery, a muddy green and grey with yellow rings around the darkness. Eden was composed but wild beneath the surface.

'No rabbit can make its way through fishing wire,' she said, taking my index finger and winding the wire around it. 'See what happens when I pull tight?' she asked, pulling the twine.

The top of my finger went purple until the wire made a cut near my fingernail. A bubble of blood balanced on my skin before scurrying down my knuckle and into my palm. Eden loosened the fishing wire and pulled it free.

'It must be big to trap whatever beast our bellies are hungry for. What if it's a lost hare that stumbles onto our little trap? Or a bleating lamb? It needs to hold it, subdued, and keep it tight so it can't escape. It needs to get lost in the fishing wire, lost enough so it can't even fumble.' She raised her eyebrow. I think she was picturing a lamb half caught and suspended in wire, bleeding and bleating until it had nothing left to give but meat. A smirk pulled at the corner of her mouth. 'What would we do if it got free? Miss out on a taste of goodness because our trap wasn't big enough?'

I looked at the beginnings of a cage in my hands. The sticks we'd picked up off the ground weren't strong enough to hold a lamb, but the fishing twine was. It would cut it to ribbons if it tried to escape.

'We're going to wrap it all up in the twine. If the little beastie tries to escape, it will bleed and give up eventually. Little beasties only have so much fight in them. You just have to apply pressure in the right place.' Eden took my bleeding finger and kissed it better. There was a smudge of blood left behind on her bottom lip that dribbled just beneath, onto her chin. She lapped it up with a flick of her tongue and closed her eyes. I wondered how I tasted in Eden's mouth. I wondered if I made her mouth water the same way she made mine water.

I imagined Mama and Eden skinning a small beast, a rabbit, and blanketing her up in a puff pastry coffin. She would make a very fine pie. My stomach groaned, and Eden smiled. Her hand wriggled up my T-shirt and squidged the pouch above my pelvis.

'We need to get that belly nice and filled up while we wait for lone strays,' she said, kissing my cheek.

'Look at my two girls,' Mama said, leaning against the doorframe. Gazing at us, she looked contented. Calm. She wore her floral number, a Sunday church dress, sunbleached from summers past, but she wore this dress draped over her body, buttons almost entirely undone. Her collarbones soaked up the sun and her breasts were free from their binding. Mama's toes played with the dusty earth on the front step as she stared.

She looked the way I'd always imagined women were supposed to look. At peace. Relaxed. A part of nature, like a stone or a stream. She was not dressed up to the nines for an unfaithful gamekeeper. Her freckles had come out with the evening sun again, just like Eden's. Mama's lips formed a soft but tired smile as she leant her head against the door. Her hair was tied back in a loose bun, but wayward strands escaped out into the breeze and played around her.

When I looked back at Eden, she was gazing at Mama. Her arms loosened around me. 'I want to keep you well fed,' she said, staring at Mama. 'I can't wait to make you something from this trap.'

'That cage looks a long way off,' Mama said, concealing

a smile at the edges of her mouth. 'So I'll keep my hunger in check.'

I looked down at my cage, which was just a few sticks twined together, and furrowed my brow. 'It's not finished yet,' I said. 'But we're building it big and strong so we can bake a pie.'

Eden nodded and leant her head on mine. She took an inhale of my scalp.

'The roads look quiet today,' Mama said. 'I was thinking of sprinkling a few rusty nails a mile down or so. Catch a stray.'

'Maybe two miles,' Eden said. 'Make it harder for them to get here. The more tired they are, the better. And it's a warm day. They'll need plenty of food and water. Keep them desperate for it.'

'What about the little back road that runs along the bottom of the pike?' Mama suggested. 'Not a lot of traffic. Mostly hikers. We'll not catch the school bus that way.'

I imagined her kicking up dust a few miles down the road and sprinkling out Papa's old nails on the tarmac beneath the beating-hot sun. Enough nails to cut into the tyres, but not enough to cause suspicion. The calm vision of flora suddenly dissipated. She was wild again, the way she was in her heart, hungry and desperate for food.

Thirty-Three

At midnight, darkness crept over the house, but moon-shine slipped between the curtains and trees. In the corner of the living room, by the ashes and soot of a once-lit hearth, I stared at one of Mama and Papa's wedding photographs. They looked happy together. Papa was wearing a shirt and a tie, buttons done up right to his collar. Sharp. He was older than Mama. A lot older. Though the picture was black and white, I could see his teeth were yellowing near his gums, his hair was thinning, and his skin was hanging off his cheekbones.

Mama had nothing but memories left to make, but his were already made.

I kept this old photograph folded beneath the couch cushions. Over the years it had become worn and faded. I touched Papa's chin with my fingers and imagined what his skin would feel like. I knew for certain his chin would have lots of stubble, but between the sprouting hairs his skin would be soft. His breath would be warm and smell like smoke. Sweet cigarette smoke on a hot summer night. He would have wrinkles like the bus driver, big ones around the edges of his mouth and his eyes. Mama called them crow's feet.

But Mama wasn't smiling in the wedding photograph. As they cut the cake she was scowling, eyes on the thick white icing. It looked sweet and chewy; the sort of icing that stays in your mouth longer than it should, making a home on the roof of your mouth and over your gums, eating away until your teeth ache.

Papa was smiling, holding Mama around her once-small waist and pulling her close as they shared the knife between their hands. His temple leant on hers, pressing against the tight perm and thin veil feathering over her features. Mama once said he chain-smoked and smelt like embers and tobacco.

I tried to feel the heat of the camera's flash firing at them while they posed with the cake.

'What do you have there?' Mama asked, creeping out from her bedroom and sitting close by. Her fingers toyed with the settled dust until they found my hands and entwined. Mama took the photograph from me and studied it. I watched her expression, hoping to see a shimmer of *something*. Anything. I wondered if, in the cold cockles of her heart, she missed Papa the way I did.

'I haven't seen this one in a long time,' she said, looking over the top of the crinkled photograph and staring at me. 'Where did you find it?' Her expression was still, mouth unmoving from its straight line.

'It was stuffed behind a couch cushion,' I said,

neglecting to say it was me that kept it there. 'I miss him, sometimes.'

'You can't miss someone you didn't truly know,' Mama said, pausing for a moment and holding back the words she was yet to speak. 'What you really mean is you miss the idea of him.' A knot folded in her brow. 'That's something he was an expert in. Loving the idea of someone. He loved the idea of me before he peeled back all the layers.' Mama pressed her hand hard on her belly.

I gazed at her, pulling the photograph from between her fingers. I settled my eyes on him again, wondering if it was really possible to tell good from bad in a simple picture of a man. I'd heard Mama say you could tell just by looking, but he looked ordinary. Plain. 'I don't understand,' I said to Mama.

'Men love the idea of women. They love *the question* about a woman. The mystery yet to be solved. Then, when he discovers she has a personality all of her own, neuroses and quirks, just like him, he decides . . .' Mama didn't finish her sentence. 'Your papa didn't love me. He wanted a wife. That was the part that made my hunger stronger than I'd ever known. I was expected to be perfect and quiet. Compliant. I've felt that my whole life but never like I did when I was with him.'

I watched her closely. Her eyes drifted across the floorboards as she rediscovered hidden coves from her past. Brow furrowed, Mama shut her eyes for a moment and thought.

'I'd never felt hunger like it, Little One.'

'Where do you think he is?' I asked, trying to picture where he was sleeping. Perhaps he was holed up in a quiet halfway house, all wrapped up, foetal and childlike.

Mama shrugged. 'Good riddance to him.' She paused, looking at the photo again. 'Do you think I look pretty here?' she asked earnestly.

'You are the *most* pretty,' I said, brushing the lines carved into her palm.

'I was only seventeen. Five or six years older than you are now. I really thought I'd met my person. I thought he was so good he'd change me, but no one ever really changes. We can be different for a while but we'll never change what is true in our bones and brains.'

'Was he a bad man?' I asked.

'He could be earnest and sweet, but his temper was short if he didn't get his own way. He had this wicked sense of humour and could make me laugh even when I was angry or sad. But he wanted me to mother him and act on his every whim. The rest of the time, he expected me to be quiet and look beautiful.'

'He doesn't look like a bad man,' I said.

Mama turned to me with a look so serious it held me still. Her hand slid over my cheek, falling to the point of my chin. Papa's chin. She pressed on the hardest point of the bone, pushing her fingernail into my skin. Mama held it between her index finger and her thumb and pinched, nails imprinting deep.

'Do you think the devil has horns?' Mama asked.

I wanted to speak, but her fingernail kept my jaw in place.

'The devil looks as ordinary as you and me.'

Eden slipped in from the bedroom, tying up Mama's dressing gown. She moved like a ghost, passing through and sitting quietly on the arm of the couch. 'Are you talking about—'

Before Eden could finish her sentence, Mama spoke again. 'I have you now,' Mama said. 'I have you both. *My people.*'

Over Mama's shoulder, I watched Eden drape herself over the arm of the couch. She sank into the cushions. All of us, within the embrace of the dark, simmered in this quiet and held our breath.

Mama pulled out an old box of photographs and showed Eden pictures of when her hair was silkier, her waist was smaller and her complexion was clearer. Eden insisted Mama was still just as beautiful, just different, more grown.

Thirty-Four

When I leant my head against the window of the school bus and tried to sleep, the jolts woke me. My skull bumped against the glass. I was trying to dream of the trap, hoping that if I wished hard enough a small rabbit or stoat would crawl inside and get caught in the twine. My mouth watered at the thought of it cased in buttery pastry and baking inside a pie.

Over the weeks, I'd come to love Eden's cooking, and I daydreamed of salt and pepper laying crushed in the pestle and mortar, of her working the dough with her knuckles, and of flour dispersing in the air like dandelion wishes when she blew it from her palms.

'You alright, Youngen?' the bus driver asked, glancing away from the steering wheel.

I nodded and pulled my feet up onto the seat. With sleep still in my eyes, the world kept its dreamlike morning haze. My eyelids were on the verge of closing, heavy, as hot air from the vent hit my face and the deep voice from the radio crackled, falling in and out of signal. We turned a slow corner and my stomach lurched.

Even though the sun was bright, it was a cold morning. I felt nauseous. The wind was rushing over the crests of the fells and pooling in the valley, and the sun was spreading across the pastures.

'You look tired,' the bus driver said, keeping his eyes on the road. We turned another corner and the faint tick of the indicator lulled me into quiet. 'You've got them big awful bags under your eyes like you've not slept.'

I took a deep breath of the petrol air and breathed out. At least it smelt nice here. There was a faint brush of his cigarette smoke too. The trees were thinning out, replaced slowly by small sandstone cottages and gardens. That meant we were closer to school.

'Bet you're staying up watching cartoons on that telly. Thing'll make your eyes go square. I tell my little nipper *only one hour of telly a night.*' The bus driver glanced at me again, waiting for me to speak. 'Is that what you kids do for fun these days? Watch the telly all day and night long?' A dry chuckle escaped his lips.

'I like to make wishing hexes,' I said. 'Out of things I find in the woods. And sometimes from things I find in the sands at the beaches when Mama takes me to Morecambe.' The bus swerved slightly and then re-adjusted itself on the road.

'Aren't you a little bit young to be getting caught up in things like that?' The bus driver's brow arched and his eyes widened.

'No,' I said. 'I make a wish on the hex and sometimes

it comes true.' I opened my school bag and rummaged around, searching for Papa's hex. It was always drifting somewhere in the furthest reaches of the back pocket. This hex was the first I'd ever wished upon.

'What've you got there, then?' he asked, brow furrowing as he looked down at the curious item I'd fished out and now held between my fingers.

The hex lay flat on my palm. I had to be gentle with it. It was four twigs twined with frays of old drift-rope, bound together in a square. Between them I'd woven old leaves and flowers that had dried up and hardened over the years. It was a brittle old thing, but it had somehow survived the savage corners of my bag, stuffed between pencils and workbooks. At the centre I'd used fishing twine to bind a small cockleshell into the weaving.

'This is the wishing hex I made for Papa. Mama calls it a tide wish because we plucked the cockleshell from the quicksand.'

'Those sands are dangerous,' he said, glancing away from the road to peer at my creation. 'And a long way from here. You should be keeping your distance.'

My stomach lurched as the bus topped a hill. I wanted to tell him that Mama had once wished for me to be washed away with the tides. Out into the sea, swept away, never found, and forgotten with the ocean spray and the depths. 'We haven't gone in a long time,' I said.

The bus driver's expression shifted as he let out a lung of air. 'Keep your wits about you, Youngen. You don't want to be getting caught in those nasty tides.'

I thought of the fast-moving tides and all the shells

they brought to shore. 'I got to pick this shell so I could make a wish for Papa.'

'Why are you putting hexes on your poor old man?' he asked, but his expression hardened. He suddenly seemed old and severe. The wrinkles and creases in his skin seemed more pronounced. I wondered what made him a person and the others strays. The bus driver could never be a stray. Not to me. I think it's because he listened to me. Really *listened*, taking in my words and remembering them.

'I made a wish to bring him back,' I said. 'Mama told me he left before my fourth birthday.'

The bus driver was quiet. He measured his words before he gave them out, like flour or butter. Children received adults' words in the smallest portions. The adults left pieces out in the fray; the pieces they thought we didn't handle well. But those left-out pieces were the ones we needed the most.

'Did it?' the bus driver asked, his hands tightening around the wheel.

I cocked my head.

'Did it bring him back?' he asked.

I looked at the hex resting in the dip of my palm and I thought of the wish I'd made. *I wish Papa would come and find me.* Beyond the details of the wedding photograph, pieces of him were slipping. His smell. The texture of his hair. The clothes he wore. The shape of his glasses. All I could hold on to was knowing he was a man who worked with his hands. He chopped wood and hunted and tinkered. His eyes were weary like the bus driver's and I had a sense he was searching for something he'd not found in life. At least, not the life he'd shared with Mama and me.

'No. It didn't,' I said.

'You know, Youngen, I lost my da when I was a young man too.'

'You did?' I asked, looking at the bus driver, eyes splashing across his face in the hope of deciphering what little pieces he was keeping from me.

'And I was an angry little thing about it too.'

'Why were you angry?'

'I felt like I'd been robbed of something. I wondered what we were supposed to be doing together at his fiftieth birthday or my fiftieth. At Christmases and weddings he never got to go to. He's the empty seat everywhere I go. I'm older than he ever got to be. Kids aren't supposed to be older or wiser than their parents. It seems wrong, doesn't it?'

I looked at the passing trees. They'd grown into such funny shapes, twisting and turning, balding as their leaves clung to their branches.

'Just keep yourself on the straight and narrow, Margot.' When he said my name, I knew he was serious. People rarely spoke my name. 'You'll be okay if you do that.'

In my mind, as I watched the winding bends of the country roads, I tried to imagine what the straight and narrow looked like. All I knew was that there was a sun rising at the end of it, bleeding out oranges and reds into the sky.

I looked at the hex in my palm, studying the drift-rope and leaves. I could do that. I could keep on the straight and narrow, walking towards the sun. I nodded and put the hex back in my school bag. The gates were just ahead, and the bus began to roll to a stop.

The bus driver took a deep breath and then heaved it out. 'Promise?' he asked, pulling up the handbrake.

'I promise.'

Thirty-Five

I'd always loved rain. It could be vicious or light on its own whim and there was no saying, at the beginning of a storm, which way it would go.

I closed my eyes as Abbie leant back in her chair and whispered to me. The rain drowned her out, breaking up her words and sounds, patting water drops against the windowpanes. Beyond our classroom, the world was grey. The oncoming humid summer kept us warm beneath the sky.

'We used to do this thing where we'd put our hands together to see whose hands were bigger. He was always surprised by how big his hands were compared to mine. Mine were little. He said they'd never grow, and he asked me to promise him to stay this small forever. He didn't want me to become a woman.' Abbie paused, looking at her fingers. 'I promised him I'd never grow up.'

As she leant back, I saw the sadness playing at the edges of her mouth. The quiver on her bottom lip. She'd already broken her promise to her papa. The last of her big teeth were coming in, popping out through her gums and squeezing into her small jaw like uneven bricks.

'You can start packing up for the day,' Mr Hill said.

Soon I'd leave this place. Check the trap, hoping there'd be food for the table. See Eden and Mama. Sit by the window in the quiet and think of Abbie. It was easier to think about her than it was to be near her. Where I could almost taste her. After all, if Mama and Eden were right and the gamekeeper had been a stray, then so was she.

As I packed my bag up with pencils, Abbie took my wrist. 'I feel quite lonely, Margot,' she said, her eyes welling up. 'I'm always by myself, unless Mam is around.'

I wanted to reach for her but I kept my arms at my side. I felt lonely sometimes too, even with Eden at the homestead.

'Mam won't stop crying. Ever. She screams. Really loud. At night while I'm trying to sleep. And sometimes she sleeps in my little bed with me because she says she doesn't want to be alone either.'

'It won't be like this forever,' I said, thinking of Mama after Papa left us. Sat at the kitchen table. I only remembered her crying once but then she put her tears away and straightened her face. After that, she never cried about Papa again. 'And you shouldn't feel lonely. You have friends. I'm your friend.' I reached into my bag and pulled out my hex. Wherever Papa was, he was not journeying his way back to me. Abbie's papa was the same, but she needed this tide wish more than I did.

'I made this when my papa left but I think you should have it.' I took the bracelet I'd made from the shoelaces pulled from the eyelets of the gamekeeper's boots and wound it round the twig frame. Then I put a quiet wish inside that he would come home for Abbie. 'You make wishes on it,' I said.

Abbie took it from me and pressed a kiss onto the cockleshell. Pulling at the cuffs of my jumper, she took me into an embrace. At first, my arms hung loose, but I wrapped them around her and held tight. Her hair smelt of apples as a loose hair by her ribbon tickled my nose. I reached my fingers high and took it. When she pulled away, I stuffed the blonde hair into my pocket.

'I want to be friends with you, Margot,' she said. 'Friends that share their secrets and talk about boys.'

*

Hidden in the forest ferns, far away from Mama and Eden, I held the strand of hair in my palm. When I held Abbie's hair up to the sunlight, it was straight and yellow. It looked like a golden thread. I opened my mouth and put it down on my tongue. It didn't taste like apples. It tasted like Abbie.

I closed my eyes. And I swallowed the small piece of her I'd taken.

Now a piece of Abbie was with her papa.

Thirty-Six

Looking at the empty trap felt like a broken promise. Over the weeks, the fishing twine had been left flesh-less. Not a rabbit. Lamb. Or stoat. Nothing but the ugly hunter footprints I'd left pressed into the mud nearby.

Eden watched me through the window. Pushing it open, she popped her head out into the breeze. 'A watched pot never boils,' she said. 'Come inside and I'll make you something warm to drink.'

'I'm hungry,' I said.

'I'm making pasta tonight. Don't worry, Little One. You'll not go hungry.'

'But I don't want pasta. I want *meat*,' I said, glaring at the empty trap. My jaws pressed together until my gums ached.

'Why don't you go to the beck or woods? Keep your-self busy until teatime. I'll start cooking soon and you'll forget all about that empty belly of yours,' she said. Eden smiled to me the way I wanted Mama to smile to me, warm and loving. I imagined her warm hands patting the chub of skin near my belly and then squeezing it tight.

I fastened my shoelaces on a nearby tree stump before heading up the dirt path towards the beck. I climbed over the fence and crossed the road. The tarmac was dusty as I made my way from one side to the other, passing over potholes and the promise of puddles. It had been quiet along these roads lately. The nails Mama had scattered miles up had brought no strays to our door. They must've been too rusty. Or the hikers were keeping themselves away from the back paths.

When I got to the beck, I slipped down the bank and sat on the stones. Hemlock was growing at the shore among the long grasses, nettles and weeds. I plucked some and stuffed it in my pocket. Mama could use it for the strays.

The woods weren't far from here. Across the beck, the clearing and treeline were only a few hundred yards away. It was the place where rabbits lived with their kits, and where the trees spoke to one another, whispers sent on the back of the wind. As I stepped over the stones and water, my calf grazed a grove of nettles on the bank. It left a light trail of little red stings over my skin, but I pushed on towards the treeline.

In the woods, the foliage blocked out the sun. It was dark and cold within the embrace of the forest. The leaves and branches shared their murmurs as I walked deeper.

'You,' a voice came. The word strained to be heard over the wilds.

I looked through the trees but there was no one there. Spots of dim light fell in through the foliage.

'Over here,' the voice came again.

I looked above the bracken. There, lying against a tree, was a wounded woman. No, not a wounded woman. A stray. The meat on my bones spoke to me. She was most certainly a stray. I knew she was because she looked lost. There was that twinkle in her eyes; a loneliness that turned people into strays. Her hair was black, tied up in a loose ponytail. Flyaway hairs escaped her hairline. She was covered in dirt and her skin had lost its colour. A backpack lay strewn at her side.

'Are you okay?' I asked, stepping over a fallen log and going towards her.

My mouth watered as I realised how pretty she was. She had the brownest eyes, like little hazelnuts, and her cheeks were round and full. I could see that, once upon a time, her cheeks had been pink where they rounded, but they'd faded grey over the hours or days.

'I'm hurt,' the wounded stray said, pulling her coat aside. She'd been using it as a blanket to stay warm. 'I've been here overnight. I've got no signal. Please.'

I looked at her stomach. Near her bellybutton, I noticed a large gash bleeding out. The stray didn't have long left and, as Mama had told me before, a stray was not a stray if it was already dead, and it would taste awful if it wasn't happy as it passed on. 'I can help you. I live close by. I can take you back to the house and get you help. Shelter. Food.' Mama and Eden would love me if I brought this stray to our homestead alive.

But the stray was fading. Her head was tipping back against the bark of the tree trunk. 'I fell onto a branch and I pulled it out. I've lost a lot of blood,' said the stray, voice faltering into a quiet whisper. She shouldn't have pulled the branch out. She should have left it lodged inside to keep the blood in her veins.

'It's okay. You're going to be fine,' I said, brushing her hair back behind her ears and wiping the gleam of sweat from her forehead. That's what Mama would do. I moved closer, sliding my hand beneath her arm and helping her to her feet. She yowled as I pulled her up. 'We have a phone. We can call for help.' I gave her hope, thinking about what hope would taste like seared into her muscles and fat.

The stray moved for her things, but I pulled her aside.

'I'll get those,' I said. 'They'll weigh you down. We have to get you back before . . .' I thought of Eden. I thought of how dominant she was when she wanted something. I wanted to be like that too. This stray, *my first real stray*, would do as she was told. I pulled her backpack over my shoulders.

We made our way back through the woods, over the treeline and towards the beck. Wading, stepping over the stones and climbing up the bank, my stray stumbled, knees muddying. Holding her wound, she wept.

'Not far to go now,' I said. 'Just the other side of that gate and you'll be safe and happy.' I was already imagining what she'd taste like once Eden had rubbed her with butter and rosemary and roasted her flesh in the oven. The skin was always my favourite. So much

133

juicier than chicken skin. The stray would fall apart in my mouth. She would fill my empty belly.

I pulled open the gate and she hobbled through, knees buckling. She fell as we faltered up the dirt path. Eden rushed out the front door, hurrying down the steps, pinny tied around her waist and cardigan pulled close to keep the evening chill from biting at her goosebumps.

'Oh my,' she gasped, rushing to our side and sliding an arm beneath the stray's shoulder. 'Let me help you up.' Eden looked back towards the house. 'Ruth, come quick!'

'I found her in the woods,' I said as Eden took the stray from me. 'She needs to be happy.'

'Thank goodness you did. Whatever would we have done if you hadn't?' Eden asked. Her puddle eyes glistened, pupils large and black and proud. *That look.* That look was all I needed. 'Let's get you inside,' she said to the stray, but the stray was almost gone. 'Margot, fetch some flowers for her hair. Let's make her comfortable. Content.'

Mama came, running faster than I'd ever seen before. She took the other side of the stray, pushing me out of reach. Whispering beneath her breath, the stray's head flopped forward. 'Please,' she said. 'I need help.'

I disappeared down the banks of the beck to fetch wildflowers and dandelions, each plucked from its stem with my bloody fingers. Mud scraped my knees as I fumbled my way back up the bank.

In the homestead, the stray whimpered. The room that kept our strays was closed off, but I heard them all inside. Eden shushed the weeping stray, whispering poetry in her ears.

'You're going to be okay,' Eden said from behind the closed door.

'I can't breathe,' the stray muttered. I wondered if those words would be her last.

Mama opened the door and slipped her head through the gap. 'Do you have the flowers?'

I nodded, dropping the bundle I'd collected from the banks into Mama's palms. Without lipstick and dancing and wine and old cassettes, Mama disappeared into the strays' room. I wondered if they plaited the flowers into her hair. Or sang her songs. I wondered if they kissed her bleeding wound better.

The stray had to be happy.

As the sun set on us, bright and burning, Mama and Eden took the stray into the dark, making her feel beautiful and free in her final few moments. I'd done the right thing, bringing the stray back to the homestead.

We would eat tonight. And we would eat well.

Thirty-Seven

There was a drop of blood left behind on Eden's ankle. It was thick and red, leaving a trail as it found the contours of her skin. It smudged and smeared over the arch of her foot as she dragged pieces of the dead stray to the chopping board. In her last moments, the stray didn't even scream. She was out like a light before she had a chance to know what was really happening.

Eden promised me she'd braided flowers into the stray's hair, but maybe they'd been so rough with her that the flowers had fallen from her plaits. I wondered if they'd tugged her hair a little too much as they brushed it through with a comb and plaited in the stems of the dandelions I'd collected from the banks of the beck. I wondered if they'd kissed her glistening forehead better as the world fell out of reach.

Mama would be inside stripping the skin from the meat and peeling the meat from the bones. The smell of blood was stronger than ever before.

*

'You did well today,' Eden said, coming close and putting her hand on my shoulder. Despite her clothes being clear of even a single speck of blood, she left a trail of crimson footprints behind her. That would be hard to get out of the wood. It would leave an auburn stain behind.

Eden, breathing heavily and standing before me, didn't smell sweet anymore. She smelt of blood and sweat. Her forehead sparkled beneath the yellow light bulb.

'Promise me she was happy,' I said. 'We can't eat them unless they're happy.'

'You're hungry, aren't you? As hungry as Mama and me?' Eden asked.

I nodded.

'And you don't want any more of those horrible soggy pasta shells or freezer chips?' she asked.

I shook my head.

A toothy smile crawled across Eden's mouth. 'She was as happy as we could make her. Comfortable even, kept inside that broken body. There's nothing we could've done for this stray. She was at death's door. Moments away from the dark. Moments away from being a useless piece of roadkill. We deserve better than roadkill, don't we?'

'Yes,' I said, but there was a twang beneath my sternum and it pounded on my flesh, trying to beat its way out from under my ribs. Something told me *No, we don't deserve better*. I tried to picture the stray falling asleep with her twisting black hair, yellow bursts of dandelion petals and the gleam of sweat across her forehead. Drifting away into a final dream.

'Your mama is hard at work now, putting her blood, sweat and tears into readying the meat so we can eat well for the next week or so. You should knock on that door, thank her, and ask her if she wants help tidying up. We should be grateful for this blessing. And you should be proud of yourself for leading the stray back here to our homestead. You, Little One, you did this.' Eden's thumb brushed my cheekbone hard. She felt warm. 'And we're so proud of you.' She relaxed a moment later and her hand pulled away. 'Off you go.' She patted my back, nudging me towards the door.

Mama usually did the bloody stuff.

Eden nudged me again, pushing me closer. My bare feet stepped in the small puddles of blood Eden had left behind. It was cold as it curdled between my toes. The door seemed bigger than it usually did when I knocked on its wooden panels.

'Mama?' I asked. From behind the door, I heard a crunch of bone. 'Mama, Eden's sent me to help.' The blood between my toes had already started to congeal and crust.

When the door opened, Mama was wearing a pair of old jeans, a faded T-shirt, yellow rubber gloves and a plastic apron. She should have been nice and clean, but her knees were red from working on all fours. There was a smudge of blood across her forehead from wiping her brow. Her breath was laboured, shoulders moving up and down. I imagined her lungs were swollen and pressing against her ribs. She was exhausted. Mama wiped a strand of hair from her face, leaving a red stain across her cheek.

'That's very generous of her,' Mama said, smiling at Eden. 'Come on in, then.' It had been so long since I'd been inside.

Mama moved aside. Looking upon the room, I was reminded of what had truly become of her and Papa's marital bedroom. The once-white walls had faded to a cigarette yellow, and the light fittings had been removed. It was an almost vacant space. There was a bed in there, but no mattress or linens adorned its slats. Over the rusted iron frame of the bed were draped the stray's skin and clothes.

There was nothing left of Papa in here. The room was bare, sun-faded wallpaper peeling at its seams. Where there once had been a thick, shaggy carpet, Mama had stretched a plastic sheet over the floorboards. The smell was a harsh mix of bleach and rotting eggs, putrid and impatient to find its way up my nose and crawl into my lungs.

A hook hung from the middle of the ceiling. From it, Mama had fastened the feet of the stray. The carcass had been stripped bare. Beneath it there was a copper basin collecting the blood. Inside, broken-up dandelions and their stems floated in circles, all twisted and twined with hair from the stray's scalp.

I didn't recognise the stray as the woman from the woods anymore.

There was a person there, but all I saw was meat. It

could have been a butcher's pig because what made her *her* had been stripped away with a carving knife and thrown in the bin.

'What do you need me to do?' I asked, looking around the room and stepping over the threshold. I wondered if this was how the room had looked when they pulled the gamekeeper limb from limb to harvest him for meat.

'You could clean up the tarp,' Mama said, pointing to a mop and bucket in the corner. 'Use the washing-up liquid from the kitchen. Fill it up. Warm and soapy.'

I took the bucket and moved to the kitchen. When I looked back, Eden was lying on the floor outside the strays' room and Mama was licking her feet. Eden giggled as the last of the blood came away from the ball of her foot, lapped up by Mama's tongue. I wondered if she would lick the floors clean too.

I filled up the bucket. Warm. Soapy. Just as Mama had asked. When I went back to the strays' room, the hot and thick blanket of iron hit me as I passed over the threshold. I realised, as I watched the carcass swing gently from side to side, that this was an abattoir. The carcass creaked and groaned.

'We're going to clean you up nice and good,' I said, reaching out to the meat. I pressed my hand onto her belly. It was soft and wet. Still warm. 'You didn't die for nothing. You're going to keep our bellies nice and filled.'

Thirty-Eight

When Eden slipped the last bone between her lips, her teeth kept the meat as it slipped out again. She was finally full. Mama and I had been finished for a while but Eden had taken her time with this meal, longer than the last. Now she'd eaten one body, she had an insatiable taste for it. She was hungrier than I'd ever seen a human. Even hungrier than Mama.

'Are you really staying forever?' I asked, nudging my cutlery to the centre of my plate. My fingers traced the edges, wiping up the last of the meaty sauce Eden had made. I put my fingers in my mouth and sucked.

Eden smiled as she dropped the bone on her plate. It met the ceramic with a chime. 'If forever is what I have left.'

'But what about the people from before? Your mama and your friends,' I said, thinking about leaving behind Mama, Abbie and the bus driver. 'Will you miss them?'

'My ma died a long, long time ago. Moments after I was born. She was the first person I killed.'

'Not the gamekeeper?' I asked, looking at Mama, but she was resting her chin in her hand, gazing at Eden. A thread of hair fell in front of her eyes but she was so lost she didn't move it. The draught played with it, tugging it left and right in the quiet.

'I could listen to your stories all day,' Mama said. 'Tell me about your ma.'

'She was called Elaine. And she was a cleaner, travelling from house to house, getting down on her knees to scrub the floors, even when she was pregnant with me. Her big round belly would touch the carpets as she sprayed and scrubbed and brushed. She was always down on her hands and knees. Never stopped working. Her waters broke on the carpet of an elderly man. Pa told me the elderly man didn't kneel to help her as she cried out. No. He watched her keel over and then told her to clean up the mess she'd made. She showed herself out and gave birth on the edge of the pavement. *You made a mess from the beginning*, Pa said to me as he tied my shoelaces before school.' Eden took a breath, swallowing her papa's words. 'He told me that every day. I think Ma was supposed to be there to clean the mess I made. He hated cleaning.'

'Did you love your papa?' I asked.

Her fingers dropped to her plate and fiddled with the bone. It moved between her fingers, which were greasy and smudged with oil from eating with her hands. 'No. But he didn't love me either. It is such a lie that we have to love our own blood.'

Mama took Eden's hand.

142

'He always said what he thought, direct, and as though every word spoken were a proven fact. He was a man with a set way of doing things. I suppose I got that from him. A desire to be dominant and unashamed and understood.'

Mama's hand dipped beneath the table. I knew she was stroking Eden's thighs because Mama used to like it when Papa did that to her. It was a comfort. 'You're a natural storyteller, Eden.'

'So was *she*, apparently. People loved Ma for her stories. And every time I met someone new, and eventually let slip that I killed Ma while I was coming out of her, touching the sun for the very first time, their faces dropped. *I'm sorry*s tumbled from their mouths like broken promises. But I felt nothing. Not sad or angry. I'd accepted that Ma was dead. Like other babies, I was covered in blood and shit, and I had taken too much of her.'

'I didn't love my mama either,' Mama said.

But I loved mine very much. I'd keep her secrets until there was nothing left of me but mulch. I'd led a stray back to our home just to feed her. Kept her belly full and warm. Watching Mama, taking in every feature on her face, her rounded eyes, her small chin, her hardened cheekbones and her Roman nose, I'd give her my beating heart if she really wanted it.

'My mama was a wicked thing. Absolutely hell-bent on getting me into my husband's marriage bed so I could give her grandchildren, but she was gone long before this one came about,' Mama said, pulling a warm smile to her mouth. 'And thank goodness too, because, Little One, you are all mine.'

'We can belong to each other,' Eden said, holding out a hand to each of us. Mama rested her palm in Eden's. I reached over the table. Eden squeezed us both tight. 'And you can stay our Little One forever.'

Eden put her stare on me and did not move it. Her eyes were large and still, shimmering beneath the light and taking in every detail of my face.

Thirty-Nine

The couch wasn't a comfortable place to sleep. My back ached where the springs pressed into my spine. There were no noises coming from Mama and Eden's room. I wondered if, while Eden dreamt, she enjoyed the bed I'd once called my own. I had slept in that room since the day of my birth. I had spent my nights there, warm and cold, listening to the rare traffic that passed us by.

I crept out from beneath my blanket and neared the bedroom. The door was ajar. They spent more time in there than ever, whispering to one another beneath the blanket, but now they slept soundly. The scent of dead stray lingered in the air still. Not even spices could overcome that smell.

Inside the bedroom, the two single cast-iron beds were pushed together, forming a nest for Mama and Eden to dream inside. Eden slept near the centre, slipping down between the gap, but Mama held on to her, wrapping arms and legs around her waist to keep her safe and warm. But secretly I think Mama was scared Eden would leave us.

I couldn't imagine life without Eden now. Even though she'd only been with us for a short time, it felt like she could slip away at any moment. And I wondered what would remain once she was gone. Mama would be silent for weeks. She would neglect herself again, consuming stray after stray after stray.

Eden was lying straight and still on the mattress. Her hair was loose, strands splayed out across her pillow. Soft curls brushed over the contours of the linens but her face was solemn. Cheeks sunken, her lips formed an apathetic line above her chin, and even her eyes, gently closed, were still beneath their lids, unmoving, undreaming.

Mama shifted, kicking the blanket away with her feet. It was warmer than usual. Humid. Closing my eyes, I pictured moving across the dark towards them, shuffling beneath the blanket and wrapping up warm. I missed the feeling of being warm inside Mama's skin.

Mama shifted again, rolling away from Eden and settling near the edge of the bed, pressing her cheek into the softness of the linens. The blankets would be like silk because they desperately needed a wash. They were always softened by use.

Eden's eyes opened and landed on me. In the dark, her pupils were large and black. 'Can't you sleep, Little One?' she whispered.

'My back hurts,' I said. 'From the couch.'

Eden sat up and came away from the mattress. Beneath

her nightgown, her skin pricked and goosebumps formed where the moonshine hit her flesh. I wanted to reach
out and touch every single bump. I couldn't stop myself.
My fingers traced her forearm, brushing up and down.

'Will I look like you when I'm older?' I whispered. 'Or
will I look like Mama?'

'You'll look like both of us,' she said, crouching down
and putting her hands through my hair. 'Being a mama
is a big job. I wasn't sure I was cut out for a daughter, but
with you . . .' Eden's knees buckled slowly and she sat
with me on the rug, still combing her fingers through
my hair. 'You're a very special little girl. You are quiet
and rarely say what you're thinking but it is written
across your face. I feel as though we've known each other
longer than our hearts have beaten.'

'I think Mama is in love with you,' I whispered. 'Even
more love than she had for Papa.'

'I think so too,' she said. 'I think we were made for
one another, formed in the womb with a string pulled
tight between us.' I pictured Eden curled up in a warm
belly, sleeping soundly, dreaming the way she was supposed to.

'Did you come looking for us?' I asked. 'I saw the
newspaper on the front seat of your car.'

Eden's fingers fell away from my hair. 'Have you been
looking through my things?' she asked.

I shook my head.

'I had a feeling about those names. I wondered if they'd
join the list of people who go astray in these parts.' Eyes
closing, Eden let her shoulders fall as a breath came from

her lips. 'I remember pressing my nose to the newspaper and smelling the letters of their names. Were they your strays, Little One?'

'I don't know,' I said. 'I can't remember.'

'Try to,' she whispered.

I furrowed my brow and closed my eyes. *Alison Blacklock. Kayley Radcliffe.* We didn't keep a ledger of names. We rarely asked for them. Names were not important. I thought back through every stray who'd come to our door, trying to picture their faces, but I couldn't quite form them. I remembered pieces of them; shapes, smells, mouths, chins, noses and eyes. 'I can't. There might have been two girls a long time ago.'

There it was again, the black in her eyes that wasn't usually there. 'I didn't know I'd find *you* here,' Eden said, fingers combing through my hair. 'Looking at the names and headlines in those newspapers, I felt called here. I have the strongest feeling that I was meant to find you and your mama.'

'Mama told me there's no reason for anything. She told me that things just happen.'

'That is where your mama and I differ in our philosophies. Everything happens for a reason. Something too big and too thoughtful for us to conceive. We're just animals, like little rabbits from the woods. Humanity, Margot, it is made up. Our empathy is waning as every second passes because it's not supposed to come so naturally to mortal creatures.'

'I don't think that's true,' I said. Something in her words was inhuman. I thought of sitting in the front seat of the school bus, and the first time the bus driver had seen me all bruised up from my brush with the bullies. I thought of Abbie. The grief she carried around with her and how it weighed her down.

'All you need to know is that I will always protect us. You and Mama were being too loud. Taking two instead of one,' Eden said, standing up. 'Only ever go for the lone stray.' Her finger pressed the tip of my nose. 'I promise you, Margot, I will make sure your belly is full and your mouth is never empty. This roof will stay over our heads because I will hold it up. I will protect you both. Mama couldn't do it on her own any longer. She needs me.'

Before Eden, Mama had been fraying at the edges like a rug coming apart, but something told me Eden wanted to tug at the threads until she wholly unravelled.

Forty

A long lunchtime led Abbie and me to the muddy corners of the school field. I'd followed her to the fence that kept us bound within and settled with her where the grasses were unruly. There was a heavy grey cloud hanging over us. We waited for rain.

Abbie's fingers were caked in mud. Dirt crushed underneath her fingernails and pasted into the grooves curving over her knuckles. When I looked at her face, she seemed different. There was something less put-together about her. The green ribbon I loved was escaping out of her hair. Blonde strands poked out from her scalp like a wildflower crushed beneath a garden stone.

Abbie's breath was heavier as she toyed with the mud. She was closer to wild than ever before but there was something beautiful about her when she was untethered like this. It was the way we were supposed to be.

I pulled a worm out from its muddy burrow and held it between my fingers. It shifted, trying to escape. 'I wonder what its name is,' I said, looking at its skin. 'I can't see any eyes.'

'They don't have any,' Abbie said, hunching her back. Her knees were brown, covered with swipes of dirt from the ground. 'They only know if it's light or dark. They don't have ears either.'

'I wonder what that's like,' I said.

'You should put it back where it belongs,' Abbie said, wiping her muddy hands on her soaked school skirt. It was grey and came down to her knees in pleats. Once, the skirt had been something so ordinary. So human. But Abbie and her mud made it seem less so.

'I don't want to,' I said, taking the worm from my fingers and holding it in my palm. I reached over to Abbie. My fingers grazed her chin, closing her mouth. 'What if I like keeping it in my hands.'

Abbie scurried around some more in the dirt, pulling out a stone from the earth. She cleared it free of mud and put it in her pocket. 'Those creatures belong in the dark. They like to burrow through the mud,' she said, taking the worm and holding it. It wiggled in her palm. She smiled, placing it down, back in the dirt. 'Can I come to yours for tea one day?' she asked, staring as the worm pushed its way back through the mud.

'Mama doesn't like me having friends over,' I said.

'Why not?' Abbie asked. 'I *always* have friends over for tea.'

I shrugged, imagining what a home-cooked meal would taste like from Abbie's table. 'Maybe I could have tea at your house one day.' I built pictures in my head. A tea table in the garden of the gamekeeper's house. Yellow napkins. Paper plates. Tumblers of sweet summer juice. I imagined Abbie's mama made the nicest food.

'Well, I want you to,' she said. 'But Mam thinks you're weird.' Her words came quick and sharp. 'She found the wishing hex you made me. The one with the shoelaces.' Abbie's fingers nervously toyed with the mud.

My body stilled. I wondered if Abbie's mama would recognise her husband's shoelaces. 'I don't understand,' I said.

'Mam took it away,' Abbie said. 'She doesn't like ugly things. I tried to fish it out of the bin after tea but the twine had cod all caught in it from the fish fingers.'

Anger took hold. A tight feeling, like I wanted to vomit. 'I hate her,' I said. 'There's nothing bad about a wish.' I hated adults. I hated adults who feared what they couldn't understand.

'Our wishes will still come true.' Abbie's hand took mine and squeezed. 'I know they will. And then, one day, we can have all the teatimes we like.'

I smiled. *Our.* Me and Abbie had an *our.*

'And when Da comes home, Mam will stop being so uptight.'

'You think he's out there somewhere?' I asked, looking up at the sky. The clouds overhead were gathering thick and hard. There was something heavy hanging over us.

Abbie stopped, looking at the ditch she'd dug out to find stones. Her scattered gaze settled on me. I saw the dark in her eyes. That grief. 'I'll never stop looking.'

Eden had told Mama to curb her hunger, and I

wondered if that was even possible. But Mama had made a big mistake. She had taken a stray someone noticed was missing. That someone was like a dog with a bone. I suddenly felt nervous around Abbie. I put my hand on my chest and took a deep breath. Something about the way Abbie reached for my hands in the mud silenced me. Her fingers coiled around mine and squeezed tight.

Forty-One

When I got off the school bus, I wandered to the banks of the beck. The slopes were slippy today from the rain. The hemlock flowering by the water's edge tickled my calves as I fumbled down the banks.

Mama loved taking from the ground. She'd always said buying something from the shop was too much of a trip and it would leave a paper trail for someone to follow. She didn't want us to be found in our quiet woodland cove off the roadside. She didn't want a single trace of herself near the towns. She wanted to live off the land. In the quiet.

Mama's silhouette lumbered over the gate and came through the grass. She sat at my side, lying down on the bank. She was wearing the dusty church dress again, but the buttons were relaxed, some left undone, and her sleeves were rolled up to her elbows.

'Do you know how old I am?' Mama asked me. The sun shone over her, bringing out her freckles. She seemed to glow in this light. Around us, drops of rainfall glittered in the grass and flora.

I studied the wrinkles on her face. I didn't see new lines each day, but every few months I noticed there were more than before, and that a few more of her hairs had turned silver. I shook my head.

Mama smiled and put her arm around me. 'I feel like a girl again.'

'Like me?'

Mama nodded. 'Just like you. Eden makes me laugh. In all my life, my lovers have never made me laugh. Not like this. She makes me want to open up the world and see all the hill's contours and the water.'

'Eden told me it was meant to be, Mama. That she was meant to find us here.'

Mama closed her eyes and took a deep breath. The beck currents rushed over the stones at our feet. 'I think it was.' When her eyes opened, she took a deep breath and spoke again. 'Years feel longer when you aren't loved the way you want to be. Or the way you're supposed to be.'

'I've always loved you,' I said, lying back and leaning my head on her shoulder.

Mama kissed my crown and squeezed my hand. 'We all need different sorts of love to make us feel whole. You'll know it too, one day. I'm not just a mother. I'm a whole person.'

I held on tighter and pushed my nose into the fibres of her clothes. Even if she smelt of rot, I held on. 'I love you, Mama,' I said.

'I know, Little One,' she said, combing my hair and dipping her toes into the water. Her hand slipped away from mine as she got up and walked across the beck's smooth stones to the other bank. Mama's feet fitted perfectly over the rocks as she found her way to the flora growing near the water's edge. Her fingers brushed over the hemlock petals, toying with the stems. She plucked some hemlock and put it in her pocket. 'Why do you need hemlock?' I asked. 'We have plenty of stray left at the house.'

'It's always good to have some at hand. Just in case,' she said, stroking the petals of the hemlock beneath her chin. 'I've been thinking about making a hex for Eden. Something like a magnet. Something to keep her close.'

'Why would you need poison to keep her close? Why not something beautiful like a fern? Or a dandelion?'

'Why would I risk it?' Mama asked, holding her dress above the babbling currents. 'Fern won't keep her near. It's not urgent enough. It needs to be something desperate. Something brutal.'

'Eden won't leave us, Mama,' I said. 'She told me so.'

Mama's arms folded. There was a small breeze going by that lifted her dress. 'What did she say to you?'

I tried to remember but all I could recall was the pale skin, the moonshine and the nightgown keeping goosebumps hidden beneath. She was like a ghost.

'Well?'

'I think she said she'd stay with us so she could keep our bellies full.'

'But what did she say about me?'

'I can't remember,' I said.

Mama rolled her eyes. 'You need to start listening properly.'

'She loves you, Mama,' I said. 'I know she does.'

'Does she love me the way I love her or does she just desire me? You have to know the difference,' Mama said. She ground her teeth. Her expression fell as the water moved at her feet. 'Your papa, he was infatuated with me, and then, just like that, he wasn't. It's a quick spark, not a slow-burning flame. I'll never make that mistake again.'

I couldn't help but think about how quickly she'd fallen out of love with the gamekeeper. I wondered if her love for Eden would keep her full. Mama stood still in the beck, loosely hanging on to a few pluckings of hemlock. Her eyes were still on the currents as they jostled over the stones to reach the river, the estuary, and eventually the sea. I stepped over the stones and wrapped my arms around her. Her palm pressed on my back and rubbed my spine, following the contours of my vertebrae.

'I know I can be selfish. My feelings get the better of me,' Mama said.

*

Mama led me back to the house. We dried our feet on the front steps with an old towel, scrubbing the mud away from the wrinkles and creases on our feet. A warm smell came through the window. Something that made this place feel like home.

Eden was cooking again. The scent of rosemary over-powered the blood. Eden smiled at Mama as we went inside. 'Breast tonight,' she said. 'I've pulled up a few turnips. They're small but they'll make a nice side.'

The meal that night was beautiful. She'd cooked the wounded stray well but I could still taste the pain the stray had felt in her final moments. My mouth didn't water quite as much as it did when the strays were happy. I thought of the stray's hazelnut eyes as I swallowed a piece of meat and recounted the steps I'd taken to bring her back to our homestead. We'd stepped over a few logs and tree roots that snaked out of the ground. We'd passed the treeline, come back across the beck, and then fumbled through the gate. I'd brought her here, where she came to hang from a meat hook until there was nothing left but bits.

We'd buried her things out the back. The ground was starting to get too full, ready to spit out the bones and trinkets the old strays had left behind. We'd have to dig a new hole soon or everything would overflow. It was all too close to the surface.

Forty-Two

Beneath the hot weekend sun, Mama, Eden and I walked the length of the beck until it forked off into the river. There was a light breeze but the currents were strong, with white foam curdling over the surface and spilling onto the banks.

We walked barefoot in the wild grass, fingers outstretched to catch the passing summer flora. The leaves came from their stems with a soft tug. We put the clippings in our hair as we walked, plaiting stems and roots into our braids.

We'd spent the morning putting a picnic together, packing all the small veggies we'd grown in our garden and a loaf of crusty bread Eden had made. There were still traces of flour through her hair that caught the sun as we walked through the glades.

Eden wore Mama's church dress. It was hanging from her shoulders. She took a deep breath and looked towards the sun. When she squinted, her eyes looked gold in the light.

Mama wore a worn-out T-shirt and a pair of bike shorts. She'd specifically said she didn't want the sunburn to tease her shoulders, but Eden had a rebuttal: she wanted us to feel the red-hot sting of sunburn so we could peel our skin away and find new freckles.

'Where are we going?' I asked, wondering where the river would lead us.

'We'll go until we find somewhere soft enough to dip,' Eden said. 'I've not swum in wild waters for so long.'

Ahead, there was a clearing. A place where the river bent into a curve, but the currents pulsed to a calm. When the sun hit the pool and the trees sprinkled new leaves onto its surface, the water looked like copper. Pine needles from upstream and newly formed scum drifted over the water. The pool forming at the bend was deep and still. It looked like ale, a rich brown with shimmers of gold.

'Do you want to come in with me?' Eden asked Mama, nipping at the buttons on her dress. 'The water will be cool.'

Mama dropped her bag in the grass by the bank and walked towards Eden. Her hands brushed Eden's forearms until they found the nape of her neck and coaxed her close for a kiss. An earnest one.

I nestled in the grass as Eden pulled Mama's T-shirt away and helped her shimmy out of her bike shorts. Eden slid out of her church dress as they walked to the river holding hands. Dipping into the pool, they swam about the clearing. Their teeth chattered out laughter as they splashed one another.

Eden took a deep breath and sank into the water. A few seconds passed. As midges skipped over the surface, Mama watched Eden's hair waver beneath. When she came back up for air, her hair soaked down her back.

'Come closer to the bank, Little One,' Mama called. 'I want you in sight.'

When I came through the grass, they were clearer. I could see their pale bodies beneath the ale-like water. They reminded me of selkies. Scattered in freckles. Embraced by soft seal skin curving in at their waists. I wondered if I'd look like that one day. Wild and beautiful.

Mama thought for a moment, dipping her palm atop the water and watching the ripples spread. 'I'm starting to get hungry again,' she said, looking at Eden.

'Contain yourself,' Eden said, smiling to herself and catching her breath on a rock. Her shoulders were in the sun, glistening where the water's reflective shimmers coated her skin.

'If we wait the afternoon out, a stray might come close. We could lead it back to the house with us,' Mama said, swimming up behind Eden and holding her tight. She kissed every drop of water on her shoulder blades.

'No more strays,' Eden said. 'Not for a few weeks. We've plenty left of the last one. The world will notice if we take and take. Consume in moderation – someone no one will notice go missing. That's how we stay safe.'

Mama pulled away. 'But I'm hungry,' she said. 'Would you deny me when my belly is empty?'

'But it's not empty,' Eden said, swimming towards her

and pressing her hand over Mama's stomach.

'Eden is right,' I said.

Mama watched Eden, dipping her mouth beneath the water.

'We're a family,' Eden said, trailing her fingers over Mama's wet cheeks. 'If someone found us, imagine what they'd do to our Little One.' When Eden spoke, Mama hung on to her every word. 'People notice more than you think. They're nosy. Always involving themselves in business that isn't their own. This is how we keep ourselves safe. From them.'

I dipped my toes into the shallows. Mama relaxed, pulling closer to Eden. Their skin looked as white as snow beneath the water. When the hot sunlight came through the clouds, they shared a kiss. This was true love; fighting and then crashing into one another again like waves.

Forty-Three

The bus driver was singing as he drove us children and changelings home, but his voice was croaky from years of smoking. It always sounded like he was singing gruffly beneath his breath. His voice was old, older than any voice I'd ever known, and as I watched him move the steering wheel, glancing at the junctions, I wondered about all the words his mouth had spoken in his life.

'Do you know every song?' I asked. 'Every song ever written?'

The bus driver smiled. The rain washed over the window, casting shadows across his face, but the wipers brushed them away. 'I know a lot of songs,' he said, slowing down to curve the length of the road. 'But I don't know all of them. There are many songs lost. Songs the villagers sang hundreds of years ago, but none of us can remember them anymore. They're gone forever.'

'If we forgot them, they mustn't have been very good,' I said.

'Things are forgotten all the time. Good and bad.

We've forgotten all the lives people have lived and all the quiet folk, but it doesn't mean they weren't important.'

I wouldn't ever forget the bus driver. He was too important. I looked at his arms. There was lots of hair poking out from his skin and a smudgy tattoo ebbing across his flesh. His body looked old but his face sometimes looked young, even with the wrinkles coming in around his eyes and mouth. I wanted to remember every line. Every bend. Every freckle. I would not forget the bus driver.

When the bus pulled in to my stop, I gathered my things. I was one of the last to be taken home. There were a few quiet changelings left in the back, but they were keeping to themselves today. It was the rain. There was something about pouring rain that made us all quiet and watchful.

'Is everything alright at home?' the bus driver asked, pulling up the handbrake and leaning over the steering wheel.

I wondered what I must look like to him. A small girl, hair covering her face, gappy teeth and laddered tights. My school jumper was just a little too tight. The bus driver noticed me. I knew he'd never forget me either.

'What do you mean?' I asked.

'Are you happy?' His hands gestured up the path, past the gate and towards the little pebble-dashed cottage.

'I'm hungry,' I said. 'I'm always hungry.'

The bus driver smiled. 'What was in that lunchbox of yours?'

'Breadsticks.' But really my belly grumbled for leftover fingers. Severed. The nails plucked from their beds.

'And you're eating your dinner?' he asked. 'You have to eat it all, lick the plate clean if you want to grow big and strong.'

I don't always get dinner, I wanted to say, but I knew that one sentence would spill more than a river of secrets from me. Secrets the bus driver didn't need to know. *The cupboards are sometimes empty and I've seen silverfish in the jars of rice we keep on our shelves. The food is running out. It's running out fast. There isn't much of the stray left at all.* 'Mama is tired a lot,' I said. 'But she makes sure my belly is full.'

The bus driver nodded. I didn't know if he believed me but my words were enough to satisfy him. Mama was right. Men always believe lies. The bus driver yawned, looking up at the house. His eyebrow cocked. 'Always found that little place very odd, you know.'

I stayed quiet, sitting on the front seat and waiting for him to let me go. The buckles on my school bag grazed my knees as my legs kicked gently to pass the seconds.

There was a pensive gaze upon the bus driver's face. 'Over the last twenty years, driving this route for the school, I've seen this home live all its different lives. Once an old woman and her cat lived there. Then the next tenant was a lone man. Then your ma and pa moved in and it wasn't long before I'd see you playing in the beck and mud by the front of the house. It's strange what you pick up about people while you're driving. You notice things a little bit more.'

It was odd to think of our home living a different life to the one it lived now.

165

'Don't let this old man bore you,' he said after a moment of quiet. 'Off you pop.' The bus driver smiled to himself.

As I hopped off the front seat and closed the door, I took a deep breath of the petrol in the air. I closed my eyes and listened to the languid sound of the school bus becoming more distant on the tarmac.

I loved that sound. It reminded me of the bus driver.

Forty-Four

When the stars came out, shimmering in the blackened sky, Mama and Eden were at odds. Eden stood on the rug in the living room, pulling her clothes back over her bare shoulders. When Mama spoke, Eden's eyes rolled back into her head. The whites of her eyes had red veins coursing through them. I wondered if she would pack her bags and leave. She seemed flighty. Exhausted with Mama's whining. Impatient. She wanted us both to do as we were told.

'I'm tired of waiting,' Mama said. 'How can you deny us what is natural? What we are craving?' Mama grabbed Eden's arm and squeezed. Her knuckles whitened.

Eden looked down at Mama's grasp and pulled herself free. 'Your belly will be full again. It will. I promise you,' Eden said. 'Just be patient.'

Mama sank into the couch and put her head in her hands. She wanted Eden to cave. Knowing she wouldn't stop until she got exactly what she wanted, Mama summoned her tears. They trickled down her cheeks. Her skin shimmered. Mama did not wipe her tears away.

Eden was always steadfast. She knelt at Mama's feet. 'I'm doing what's best for us,' she said, brushing her thumb over Mama's skin to wipe away the crocodile tears. 'I'm looking after you.'

'You don't know what's best for me,' Mama said through gritted teeth. 'Maybe you don't know me as well as you think you do.' Her jaw strained. Biting her tongue, she pressed her teeth hard into her own flesh. Mama wanted blood. Her fingers curled over her scalp and clutched onto her roots. This was Mama's anger. She tried to contain it, but she was never able to. It always slipped out.

'Listen to me, Ruth,' Eden said. 'I'm just trying to love you. And protect you.'

'Eden wants to keep us safe. What if someone notices us taking lots of strays for our dinner? They'll follow the smoke to our chimney, Mama. Abbie talks about her papa at school all the time. She won't let him go.' The words came tumbling out before I could stop them.

Mama's head lifted from her hands and I saw the deep black of her eyes. She was wolfish as she leant forward, hurtling off the couch towards me. Her fist took my school collar. 'What have you said to her?' Mama spat. 'That stupid little stray friend of yours.'

'Nothing,' I said.

'She will be our next one if you don't nip this in the bud. I don't want you talking to her.'

'But she's my friend,' I said.

'What did you just say to me?' Mama asked. But she didn't want an answer. She wanted her Little One to cower, obedient and silent. 'You're not to make friends.

You're not to draw attention to yourself like this. You're supposed to go unnoticed.' Mama bit down on her bottom lip with the sharpened edges of her two front teeth.

I kept my head low before glancing at Eden. *Help me. Do something.*

'Look at me,' Mama said, pulling my chin up and holding it tight between her fingers. Then my cheek stung. It was hot and crackling. Mama left a clean slap across my cheek. The sort of slap that shocks you into quiet. My ears rang and around me the world blurred as I pressed my hand over the mark she'd left behind, blushing and red. It felt like a thousand tiny bee stings.

One of Mama's special kisses.

'Ruth,' Eden hissed. But the world was a haze, coming back to me in pieces. 'Come to me.' Eden took her hand and pulled her into an embrace. Her fingers moved through Mama's hair, tugging at the knots until they came free.

'I didn't want to hit her,' Mama said, weeping. 'You see how she says things just to spite me?'

'I'm sorry, Mama,' I said, my hand still perched on my cheek. 'I haven't said anything to the stray. I promise.' My eyes watered, bubbling over the crests of my cheeks.

'Don't speak to your mama,' Eden said, as though Mama were hers and not mine. Eden's voice was steady. Together, they seemed to float at the centre of the rug, bare feet brushing the fibres. They wanted to become one body. One set of lungs and one heart to share while it beat the blood about their arteries.

I felt the unspoken words in the room. Mama didn't

want me. She only wanted Eden. There was not enough room in her heart for the both of us. I wondered what use I was now that she had Eden. If it was her and Eden that would beckon strays to this homestead, and tempt them into their bellies.

'You are the most important thing in my life,' Mama whispered to Eden as they held each other. 'I don't want you to leave me now you've seen this ugliness.'

'You are whole and complicated. You are a *real* human. Not a piece of meat. I love all of you.' The words sounded rehearsed. 'You can show me the blackest part of your heart and I will not flinch.'

I stepped out the front door. The sun's heat beat down on my back as I stole a glance at Mama and Eden. Their hands explored one another's bodies and they found themselves fumbling into their bedroom, crashing from wall to wall, lips meeting, teeth biting.

Forgotten, I slipped out into the wild.

*

My fingers pruned from hours spent soaking in the beck. Midnight had come and passed. Walking back towards the house, through the gate and the long grass, I bounced over the nettles and collected little pink stings on my ankles. I stopped on my way to the door.

There was something in the trap.

A little rabbit was fumbling around in the fishing wire to fetch the carrot I'd left knotted inside.

It was already bleeding. Tomorrow we would feast.

Forty-Five

The meal before me looked beautiful. Mama had washed our plates until they shone. The faded silver edges of the china shimmered beneath the candlelight. At the centre of the plate, a quarter-slice of pie surrounded itself with vegetables. Long green beans, cut-up carrots and roasted potatoes. The pastry was puffed up and copper, crowned with a perfect golden-brown crust. It crackled as I pulled away a forkful.

When I took my first bite, I closed my eyes. From inside, cream sauce spilt out. The rabbit's meat was tender. It was perfect. Even more beautiful than any stray we'd eaten over the years. I chewed and swallowed.

'Do you like it?' Eden asked me. 'I wanted to savour the last of the stray we have. Keep it for a rainy day. So, Mrs Rabbit will have to do.'

I nodded as I took another forkful.

'Don't forget your vegetables,' Mama said, poking her fork over my carrots.

I shovelled up some vegetables and put them in my

mouth. Mama and Eden hardly touched theirs. The meals sat patiently on their plates as they watched me eat, like they knew something I didn't.

'What?' I asked.

'Well, it was your rabbit,' Eden said. 'We wanted you to enjoy the food you helped put on this table.' She smiled, resting her chin in the curve of her palm.

Mama smiled too, but it was reluctant.

For the first time, I noticed my portion was as large as theirs. They had shared their spoils with me. 'I love you,' I said. 'I wish to never grow up. I want things to stay this way forever.'

Mama summoned a stiff smile and took the cutlery in her hands. Though she closed her eyes with delight as she took that first bite, she only wanted stray. Of that, I was certain.

'I'm sorry, Mama,' I said. 'I'm sorry I wasn't careful enough at school.'

'I'm sure you've learnt your lesson,' she said, not looking up from her meal.

I had learnt my lesson. There was a bruise on my cheekbone to show for it. And it still hurt when I prodded it with my finger. Blue and purple and brown.

'That's done now, though. Isn't it?' Eden said, taking Mama's hand and kissing her knuckles. 'Families fight all the time. It's only natural, stuck under this little roof, all cramped in together. A few bruises are bound to pop up now and then. Proof that we love each other, still.'

'I really am sorry,' I said.

'You're forgiven, Margot,' Eden said. 'I forgive you and Mama forgives you too.'

I ate the rest of my pie and licked the plate clean. The cream was cold on the surface of the plate by the end of the meal, but it still tasted just as good. I'd be putting another carrot in the trap tomorrow morning. 'I didn't know rabbit would be this nice,' I said.

'Oh, this is nothing. Have you tried one of their kits before? The babies are the most tender,' Eden said, closing her eyes and imagining a little baby rabbit in her mouth. I felt a pang of guilt go through me as I shuffled uncomfortably in my seat. 'I haven't had a kit in an awfully long time. Hard little buggers to catch. But worth the fuss. To feel a little baby inside you is like nothing else.' Eden put her eyes on me and did not move them. They came with the weight of stone as they fixed on my cheeks. Mama watched her intently.

I remembered that day at school where we children had stumbled in to find little kits hung upon our coat pegs. The memory brought with it the smell. Iron.

This was the secret I'd carried with me.

I remembered catching those kits while it was dark. Leaving little traps. Rusty nails from Papa's toolbox. Old fishing wire. Rat poison from the cupboards. Some of them were still too young to know how to use those little legs. I cornered them in shallow burrows and warrens deep in the woods and let little Marcus take the fall. I'd wanted to scare the boys from the back of the bus. But they delighted in the blood and bodies.

'Tell us one of your stories,' Mama said, dropping her knife and fork on the table.

Eden's eyes scanned the ceiling as she searched for something. 'Do you remember the story of the rabbit woman and how she first made flour?'

I nodded.

The candlelight flickered over Eden's skin. She looked like fire. 'There's more to that story. The rabbit woman stayed in the burrow near the forest clearing and continued to live out her days. She had created flour from bone. And from her flour, she made the most beautiful cakes and pies. She used elderflower, pine and snowdrops to flavour them. Anything she could find, really. Even nettles. Early in the mornings, she crawled out from her burrow, a shadow of the person she'd once been, and made for the markets to sell her cakes and wares.' Eden took a breath. 'Creature folk came from far and wide to taste her delicacies. She told them of her flour, keeping the bones it was made with a secret. She showed them the fine, soft powder, letting people rub it between their fingertips and dab it on their mouths. The world marvelled.'

'What happened next?' I asked, leaning over the table.

'She enjoyed watching people eat her cakes and pies. If they'd known it was made from their kin, they would have spat it out into the dirt, but they kept coming back and stuffing their faces. The rabbit woman knew that people were animals.'

I tilted my head.

Mama smiled.

'The rabbit woman kept to her burrow, waiting for other rabbits and kits to pass her by. When they did, she'd bring them in from the cold and keep them warm by a fire. It wasn't long before their furs were hung to dry out, their meat was being roasted for the pies, and their bones were being filed down into flour. She stayed in her burrow forever.' Eden paused for a sip of her wine. 'If they'd only known what they were eating,' she laughed.

*

The world had darkened and the candles were blown out. Unclean plates were left upon the tablecloth. Embers simmering in the hearth crackled.

'How did you first hear the story of the rabbit woman?' I asked Eden as she pulled a blanket over my shoulders and snuggled me into the couch cushions.

'I've travelled for a very long time,' she said. 'I was born in a small town and I couldn't wait to leave. All that time, I just needed a reason to settle.' Her hand snaked through the blankets and held mine. 'I've met so many people in my life.' There was sadness in her voice. A grief. 'But none of them will remember who I am, whether I was a passing face or a lover. But Ruth will remember me forever.'

'Where have you been?' I asked. 'Have you travelled far?'

'I've walked the banks of the rivers in France. I've touched the peaks of mountains beyond Europe. I've been to the street markets of Bangkok and tried flavours that don't exist here yet.'

'I've never left this place.'

'Let me tell you the only truth you need to know. The scenery looks different but the people are all the same.' Then she closed her mouth and sat at the end of the sofa. 'Greedy. Self-righteous. Cowardly. Hungry to be loved and wanted. Attention starved.' Her silhouette was like a shadow. Eden was dark until she turned her head. I saw the twinkle that always shone in her eyes, morning or night. Light or dark. 'Nothing mattered until I met her.' Her cheeks went red. That wasn't supposed to slip out, but it was shared with me, secret or not. Though she didn't hide her love for Mama, that confession was a precious, quiet thought.

'I wish I could see the things you've seen. And hear the stories you've heard.' I rolled over and snuggled into my blanket.

'Goodnight,' Eden said. Her fingers caressed my forehead, pushing wayward hairs behind my ear. Her skin was warm, touching the edges of the bruise forming on my cheek. At her touch, the bruise ached.

'Night.'

'What will you dream of?' she asked, standing up and brushing down her dress.

I squeezed my eyes shut. 'I dream of the strays.'

There was a groan on the floorboard as Eden stopped in her tracks.

'Last night,' I whispered, 'I saw the gamekeeper. There were pieces of him missing. Fingers and toes. And his eyes were large. He said he missed *his Abbie*. And I told him she was mine now and that I would look after her.' The words had fallen out before I could stop them.

Eden's breath was heavy. 'Abbie,' she whispered, feeling the shape of the name in her mouth. 'She sounds like trouble to me. I wonder if one day you'll bring her over for tea.' Eden's mouth formed a wicked smile.

Looking at my toes, I shook my head.

'Don't you think she'd enjoy a nice broth? Meat stewed in stock made from her father's bones?'

I bit down on my tongue. Hard. I wanted it to burst. 'I don't want her to come over. I don't even want to be her friend.'

'No?' Eden asked, moving slowly in the dark. 'Then she's not *yours*, is she?' Her breath was cool on my cheeks. 'You're to leave her be. Or I might bake her in a pie.' There it was again – the playful smile pulling at the corner of her mouth. Eden left a kiss on my cheek. Her lips lingered on my skin, leaving the graze of her teeth as she closed her mouth. 'Goodnight, Little One.'

'Goodnight.'

Eden walked back to the bedroom and closed the door behind her. I heard her crawl into bed and share whispers with Mama. As I fell into a deep slumber, I wondered if it would be another night of blackness or if I would chase the strays into the shadowy corners again.

Forty-Six

A rainy Sunday hung over our homestead.

When I looked out at the rain, it reminded me of Abbie. She always smelt like rain, as though she'd been out in a storm and got soaked. I remembered a time when we'd been ushered in from the playground and her hair was wet, clinging to her cheeks and neck. She looked like something from a storybook. Her eyes were like rain, too. A muddy blue, made of grey puddles and splashes.

'What are you thinking of?' Mama asked, coming to the window and sitting with me. Her fingers combed through my hair. They slid through because it was greasy near my scalp.

'Nothing,' I said.

Mama yanked on the ends of my hair. 'Don't lie to me.'

'I'm thinking of Abbie,' I said. 'She loves the rain.' My fingernail played with a stray splinter on the window-pane. It was sharp and pointed. 'But I won't speak to her at school anymore, Mama. I promise.' I missed her even when no time had passed. Even when I knew I'd see her the very next day.

'Don't play with the splinters,' Mama said, pulling my fingers away and kissing them. Her mouth was soft and warm. 'You know to keep well away from her. Take those feelings and hide them. Push them down. Keep them in the dark. Keep them where no one can see them.'

'It hurts when I try to forget her,' I said.

'I know,' Mama said. Her face was still, watching the rain too. 'I've had to do that before. Put my heartbreak somewhere I could not see it. It's sometimes for the best.'

'Papa?' I asked.

Mama nodded and brushed my hair away from my face.

'He's forgotten about us, hasn't he?' I asked.

'It's hard to do it all on your own. Sometimes I don't want to anymore.' Mama leant her forehead against the window. The sound of the rain was like small stones hitting the glass. 'I've been so hungry. And only now I have Eden do I feel like I can fill the space in here.' Mama paused, pressing her hand above her ribcage. 'But the space just keeps getting bigger.'

'Bigger?'

'I think there's only one thing that will fill it for good, but sometimes I worry nothing will ever be enough. That my eyes will wander for the next stray. And then the next. Until there isn't another human left alive.' Mama paused. 'I'll be alone on this earth. And the hole will keep getting bigger and bigger.'

Footsteps came through the home. Eden was light on her feet as she wiped down her muddy knees and slid her hands over Mama's belly. She pressed a kiss on Mama's blushing cheek. 'What are my girls talking about?'

'Mama is hungry again,' I said.

'I want a stray,' she said. 'It's not just the taste. It's how you catch them and prepare them. It's exploring their wishes and dreams and regrets.'

'I miss it too,' Eden said.

Together, we looked out. Warm days were shy. Rain had overtaken the sun.

'We'll have another stray again soon, I promise,' Eden said earnestly. 'I cross my heart.'

'Hope to die,' Mama said, turning to face Eden. Their lips were close enough to touch.

'Stick a needle in my eye,' Eden whispered to Mama's mouth. 'We'll eat well again soon, my Ruth. We will.'

I imagined Abbie at the bottom of the path, chasing up the road, looking for her papa. When I pictured her, she wasn't wearing a raincoat. She was letting herself get soaked. Then, just like that, as eager as I was to see her face again, she vanished in the rain and mist.

That night, I knew I'd spend my whole sleep thinking of her and that green ribbon she always wore. My belly rumbled, and all of a sudden I wondered what she would taste like.

Forty-Seven

The rain didn't stop that day. It carried through until Monday. From my little plastic chair, I watched the clock hands move. Morning to afternoon. I paid no mind to the changeling boys or to Mr Hill, even when the boys threw the pointed ends of their protractors at the back of my head.

I watched Abbie all the way through times tables. All the way through acrostic poems. All the way through PE – even when the boys tripped me over with their hockey sticks. Abbie's white polo shirt was filling out around her arms. Her chin was more rounded, and her thighs filled her shorts. She'd been eating. With every precise move, she was slow and thoughtful.

Abbie never cried. Her eyes had watered and there had been a few times I'd caught her swallow a lump in her throat, but she never cried. Not once. She was stone. More changeling than child. Still and quiet and absorbing. If Mama had her way, and we took her as a stray, she would taste delicious, even in her grief. But that was a terrible thought.

In the last few moments of the day, we walked towards the school gate. I imagined her sandstone cottage on the hill. Old. It should have been an expensive home, but it was falling apart, giving itself to decay. There was a cracked window near the front door. There was mail stuffed into the letterbox. I pictured bills piling up. Left unopened. Its state of repair had got worse since her papa had disappeared.

Once, Abbie had been the prettiest girl in school, with her well-placed green ribbon and her beautiful hair. Boys liked the way her thighs didn't touch and parents remarked on how thin she was, saying she looked just like her mam. Spindly but bonnie. Saying how she'd break hearts and how her mam must struggle to keep the boys away.

Even though people noted she was rounder, to me, she was just as beautiful. I took her hand. 'We still have half an hour before my bus goes,' I said. 'Do you want to go to the trees?'

Abbie nodded. Together, we followed the mossy wall all the way to the treeline near the school gate. Beneath it, we sought shelter from the rain. 'Mam's started to put all my da's things in boxes. Soon they'll be in the loft. Getting dusty. He hated dust.'

But the gamekeeper hadn't hated dust. He'd loved his back pressed against our dusty kitchen table. Him and Mama, wrapped up in one another, had reached their hands towards the window on a sunny day and caught the dust motes between their fingertips. Boys and men always lied about the silliest things instead of saying what they really thought.

'I wonder if mams and das really love each other at all,' she said. 'They always shouted and cursed but now Mam can only remember the good bits.'

Mama had told me she loved me. Eden had told me she loved me. Papa had told me he loved me. But it had all started to fray and lose its meaning, like a wave curling, crashing, and then becoming nothing at all as it disappeared back out to sea.

'Sometimes,' Abbie said, 'I think about you in ways I'm not supposed to. The way I'm supposed to think about boys. I imagine us together, in the woods or in a kitchen. Holding hands and stuff.'

I had imagined that too. Holding hands, walking by the beck and following footpaths until our feet took us to the break of the estuaries.

'And I thought about putting a kiss on your cheek and on your nose,' Abbie said, anxiously playing with the cuff of her school shirt.

I took Abbie's hand and squeezed. Mama wanted a new stray, but it could never be Abbie. Even if I had thought non-stop about the strand of blonde hair that sat at the bottom of my stomach. 'Maybe one day we will live together,' I said. 'And we can hold hands all day. As much as we please.'

'I want to go to the city. I don't want to live here anymore. It's a strange place. It gobbles people up.' Abbie's hand was small, nothing like her papa's. The pang of guilt came again. It felt like insects feasting on my chest. Woodlice. And biting ants. And nettle stings all at once.

She twined her fingers with mine, unaware that I was the monster that had eaten her papa's fingers. Each of her fingers was red and plump from the rushing blood in her veins. I wondered if I'd always feel this way; if I'd forever crave the meat on her bones.

Forty-Eight

The bus driver didn't sing on this journey. He didn't even play music. He smoked a cigarette out the window and listened to the quiet of the passing roads and the world beyond. There was a light rain cloud following our route. I was quiet too, listening to the patter of rain on the windscreen. His brow furrowed and he took deep breaths of smoke before letting a black ashen cloud out through his mouth.

It was one of those rare occasions when I was the last child on the school bus. A summer bug had kept some of the children away from their desks and tucked up warm in their beds. The exhaust coughed and spluttered as we pulled to a stop outside the gate near the beck. The bus was an old thing and it filled the air with that musty petrol smell.

'Do you want me to walk you up?' the bus driver said, pulling up the handbrake and dropping his cigarette outside the window. He'd never offered that before.

'I don't need walking,' I said, clutching onto my bag. 'I can go by myself.'

He kept a serious look on his face. Glancing at me, he cast a straight line over his mouth. Maybe he could see the bruise. The one left by Mama's hand. Even though it had faded, there was a look upon his face as though he could see the just-as-juicy, just-as-purple smudge kept hidden by my rosy cheeks.

I wondered if he could smell the strays from here, the room where we hung their skin and meat before we ate it. It harboured the scent of blood and rotten eggs.

'I wanted to make sure everything was okay,' he said. 'Speak to a parent.'

'Everything's fine,' I said. If Mama put her eyes on him, she would think he was a stray. And I'd never seen her so hungry, champing at the bit for flesh and blood. 'You don't want to come inside.'

'Why is that, Margot?'

'It's not very tidy. Mama is very house-proud. She wouldn't want anyone to see it like this.'

'Is that your mama up there?' he asked, pointing to a slender figure looking through the open door. Eden stood on the top step, dress blowing in the wind. It was another of Mama's dresses. A sundress. Lacy and light. The breeze carried it around as Eden stood resolute, arms crossed.

Looking back at the bus driver, I shook my head.

'Who's that, then?'

'That's Eden.' I twiddled my fingers around my school bag. 'Mama is in love with her.' I watched Eden from afar. She might have been sizing him up, wondering whether to bake him in a pie or soak him down into a stew. I pictured him, hanging from the hook, being skinned with Mama's knife. I would have to clean it all up. I would have to take his smoke-infused clothes and hide them in a hole in our garden. 'I'd tell you if something was wrong,' I said, holding his stare. 'I promise.' But I wouldn't. Not if my broken promise would keep him safe. 'I'll see you tomorrow.'

I opened the door and hopped out into the shallow puddles by the gate. The rain was hard now, hitting the ground and forming pools on the pathway. Behind me, the bus drove away. I turned and watched it get lost in the rain.

Eden was waiting, kept dry by the shelter of the homestead.

'He kept you late,' she said. 'What was that about?'

'He was just asking about homework. I was doing it on the bus with him.'

'And what homework is that? Maybe it's something I can help with.' The rain soaked me through. Eden leant over me, waiting for an answer.

'Poems. We're doing acrostic poems at school.'

'And why do you think a bus driver could help you with writing a poem? A measly stray.'

'He knows lots of things about the world. He knows about music. And about people,' I said.

Eden scoffed and stepped aside. When I came through the door, I left my shoes and coat by the hooks and curled up on the couch to stay warm. I pulled the blanket around my shoulders and brought my knees to my chin.

'Can we light the fire?' I asked.

Eden sat at the foot of the couch. 'It's all soaked,' she said, pointing to the pile of logs dripping wet from a chimney leak. 'Your mama is out trying to find some sticks we can dry off in the oven to keep us warm. She's all alone in the woods but who knows what she might bring back to surprise us.'

Eden licked her lips and watched the rain pour. When Mama returned, she came empty-handed.

Forty-Nine

In the dream, I saw the severed fingers trail across the floor. The very first severed fingers I could remember from my memories. The girl with the purple nail polish and the nervous boy. The nervous boy who knew too well that something bad was about to happen to him, but he wasn't quite sure what.

I followed the trail of fingers from the couch and picked them up one by one.

One finger. Two fingers. Three fingers.

My footsteps were louder in the dark.

Four fingers.

I think there was something standing in the corner but it was too dark to see.

Five fingers.

The last finger was at my feet. It lay there for the stagnant air to pluck it bare. I picked it up.

Six fingers.

When I looked up, standing in the dark shadow of the house, there they were: the girl with the spaghetti straps and purple nail polish and the nervous boy. They wanted to speak but before the words could come, I woke.

Fifty

As days slipped through our fingers, Mama stopped putting me to bed. I missed the smell she carried with her. It was something like smoke. Something like meat. Something like lipstick.

I watched Mama and Eden from the windowsill. They cosied on the couch watching the telly as it dithered between channels. But Mama was restless. She drifted from the couch, where she lay entangled in Eden's limbs, and went to the bedroom. The door shut firmly behind her.

Eden watched me from the couch. My shadowy corner felt colder when her eyes scattered on my forehead, then trailed down my nose. Her eyes dropped to my chin and jaw, then her gaze settled on my stomach.

'You didn't finish your meal,' she said.

'I wasn't hungry,' I said, but that was a lie. I was hungry. In fact, I hadn't stopped thinking of Abbie's single strand of hair, hoping it was still somewhere in my stomach, tickling my organs. If that strand was still there, I knew Abbie would always be with me.

The strand was like the twine I'd used to make hexes, but now, bound by her thread, I was the hex. A wish pulling us closer. Abbie made me think that taking strays for ourselves and our hunger was wrong. A terrible thing to want, to hunger for.

'You'll get too skinny if you don't watch yourself,' Eden said. 'Nobody wants a weedy little thing.'

I looked down and poked my belly. I wasn't skinny but I would be if I stopped eating altogether. I closed my eyes and imagined drinking from Eden's skull, dipping my fingers into her fracture just as Mama had done with her first stray. She would taste wonderful. Her thoughts would be otherworldly.

'Come to bed,' Eden said, patting the sofa cushion. 'It's time for you to rest.'

I moved to the couch. As I sank into the cushions, Eden slid closer, brushing my hair behind my ears. She spent a long time studying my face. Memorising the details. The gap between my two front teeth. My chin. My freckles. The exact shade of red surfacing on my cheeks. The lines of my skull. She knew me inside out.

'We don't take strays the way we used to,' I whispered.

Eden's fingers lingered on my skin. Slender and pointed, they scraped my forehead as they cleared the hair from my face. 'Taking in every hitch-hiker and hippy that crosses the trail? Now, that's a dangerous game. We have to be selective and discreet. You know that.' Eden kissed my head and pressed her thumb on my cheek, seeing how far it would sink in. Through my flesh, her thumb pressed onto my tongue. 'So skinny. You used to have such life in your cheeks, but not anymore. We'll have to sort that out, now, won't we?' She was looking at me differently. Her eyes were more focused.

I thought back to the day she'd patted a daub of flour on my nose and somehow I knew she was thinking of that same day too.

Eden stood and walked towards the hearth, staring at the embers of the fire as they faded into the dark. She sighed as she fell to her knees, dipped her fingers in the soot and inhaled the smoke. 'I've always loved the smell of after-fire,' she said, turning back to me. 'Sit up.'

I shuffled up, leaning my back against the arm of the chair.

Eden settled at my side. She pressed her finger to my nose and smiled. 'We are family now. You belong to us.'

But you are still a stranger, I thought. *Someone I've known only for a few months.* 'Sometimes I wonder, if I went missing, would anyone notice I was gone?' I asked. 'Would *you* notice I was gone?'

Eden cocked her head, brow knotted. 'Why do you say that?'

I shrugged. 'It's just something I think about.'

'Don't, my Little One,' she whispered. 'Think only of nice things. Happy things. Juicy rabbits and their kits. A full trap. The forest breeze. Fill that belly of yours. Stay nice and juicy. Healthy.'

I nodded, rolling into the embrace of the couch cushions and watching the hearth cool down from a day of burning hot coals.

When Eden left me and closed the bedroom door behind her, I slipped off the couch and pulled my blanket towards the hearth. There were still traces of heat left by the embers. I watched the fire go out, fading from orange to an almost black.

Before Eden, we hadn't really used the fire all that much. Mama thought the smoke from our chimney drew too much attention, but now we all burnt in here. The hearth was lit every night. The house smelt of fire. And ash.

I blew on the embers to keep the fire alive and though it flickered, trying to come back to life, the light was quickly snuffed out.

Fifty-One

I felt it first below my belly. A throbbing pain that came like ripples. Something warm ran down my legs. It was sticky and clung to my skirt and thighs. Cramp pulsed from inside and pushed out into my back in pangs. Sitting at my desk, a lump formed in my throat, contracting until tears perched at the edges of my eyes. Each drop fell into my workbook and smudged my graphite scribbles. Now my words bled over the lines.

Mr Hill knelt down close enough to feel the hot of my breath on his cheek. 'What's wrong?' he asked, looking at the workbook and furrowing his brow at the smudges.

'It hurts,' I said. My cheeks went red. I couldn't find the words to describe where it hurt. 'Can I go to the bathroom?'

'I want you to finish these sums first,' he said, tapping his finger on my workbook.

'Please,' I said, scraping up rogue spots of blood from my thighs. I held up my fingers. 'I think there's something wrong.'

Mr Hill's face paled. White as a sheet. He stepped back, putting space between us. I realised that he was more unprepared than I was.

The pain passed through my groin again. I wondered if this was what growing up felt like. Not just the pain in my gums from where my new molars were coming in, or the shooting pains up and down my legs and arms, but this new pain in my middle. Growing up hurt.

Mr Hill had briefly taught us about periods. In passing. I remember he'd shuffled his feet uncomfortably across the carpet and coughed back the words. The *it's perfectly normal*s and the *this is what a pad is*, but not how to use it. *Tampons are impure.* He'd told us we would bleed. And that pain was normal. *You must still come to school. No matter how much you bloat, or vomit, or faint. It's normal for a woman.*

Mr Hill wordlessly excused me from my seat. I left behind smudges of blood on the chair. I used my coat to cover up my legs as I passed around the edges of the classroom towards the door. Moments later, I lurched into a cubicle and hurled myself over a toilet seat. I vomited up what little food was in my belly, hoping with all my heart that Abbie's strand of hair was kept safe somewhere inside my intestines.

My mouth tasted like acid.

Mama had told me that, when she'd started her period, she couldn't stand the sight of food. She told me my breasts would swell, my thighs would grow like beanstalks and my hips would widen like the door to a hollow tree. She promised me I would shift and change, and that everything would stretch and grow, but nothing would be the right shape or size for a long time.

I went to the mirror and splashed my face with water. When I caught my reflection, I was a thing half-formed and broken. Barely even human. My skin had turned a shade of apple green.

There was a gentle knock on the door. A short, stout woman edged around the corner. She had tight curls and a warm smile. I'd seen her before in the main office. Roz. I think her name was Roz. 'Mr Hill told me what happened,' she said. 'I just came to give you some bits and pieces to help.'

'I want to go home,' I said. 'I want Mama.'

She pulled a tissue from the canvas bag slung over her shoulder and wiped a stray smudge of vomit from my school jumper. 'I know, sweetie. If it were up to me, I'd have you wrapped up in a blanket, with some beans on toast and cartoons.' She stopped and produced a pad from her back pocket. 'Do you know how to use one of these?' she asked.

'I think so,' I said, recalling Mama's fingers peeling back the layers of cotton and plastic when she had bled before.

She opened the pad and pulled away the stickers. 'This middle bit goes around the bottom part of your knickers,' she said. 'Nice and easy. Do you want to go into one of those cubicles and just wipe yourself up? You can have this one. I keep lots of spares in the office if you ever forget them.'

I took the pad out of her hands and went into the cubicle. As I pulled my knickers down, there were thick clots of blood nesting over the fabric. I wiped it all away, along with the blood on my legs too. 'It really hurts,' I said through the door.

'I know, sweetie,' she said. 'If it's really bad, you get your mam to book you a doctor's appointment.'

Even when I'd been so sick that I'd felt like I was at death's door, Mama had never taken me to the doctor's. She hated how they poked, prodded, probed and asked their silly questions.

'I have a hot-water bottle for you to take into class. I've already told Mr Hill you can keep it with you while you work.'

When I came out of the cubicle, she was already equipped with a wet paper towel and the hot-water bottle beneath her arm. She knelt down on the floor, smiling when her eyes found mine. 'You've missed a spot. Can I wipe it up?' she asked, pointing to my knee.

I nodded.

Roz wiped away the smudge of blood across my knee and smiled when it was all gone. 'I got you something,' she said. 'I give it to my daughters when it's their time of the month too. I have a stash in my desk drawer just in case.'

I looked up at her. 'You got me something?'

'Don't tell anyone,' she said. From her bag, she pulled out a bar of chocolate. 'It doesn't matter what age you are: if you have your period, you deserve chocolate. You remember that.'

I held out my hands.

'It's dark chocolate,' she said, opening the packet. 'It's really good for you if you're menstruating. It's got lots of good things that make the pain a bit easier and it will keep you energised.'

Chocolate was a rare treat in our home. Mama liked to live from the land where she could. I took the chocolate bar between my fingers and pulled away the rest of the packet before taking a nibble. It was sweet but bitter. 'Thank you,' I said, looking up at Roz. I stepped forward and wrapped my arms around her waist.

'Let's get you back to class,' she said, patting my back.

As she walked me back through the halls, I kept quiet. The thick sweetness of chocolate subsided as I licked it away from my teeth. As though it had crawled up from between my legs to my throat, I tasted blood in my mouth. Sour and salty. I wondered if Mama would want to taste it too.

*

'It hurts,' I said, holding my belly. My mouth watered, lapping up spit. Something wanted to come up and out from my belly. 'I'm hungry too.' My voice trembled as a thick lump formed in my throat. The pain came through me again, first a dull ache at the bottom of my spine, but then a sharp pang through my groin. It made me queasy.

'Hush,' Mama said. She was tired today. Impatient. 'Get yourself off the couch – I don't want you leaving stains all over the cushions.'

199

'I'll sort it,' Eden said, leaving a weightless kiss on Mama's cheek. 'Come with me,' she said, moving towards me and nipping at my toes with her fingernails. They were sharp. Sharp enough to leave a beautiful, curved indent in my skin.

I rolled off the couch and followed her to the bathroom. The pain was tidal, coming in and out of my body.

'Does it ever stop hurting?' I asked.

Shaking her head, Eden's lips downturned. 'Mine are so bad I'm sick. Sometimes I tremble, and my body goes to sleep. It's just how it is.'

'Do the boys know about this?' I asked. 'Do they know it hurts this much?'

'Of course they know, but it's not real pain to them. Pretend-pain. Not as painful as their pain.' Her fingers turned the tap and water came gushing from the spout. 'You need to get the stain out of these,' she said, hanging the knickers off the edge of her finger.

I reached for them, pulling them away from her hand.

'Pop them under the tap,' Eden said.

Throwing them beneath the water, I watched them soak, but the blood stayed exactly where it was.

Eden nudged me aside, rolling up her sleeves and taking my hands. She wove them beneath the water.

'It's cold,' I said. 'My fingers are tingling.'

'You'll get used to it,' she said. Our fingers entwined, I watched them turn red together. The blood rushed to our fingertips. 'Hold it still beneath. Imagine it's skin. Stretch it out wide beneath the gush of the water.'

Fifty-Two

The window was open on the bus and the afternoon air was warm. Each time the bus driver pressed down on the accelerator, my heart beat faster. We were almost home. The song from the radio was escaping out into the wilds and being carried across the wind towards the forest. The bus driver sang to himself. 'Do you know this one, Youngen?' he asked. 'It's one of my favourites.'

I shook my head.

His words listed as I stared out at the hills and traced their shapes on the air. The world outside seemed un-touched. I imagined the taste of the dirt in my mouth, fresh and clear. That's where the gamekeeper had ridden his quad bike.

'Youngen?' the bus driver asked again. 'What are you thinking about?'

'I wish I went to the fells more often,' I said. 'I once knew someone who loved it there. I mostly go to the wood or the beck.'

'There are becks and woods on the fells,' he said. 'If you know the right places.'

'But the changeling boys from the village creep around them,' I said.

'Those boys are nothing but trouble. You stay well away.'

'I know,' I said. 'The wood near my house is safe, though. I think they're afraid of the wood.' I was the only danger in that wood. I would climb the trees and pick at the moss growing on the bark. While I waited and watched, I'd press it into my skin so I blended with the world. I'd smother mud across my face and wait for the ants and woodlice to roam my skin, hoping the changeling boys would venture far enough into the dark so I could catch them. Passing the time, I'd watch the ants trailing the peaks and valleys of my skin until they got lost. Ladybirds had even slept on my nose to rest their wings.

'Be careful if you're heading up to the woods. I've always wanted to give those boys a taste of their own medicine,' the bus driver confessed.

I wanted to as well. I wanted to ram their penknives into their bellies and cut them open. Leave them to hang from the trees like the kits on the cloakroom hooks. I'd never eaten a changeling boy before. They would probably be poisonous.

For the first time, thoughts like this didn't sit well in my head. They sank with a weight. Guilt.

'Their parents don't know they've produced these little ne'er-do-wells.' The bus driver paused. 'You have to try to put good into the world, otherwise everyone's putting bad into the world. Someone has to swallow their pride and make things okay.'

'Can you do something good by doing something bad?' I asked. 'Like if I took away something bad, would that be a good thing?'

'It depends,' he said. 'Everything has its place in the world.'

'That doesn't seem fair,' I said. 'That people can just be bad and it's okay because it has its place.'

'It's not fair,' he said. 'But if you spent your whole life, all those years, thinking about getting rid of the bad things, you'd not be very happy, would you? I think we all deserve a small piece of happy. Life's hard enough.'

'But what if I find a way to stop something bad?' I asked. The bus curved around the edges of the woods. We weren't far from home now.

'What's this bad thing you're so worried about?' He eyed me as he turned the steering wheel.

'Nothing, really. Just school things,' I lied.

'Well, it's not up to you on your own. There are grown-ups who get rid of bad things. Police officers for bad people. Doctors for bad diseases. Farmers for food shortages. And schoolteachers for little ne'er-do-wells.'

The bus wove along the small roads and bumped over the potholes. Now and then we'd pull to a stop and drop off another tired child. The bus driver sang once we were on the road again. When he sang to himself, he was thinking of his daughter – I could tell. I tried to picture him younger, with a child about my size, in a small car with a heap of cassette tapes.

I watched him pull a cigarette out from the glovebox and light it as we followed the bend in the road. His sleeves were rolled up. My eyes wandered across the tattoos twining around his arms. Each one was fuzzy. Old. Illegible.

'I used to live in the city,' he said. 'You see those little smudges of grey and black on the horizon?' He pointed over his wheel beyond the hills. 'That's Carlisle. About fifty minutes' drive away from here. It's a small place. Not got a lot of charm. But I called it home once.'

'Why did you come to the countryside?' I asked.

'I wanted to be alone with my thoughts. You can have too much nice food and too much good music. Sometimes you just need nothing.'

'I want to go to the city one day,' I said.

'I promise you that you'll want to come back.'

'Maybe,' I said.

'Even with the cold and the loneliness, this place is better by far,' the bus driver said, breathing out a puff of smoke. 'Even with the folk who come and get lost on the trails without the right boots and equipment.'

'My friend Abbie thinks the ground swallows them up.'

'She's right. Foolish city folk come without the right tools to get them through the wet seasons. I've always thought it's the rural world's way of biting back a bit at the cities as they try to expand out into the wilds. These rural parts are perfect for their pretty holidays with their families until they see an old farmer or a village odd bod. Then they come up here and trash the place with their litter and their left-behind tents.'

'If I see one, I'll make sure to send them back where they came from,' I said, folding my arms and thinking of the strays we'd encountered. The lost ones. The hurt ones. The strange ones.

The bus crawled to a stop. I slid off my seat and clambered down the steps until my feet hit the ground.

'See you tomorrow,' he said. His smile faded from his lips.

'See you tomorrow,' I said as the bus pulled away.

Fifty-Three

The woods were quiet. Even the ceaseless whispering between trees had quietened to watch the forest floor. There were no rabbits. And even when I turned the mossy stone by the fallen tree, the cluster of woodlice was nowhere to be seen.

Every creature was hiding from me.

I kept behind the tree, sitting between its roots and imagining they were arms. There, I sang beneath my breath, whispering a melody and telling the hidden creatures the story of the rabbit woman.

'D'you know the story of the rabbit woman?' I asked, but there wasn't a sound in the wood. Not even a twig snapping. But it felt like something was creeping up on me. 'And how she made flour for the very first time. When humans still worshipped the land and kissed the roots growing from the soil.' Above me, sunlight broke through the foliage. 'Once, there was a rabbit woman who lived in a hole in the hills. She lived there like a rabbit.' I smiled at the thought and then plucked a flower from the grass. I held it in my palm, pressing my fingers over the almost-budded petals. 'She ate the mushrooms she foraged from the land. But a hunter had come down her burrow and stolen away with her fur.'

I used my fingernails to break open the bud. Looking into the petals, I found a small fly hiding between the folds.

'Did you know that women back then had fur?' I smiled and put the flower back down on the ground, hoping its roots would find their way back to the stem. If I returned here in a week, its petals would have browned and crinkled, and the flower would be no more. 'Having her furs stolen harmed her so. The person she used to be was gone, pulled apart and spread to places she couldn't reach. Something in the alchemy of her blood changed.'

A twig snapped. I lurched behind the trunk of the great tree and peered around the other side.

A woman, taller than me, with a young face and a soft smile hovered beneath the dark of a tree. 'I didn't mean to frighten you.'

A stray.

'My mam used to tell me this one,' she said. 'Over and over.'

'It was anger,' I mustered, 'that changed in her. It had broken free and now it controlled her.'

'*Why did it have to be me?*' The stray echoed the words of the story. 'But she was simply in the wrong place, at the wrong time, with the wrong person.'

I wandered to her side. Maybe she wasn't a stray after all. Maybe she was just like me.

'One day,' the stray said, 'when the sun was at its highest point in the sky and the heat was beating down onto the beck, she brought the women of the burrows out to the pastures. She held the hunter to the rock. Her mam took his hand. Her sister took his toes. The other women took one finger each. When they set him free, the sun was warm. They took the bones they'd gathered, ground them and watered them into mulch, and the pain watered the earth. The rabbit woman grew the harvest crop to feed the burrow sisters.'

'That's not how it goes,' I said.

The stray watched me. 'My mam told me that bedtime story every night before I slept.'

'Margot?' The echo of my name disturbed the quiet. Mama was coming through the forest to find me.

'You have to go,' I said.

The woman furrowed her brow.

'Leave my forest!' I shouted, baring my gappy teeth. 'Get away, now.' Mama would make her a stray. She wouldn't have skin, or eyes, or a mouth left to tell her stories. There would be nothing but bone dust.

The woman was still.

'Get away or I'll pull out your teeth,' I said. Between my fingers, I took a sharp stone from the ground and pelted her feet.

Watching me, the woman stumbled back. Into the ferns she disappeared with no idea how lucky she was to walk away with the skin still bound to her back. With a mind still to remember her bedtime stories.

Fifty-Four

The weekend brought tears. Mama wept but the rain almost drowned her out. I watched from the window as she curled her fists in the mud and shouted to the open sky. Through the glass, she seemed like another creature. I leant closer and listened. She murmured to herself between the sobs, something I'd heard her do once before when Papa had upset her. Almost soaked through, her church dress looked like skin as it stuck to her flesh.

The house felt emptier when she wept, as if the items we loved slowly made their way off the shelves to hide. But Mama, even in the rows she'd shared with Papa, had never been left so distraught. Eden brought something out in Mama that Papa never could. A torment.

'She doesn't keep her heartbreak locked away, does she?' Eden asked, sighing and leaning against the wall. 'I'm scared she will leave me,' she said, putting her hand on my shoulder. 'All I did was deny her a stray.'

'She's hungry,' I said, nestling into Eden's warm belly.

'She's insatiable,' Eden said. 'And she won't listen to me, Little One. She thinks the world is there to fill her stomach. But it's not. She must be more cunning.'

I kept my eyes on Mama, who now lay in the puddles of mud at the front of the house. Eden disappeared from my side. Her footsteps took her to the bedroom she shared with Mama. The door shut with a slam.

I moved from the windowsill and out to the rain, where heavy drops of water hit the ground like stones. It ran down my scalp and spine, absorbing into the threads of my school jumper. This was a wash long overdue.

'Mama?' I asked.

'What?' She rolled over in the mud and looked up at the sky, arms outstretched and smeared with dirt. 'What do you want?'

'Come inside. You'll catch a cold,' I said.

Mama laughed, baring her teeth.

'Please, Mama.' I sat in the mud close by. The puddle was cold. 'I don't want to leave you out here all alone.'

'That word,' she said. '*Leave.*' Mama sat up and held my chin between her pointed fingers. Her nails dug into my skin. 'It's such a dirty word. Take it out of your mouth and never put it back there. Not ever again. No one can *leave* this place.'

'Eden is afraid too,' I said, wrapping my arm around her and pulling her close. She was shivering from the cold. The fabric was forged to her skin.

'I'm sick of it,' Mama snapped. 'I've changed for her. I don't take anything I want anymore. And she doesn't know this hunger that *we* feel. The emptiness.'

'Eden doesn't want you to change, Mama. She doesn't want to stop you from taking in strays,' I said. 'She just wants us to slow down.'

'She doesn't have an empty belly,' Mama said, gripping her belly between her fingers and squeezing tight. 'Not the hunger that *I* know.'

Together, we soaked. The chill of the air kept us cool.

'Come inside,' I whispered, touching her hair. It draped down my fingers, split ends getting lost in the puddle on the ground.

The grey cloud above got darker. It let out a rumble of thunder and a cut of sheet lightning.

'Why don't we just eat normal food? Eden can make something with dumplings,' I said, but Mama looked at me with disgust.

'No. I'm not settling anymore. I want to hunt.'

I quietened. I didn't want to eat strays anymore. Maybe somewhere, deep down, Mama knew that.

'You agree with her? That we should not sate our hunger?' Mama's words came as a whisper through the rain. She took my wrist in her hand and watched my veins. She stared at them, tracing each faint blue line with her fingernail. Pressing her thumb on my pulse and closing her eyes, she listened. 'Your pulse sounds the same as your papa's. Soft beats. Easily snuffed out.'

'Don't say that,' I said, pulling my wrist away.

Mama's eyes opened. 'Do you want to know something? From when you were small, your brain couldn't seem to keep hold of memories. Everything slipped through the cracks. He noticed it more to begin with.'

'I remember things, Mama,' I said.

'Is that so?' she asked, her face straightening. Mama's gaze lingered, sharp. She measured her words before speaking them. 'You said he was the best food you'd ever eaten.'

I stopped. Even though the rain hit the ground, the world went silent. In an instant, the memories I had – the scent of cigarette smoke, the scratchy jumpers and the tired smile – all of it dispersed.

'I bet you don't even remember what I turned him into,' she said, pulling her hands away and studying my face. 'But you thought he was delicious.'

'Don't lie, Mama,' I said, stumbling back through the puddles.

'I'm not lying. Cross my heart,' she said, passing her fingers over my chest like a cross-stitch.

My stomach twined in knots.

'Wrapped in pastry, he made the most beautiful pie. The pastry was crisp. Buttery. The meat was tender and we ate every single piece of him in just one day. We *feasted*. There wasn't even a scrap of meat left on his ribs. You licked the plate clean. And you *loved* it. I formed you, Little One. With my own flesh, I formed you in my womb. We're made of the same cloth. You feel this hunger the same way I do.'

Words dried up in my throat.

'Because he was a little rat, no one questioned where he was and why he'd left. He was a stray from the start.' Mama laughed as she rolled back into the puddle. 'I was never going to let him leave. When you love someone, you promise to love *all* of them. Even the ugly bits. But he couldn't. He took one look at the hunger and . . .' Her words trailed off. The sound of the rain came back again. Harder than before. When I looked up at the window, Eden was watching over us, a straight line across her mouth. 'And sometimes, when I look at you, I see him. And it makes me hungry all over again. It makes me want to exhume his bones and lick them clean. It makes me hunger to taste the meat that fell away from his bones. To feel the break of his tendons like the sharp snap of an elastic band.'

Standing, I dragged myself back to the steps of the house, holding the pouch of my belly as it lurched. I left a trail of wet footprints as I went to the bathroom.

I vomited. And vomited again. And I didn't stop until I fell asleep on the tiles in a pool of my own bile.

We consumed him. Wrapped him in buttery pastry. And I grieved a man of blood and bone who had steadily been digested through my intestines. Years ago.

When I came out from the bathroom, midnight had swept over the world. Mama and Eden made love behind their door.

I wanted to pull off my skin and hang it out to dry like linens. I shivered, cold and damp, wiping the mud from my body.

'I ate my papa,' I whispered.

Fifty-Five

'Bath time,' Mama shouted from the bathroom. The tap went silent as she stopped the water gushing out from its spout. I hopped off the couch and wandered towards the sound of her call. Mama leant against the doorframe. A soft smile played with either side of her lips, like a sewing needle pulling threads tight through a seam.

'Let's get you squeaky clean,' she said, running her hands through my hair and tapping my nose with her fingertip. 'You're a greasy thing, Little One.' Mama had woken in a good mood today, but she couldn't take back the secret she'd shared with me about Papa. Beneath the smile, there was regret. Mama hid that well most of the time, but today I could feel it. Her eyes were hollow, stuck on me. She leant her head down and pressed her nose upon my crown. Taking a deep breath, she told me, 'You smell like rotten meat.'

'I can't help it,' I said.

'Can I sit and talk with you?' she asked. 'The way we used to?'

I couldn't remember those times from *the way we used to*. I wondered if it was a time so long ago that I couldn't remember it at all; a time I couldn't yet speak or see properly, with only a few teeth and toes. Perhaps she meant when I was inside her, safe and sound in her warm belly. When I was only the idea of a person. Papa had once said she spoke to her belly even though I'd made it large and bloated and *ugly*. From the stories I'd heard, he'd hated when Mama was pregnant. He'd called her a heifer once but she'd slapped him clean across the cheek for it.

Mama locked the door. The bathroom tiles were cold at my feet, but the air was steamy. It was humid. Close like thunder. I pulled off my school jumper, and then my shirt too. It crinkled over my ears. I pulled my knickers down to my ankles.

When I dipped my toes in the water, my skin went red, blushing. 'It's too hot,' I said, looking back at Mama. She sat on the floor and watched me hunch over the bath. 'I'll boil.'

'You'll get used to it,' Mama said.

I slipped in, squeezing my eyes shut and biting my top lip with my bottom teeth. The heat scorched my skin, but I kept myself from weeping by holding the cry behind my teeth, anchoring it at the back of my throat.

'Eden's told me to try something new. To get my anger out,' Mama said as I pooled a small coin of shampoo into the centre of my palm. 'Drawing,' she said. 'She went to the hearth of the fire and got down on her hands

215

and knees, collecting long strips of charcoal from the burnt-up logs. Her knees were ever so sooty. Then she went out to the beck today and used something she'd made to make mulch out of old bills and newspapers. At first I thought it was a tambourine, a large circle of netting held tight by a circular wooden frame. She tore up our old bits and pieces into shreds and dropped them into the *thing*. Then she dipped the frame underwater, and pulled it back up once the mulch inside was wet and crushed down. She made us our own paper, Little One.' Mama held up the paper, marvelling. But all I saw were thick and clumsy sheets. Her fingerprints drifted over the tops and brushed the sides of the paper. I hoped she'd give herself a paper cut.

Scrubbing the suds around my hair, I watched Mama. 'She's so clever,' Mama said.

I dipped under the surface and held my breath. It was still too hot. Beneath their lids, my eyes stung. Mama spoke, but her words drawled, slipping from one to the next senselessly. The cold nipped at my shoulders and nose when I came back up for air.

'Can I draw you?' Mama asked, shuffling closer to the bath and brushing my clumps of wet hair aside.

'Don't you want to draw Eden?'

'You are my Little One,' she said, kissing my nose. 'You were once warm inside me. Curled up. Quiet.' Mama smiled. 'Do you want to try to remember how it felt?'

I nodded.

'Hold your breath,' she whispered in my ear. Her palm

came to my head and pushed me beneath the surface of the water.

I slipped under again and held my breath. My heartbeat slowed.

Her words were broken in pieces. I tried to string them together. *Nice and warm. All curled up. Quiet. Well behaved and predictable. Obedient.*

My head began to hurt. I held my nose but my lungs craved air.

'Stay,' Mama said. 'Just for a second longer.'

I counted. *One stray. Two stray. Three stray. Four. Five stray. Six stray. Seven stray more.* When I re-emerged, Mama gazed at me. I tried to catch my breath, letting my belly heave in and out.

'Remember what I told you about lungs?' she asked. 'Just let me cut a little bit of skin free and they'd blow up to be the biggest balloons you'd ever see. They look like wings.' Mama shuffled back to sitting and pulled her charcoal and paper to her lap. 'Now sit very still,' she said.

'Can I tell you something, Mama?' I asked.

Mama nodded.

'It was me. I put the baby rabbits on the coat hooks at school.'

The pencil stopped scratching against the paper. Silence came. Mama fixed her eyes on my face. For the first time, she recognised something pure in me.

'The baby kits that they found on the coat hooks at school. They blamed Marcus for it, but it was me. I went to the woods and caught them. I wandered close to the almond stone and once I found the road I followed it to the school. I was in and out. Home by sun-up.' I wanted to be punished, but Mama looked at me with wonder for a moment. 'I wanted to feel what you felt when you dipped your fingers into the skull of your first stray, Mama. I wanted to feel *full*. But I didn't feel anything like that. I felt like everything had been scraped out from inside of me.'

Mama sat, watching me from the tiles and keeping her distance. 'Just stay very still,' she whispered, eyes wide.

She soaked in each second, studying my anatomy. The strange curves and twists of my body. The slight hunch at the top of my spine and my ribs bumping beneath my skin. When she was finished, she marvelled at her work, but it was a poor imitation of me. Maybe she was drawing the changeling she saw inside. The monster. Maybe that's what I really looked like. Monstrous, with sharp, cutting lines defining every feature.

After I finished getting clean, Mama made me sit with her while she had her bath too. Even away from the water, wrapped up in a warm towel, I felt as though every inch of me was being studied and recorded. We said nothing to one another as I watched her rub soap onto her skin. Bubbles formed. Every curve on her body escaped the water.

After she'd lathered her hair in soap and scrubbed it clean, she looked at me. After what felt like hours of silence, she spoke. 'Tomorrow, Little One, go to the woods and bring home a stray. You have no idea how

hungry I am. We've gone long enough without food.'
Mama paused, letting a thought wash over her. 'I know
how capable you are now. Resourceful and cunning,
just like me. Prove yourself useful, Little One.' Her
voice was calm, in control – the way she had spoken to
the gamekeeper the night she made him a stray. Her
eyes were large as they fixed themselves upon me. Her
wet hand crept from the water and brushed my cheek.
'Sometimes I try to imagine what life would be like
without you, Little One. What would have happened if
I'd never met your papa. If you'd have still haunted me
anyway.' Mama took a deep breath, poising herself to
speak, but her mouth stayed closed.

The silence hung in the air.

Tell me you love me, Mama.

Mama was silent, watching me as she slipped her chin
beneath the water. Her toes teased the spout, catching
cold drops of water before they could submerge.

'I'll bring you a stray, Mama.'

'Make sure it's nice and big, so there's plenty to go
around.'

I smiled to her and she smiled back before dipping
her head below the water. I went to the side of the bath
and put my fingers inside, touching her shoulders and
her arms with my fingertip. The water was tepid. When
she blew me a kiss from beneath the water, bubbles
broke the surface.

Fifty-Six

I can't remember the last time Mama held me. I missed her stray hairs tickling my nose when she held me tight, lip grazing the ridge of my forehead.

At the crack of dawn, the sun hid beneath a grey cloud. I pulled away the blanket and my feet fell into my boots, sockless and cold. Mama and Eden were fast asleep, their door soundly closed, keeping them safe from the world. I imagined crawling between them, burrowing deep into the warm blanket and weaving my limbs between theirs.

This stray could fix everything. Make everything go back to the way it was before – when it was just me and Mama. There wasn't enough love to go around. It was finite and I wanted it all for myself.

I looked out over the pastures beyond the window and the wood. Even from our homestead, the forest seemed endless, with its farthest point reaching out to the moon and stars. It was there, where the trees were dense and thick, I'd find my stray. Somewhere no one would notice them go missing.

I did the buttons of my raincoat up as I stepped over the threshold of the front door. I imagined Mama and Eden warm in each other's arms and wrapped tight between the soft bed linens. I imagined they dreamt together of the strays I would bring to them.

Knowing the wood was vast and quiet, I'd have to find a lone walker. Sometimes it took weeks to find them foolishly pushing on through the ferns and bracken, getting lost in the great wide wood.

Beyond the front door, the air was moist and humid, carrying a weight on its back. As I climbed over the gate and jumped from bank to bank, over the beck and towards the treeline, I wondered what my catch would look like. Would he be an old and wiry man? Or would she be a short and stout woman? Reminiscing about our other strays, I tried to hold on to the details.

Mama would want a woman. *A girl*. Young. Someone who didn't know any better. Someone trusting. Someone a little bit broken. A girl she could kiss softly on the lips. A stray who needed Mama and would whisper prayers into her mouth so they could be eaten up. A girl who would come willingly, with no questions asked.

Beneath the canopy of the forest, I wandered until the shadows milked my skin – a place far from the beaten path. Lost strays always *needed something*; a point in the right direction, someone to help them with an injury, someone to talk them down from the ledge.

A few thousand paces into the wood, there was a large

mossy rock shaped like an almond. I climbed to the top and watched between the trees. If I waited patiently, nature would reward me. Nature would share with me her spoils. I watched between the trunks for passing figures.

I waited, lying over the top of the rock, bellybutton looking up at the sky, and wished hard for a stray to come deep into the wood and follow me home. Hours went by, quiet and lonely. I passed my time fussing with the tufts of moss that clutched to the back of the rock and all the insects that lived within its softness.

Footsteps echoed quietly over the ground as rain began to fall. I imagined each drop spindling into the soil to feed the trees. I slid down from my perch and hid behind the standing stone and its great shadow. Watching, waiting and listening. Somewhere in this wood, somewhere close by, there was an oncoming stray.

The crunch beneath the stray's shoes became louder as it left behind deep prints of old walking boots in the mud.

I peered over the rock. A man stood between the ferns, but he wasn't wiry or old. He was stuck somewhere between old and young. Cheeks filled out on his face. His head was propped up on a wide neck. Hair sprouted from his chin, unkempt and bushy. The smell of sweat pulsed from his skin. Broad shoulders curved over his arms, and muscles filled a tight T-shirt. He stopped close by in the evergreen and watched me.

'You okay?' he shouted, keeping his distance. 'Where's your mam and da?'

'They're ahead on the trail,' I said, looking to where he would forge his path.

'Why are you all on your lonesome?' he asked, stepping closer. Beneath his feet, twigs snapped and fallen leaves crinkled.

'I felt like being alone,' I said. 'I much prefer being alone.'

The stray grimaced as he pulled out his water bottle and took a drink. He wasn't biting. I needed him to bite.

'Are you alone too?' I asked. 'Like me?'

The man nodded.

My eyes followed his features. Now he'd stopped to catch his breath, I noticed his eyes were brown. His breathing was laboured. This was a man who rarely strayed from his home. A man in search of new adventure.

'Are you okay?' I asked, looking into the bark brown of his eyes. 'You seem tired. We have warm food at home. I'm sure Mama won't mind sharing.'

The man shook his head. 'Don't need no food,' he said. 'I've got loads in my bag.'

'Will you make it to the end of the trail? There are still a few hours of walking until you reach the treeline.'

'I'll be on my way,' he said.

I stepped forward, blocking his path. 'You can't go,' I blurted out. I wondered if he could hear the guilt behind my desperation. Maybe he knew I was the sort of rotten heart that could lead him somewhere he'd never come back from.

The man cocked his head, watching me. He was speechless.

'I don't think I want to be alone anymore,' I said.

'Your ma and pa will be back soon.'

223

'But what if they don't come back for me? I've never been this far from our house. That's why I'm waiting by this rock,' I said. An uncomfortable twist came through my chest like a tree root's wooded fingers winding around my sternum.

'Do you want me to call someone for you?' he asked, but it was a reluctant offering.

'They don't have phones. We have a house phone, but it doesn't work very well. The cord has been bitten at. By our pet.' I was adding too much detail. Lies had to be abstract. Discreet. Simple. Maybe I wanted him to escape.

The man raised an eyebrow. 'They'll be back. Just stay put.' He pressed on, striding back towards the trail.

'I'm scared they won't be,' I said. 'Please.' My words echoed into the woods.

The brown-eyed man kept walking.

I kept pace, dragging close behind his heels. 'Please,' I said again, tugging at his jogging bottoms. 'I'm scared she won't come back. The least you could do is walk me back to my house. It's on the way. I wouldn't be any trouble.'

'They'll be back. Wait by the rock,' he said, pushing me off.

'Come back,' I said, watching him disappear into the thick of the ferns and trees. Soon he was gone. There was no trace of his head bobbing above the curve of the earth. He'd been eaten up by the trees.

I waited until it was dark, but no more strays came that day. Perched on the rock, I fiddled with the moss, disturbing the ants and woodlice until they came crawling from their beds. When the stars woke in the darkened sky, I followed the path back home. I found the brown-eyed man's footprints deep in the soil. The soles of his feet had been heavy as they marked the crust of the dirt. Eventually, they curved off and disappeared.

When I got to the treeline, even from a great distance, with the dark of the forest at my back, I spotted the small yellow lights shining from our windows.

Impatient and hungry, Mama and Eden would be waiting for their stray. I closed my eyes and made a wish that they would be forgiving. As I paced through the clearing and over the road, I wondered if I'd tell them the stray had slipped away or if I'd lie and tell them that no stray had come through the forest.

As I reached the bottom of the steps, I closed my eyes and took a deep breath in. I held my breath inside my body. It was like an iron weight sinking to the bottom of my stomach. I climbed the first step and rehearsed my lie.

No stray came to the wood today. I'm sorry you'll go hungry, Mama.

I took the second step and rehearsed my apology again. Climbing the last step, I looked through the glass. Their two faces looked up eagerly as they embraced one another.

I was alone. No stray had followed me back to the homestead. I wasn't ready to face them. I had not proved myself to Mama.

Fifty-Seven

'When you were small, you were so easy to love. You'd do anything for me. Every word I spoke was gospel and you looked at me like I was the most beautiful woman in the world. But something has changed, Little One,' Mama whispered, careful and quiet. 'And I'm wondering if it's quite possible I don't love you the same anymore.'

The words gently tugged me from my slumber.

'Mama?' I croaked, sitting up from the couch cushions and pulling the blanket around my shoulders. Her blonde hair glittered in the gleam of moonlight slipping in between the curtains.

'Go back to sleep,' Mama whispered. Her voice seemed different somehow. She sounded young. Warm. The tired groan that hissed at the back of her throat dissipated for a moment and only the girl within was left behind. Her expression was relaxed, skin as smooth as cow's milk. Shoulders down, she was calm, and her hair was free from binding. I wondered if this was who Mama really was. The piece of herself she kept secret.

I rubbed my eyes. The firm knot bedded in my throat tightened. It was thick and hard and heavy and growing. My lungs stopped. More than anything, I wanted to tell her I'd heard the words she'd spoken. But *everything*, all the sentences and words and feelings, stayed lodged at the back of my throat. Trapped.

Mama's eyes glimmered. She only had enough love inside her to give to one person. Just one.

And Mama was in love. Desperately in love. But she wasn't in love with me. And I don't think I was in love with her either.

*

Dust motes on the windowsill whispered to me. They often spoke in soft patterns, breathing secrets into my ears. I couldn't understand the language, but the language of the dust could seemingly understand me.

If I stayed put forever, I would turn to dust too. Every dead skin cell would break down until it was nothing. When I listened to the world this way, it made me feel how I felt with Abbie – like I was small and other things didn't matter. The cosmos was quiet around me and her.

Mama watched me from the couch. I felt her eyes rest on the back of my head, still angered because, in spite of my best efforts, I could not bring a stray home to our doorstep. Because maybe we weren't made from the same cloth. And now she was realising it.

Sombre humming came from the kitchen. Eden was

cooking. The soft clattering of pots hitting the stove echoed.

The absence of conversation was eating us up.

I imagined the meal we'd have that night. It wouldn't be floppy, soggy pasta shells – Eden made sure of that always. Still, it would be something simple and plain.

'How about another bottle?' Mama said, getting up from the couch and walking to the kitchen. The glass slide of a wine bottle pulled from a cupboard.

'Yes, love,' Eden said. She was quiet tonight. Quieter than usual. Her mind was wandering and her sentences were stuck behind her teeth, but Mama hadn't noticed.

I glanced over my shoulder and stared at Mama and Eden together. They embraced. Their free fingers explored one another, fiddling with buttons and tracing shapes on bare skin. Their other hands were burdened with glasses of wine. I knew at the end of the night their mouths would have a black ring on the inside of their lips and it would taste and smell of sour wine.

'I'm hungry,' Mama whispered in Eden's ear. I heard her words even from the windowsill. 'Hungry as Saturn devouring his son.'

I tilted my head. Mama smiled when she saw me looking over my shoulder.

'Do you know the story, Little One? Of Saturn and his son?' Mama said.

I shook my head.

'A master of time feared his only child. His son would grow bigger and stronger than he himself ever was. More handsome, too.' Mama bit off the words.

Eden's hand slithered onto Mama's lap as they took their seats close by.

'And one day the master of time took his son between his palms and tasted him. One bite at a time. Until there was nothing left.' There was a smile on Mama's face.

I watched Mama and Eden, wondering if Abbie and I would hold each other like that one day, middle-aged and hungry and drinking wine like grown-ups.

Mama was wearing her black jumper, the fluffy one, and her old jeans. She'd even straightened her hair and put on lipstick just in case a stray visited our door. Behind her lips that horrid smile hid, waiting for the next meal.

'We can wait just a little bit longer for the perfect stray. We can drink wine instead and tell our stories,' Eden said, chiming her glass against Mama's. 'Not folk tales. Real stories. Maybe something about me. Something more than Saturn and his son.'

Mama perked up.

'Little One,' Eden said, 'come listen.'

I wandered to the dining table and took my seat next to her.

'Listen to Eden, Margot,' Mama said. 'And don't utter a word.'

'I want to tell you something. A confession. A story. A secret chapter of my life,' Eden said.

'Oh yes,' Mama cooed, fingers spilling over Eden's knuckles. They always had to *touch*. 'Tell me.' Mama spoke softly, as though her whispers were promised for the ears of a sleeping bairn.

'I've taken another stray before. Only once. And it was a very long time ago. God, I was so young. Just a girl, really. Fifteen years old. But I didn't call this feast a stray like you do.'

There was fire in Mama's eyes. A newborn hunger.

'It was a little baby called Bobby. The nurse pulled him out from my insides. He was fresh and new, covered in a slick liquid. Creamy and waxy and white and delicious. He tore my skin in so many places. That's the thing with babies, they're destructive little things before they're even out of you.' Eden sucked up a deep breath, taking in the grief.

I seized my chair, fingers coiling around the edges of the seat. The hair at the back of my neck stood on end and goosebumps formed on my arms.

Eden stayed very still. Her eyes fixed on me, round and old and moonlike. 'My body was broken. My body was a stranger. But my father wanted me to bring the baby to term and then he wanted me to give him up. To this *lovely* married couple. This *pretty*, *perfect*, disgusting family. They lived in a suburb, rich, with a nice car, with money to keep them warm at night. They were a husband and wife, a couple who couldn't form their own child in the womb.'

Mama's hand tightened around Eden's.

'So do you know what I did? In front of all the nurses and doctors, using only my finger and my thumb, I picked my baby up by his big toe and I lowered the whole bairn between my jaws and swallowed him whole.' Eden smiled wickedly. Throwing her head back, her lips parted and she laughed. The scent of red wine washed the air. It was sickly and sweet. Rich. 'I gobbled him up in one bite.' Eden's laughter was infectious. I wondered if she had truly eaten her little one. I imagined her jaw unhinging, inhuman and serpentine, opening wide enough to fit a chubby baby in just one bite.

Sipping on her wine, Mama laughed too. Her gaze moved across the table and settled on me. Her mouth parted and her pupils dilated, big and black. Mama nibbled at her fingernails, pulling strips of skin free and chewing on them.

'I just wanted to freeze him. Keep him all to myself, so he couldn't grow or shapeshift. So he could stay perfect forever.' Eden sighed, swallowing her laughter and toying with the stem of her wine glass. Her smile dropped, sobering. 'After Bobby, I ran far away. To different shores. I couldn't be *there* anymore. I didn't want to see the oh-so-perfect family that took my son. I was fifteen and somehow it was all my fault. But the man who put that young boy inside me, he was much older. And nobody cared who he was. Just that *I'd* ruined myself.' She paused for a breath. 'Bobby wouldn't have been like him. He would have been like me.'

It was the first time I'd seen something broken inside Eden. Something that couldn't be mended. She carried something terrible with her. She kept her grief subdued and quiet – so much so, it had begun to rot.

'I worked in odd market stalls for years in far-off foreign cities. I travelled by boat, tracking coastlines and beaches west to east and north to south. Then I came back here, to England, and I found you. There was this newspaper left on an old bus in Brixton. The article was about your strays. *The missing girls*. But something in me knew this was where I was supposed to be. That the wood wasn't gobbling up the lost hikers. I knew I would find *something* or *someone* here.'

'You don't have to run anymore,' Mama said, taking Eden's hands. 'Here, in this homestead, with me, you never have to curb your hunger.'

I wondered what Bobby looked like – if he'd grown to look like the family he'd inherited. Or if Eden had truly gobbled him up, jaw prised open, ready for meat.

I imagined he'd be almost twenty years old, living with his normal family. He'd have gone to a big school. Maybe even university.

I wondered if he looked like Eden – the way she promised me I'd one day look like her too.

Fifty-Eight

The school bus was silent in the morning. The boys slept at the back of the bus, heads leaning on one another's shoulders, blades in sheaths. When I caught a glimpse of them in the rear-view mirror, for the first time they seemed peaceful. Sleeping children were not the monsters I sometimes thought they were. Tangled, they lay entwined in each other's limbs like tree roots. Their pink cheeks brushed against one another. I imagined their breath smelt like bark, mud and smoke. This was the way human children were supposed to be.

I enjoyed the quiet vibrations of the bus window against my head and I followed the words of the bus driver's music. To me, he was a church. Calm, wise and quiet. Most wouldn't realise that because he didn't look like a church, but he was.

I looked at the rear-view mirror again. I imagined Abbie, legs tangled up in the limbs of a changeling boy as she slumbered. My heart thumped hard as I imagined Patrick's fingers moving across her hairline and gently tugging at her ribbon. It was my ribbon to tug at.

I took a breath and closed my eyes. When I opened them again, the sleeping boys remained, but Abbie was gone. She was safe. Somewhere else. Away from us.

*

At lunch, Abbie and I stole away to the edge of the playground. The bark in the pit beneath our knees scuffed our skin and dampened our skirts but we nestled in together, warm.

'Patrick asked me out,' Abbie said, toying with a damp piece of bark. 'He came right up to me in maths and asked me if I wanted to go to the tuck shop with him after school. He said he'd show me the knife he stole from his da.'

'Only small boys use little penknives,' I said, thinking of Mama's blades at home.

'Mam wants me to go out with him,' she said, putting her hair behind her ear. 'She said he's a dish, but I don't really know what that means. She likes the way his hair curls up. It reminds her of Da.'

I watched her fingers get muddier as she nervously played with the bark. 'Do you like him?' I asked. 'Like, *like*-like him?'

Her fingers stopped toying for a moment. 'When he came up to me, he pulled my homework right out of my hands and told me to look at him. Right in the eyes. Then he fiddled with my ribbon. He pulled it to the side. Straightened it up.' She didn't answer my question.

I wondered what creature Patrick had killed most recently with his boyish little penknife. It could have been a stoat. Or a fox-child. Or a kit. It was easy to picture him with blood and mud smothered across his chin and lips, with his teeth half buried into a kit's coat.

'Mam said she would play dress-up with me. Get me a nice white dress so I could imagine getting married because she and Da met at primary school too.'

'I don't think you should marry him. You'll get bored with him quickly.'

'Mam told me she wants me to fall in love with a boy. She said falling in love will make me happy.'

'You don't have to love anyone,' I said. 'Especially not him.' Over Abbie's shoulder, in the corner of the play-ground, Patrick watched us. Surrounded by his coven of changelings, he started towards us. 'He's coming over,' I whispered to her.

'What should I say?' Abbie said, eyes wide.

'Tell him to go away.' I held her hand. An unspoken promise was made; she would tell him to go away so we could be together in the bark pit forever, talking about the world and making our wishes.

'Abbie!' Patrick shouted as he neared.

'What?' Abbie asked, looking over her shoulder and standing from the bark pit.

Patrick bundled towards us and knelt down next to Abbie. His hands travelled up her legs from her ankles as he patted away the bark. When it came away, pink imprints were still embedded in her skin. 'Girls should be prim,' he said.

'I like the bark,' she said. 'It makes me feel like a tree.'

The changeling boys stifled their laughter.

Patrick got to his feet. 'Did you bring money for the tuck shop?' he asked.

Abbie paused, glancing at me. She looked back to Patrick. 'I'm not going to the tuck shop with you,' she said.

I couldn't stop it. My cheeks were burning hot. A smile appeared.

Patrick narrowed his eyes. 'What are you smiling about, *freak*?'

I narrowed my eyes.

'Don't call her a freak,' Abbie said. 'She's my friend.'

'Freak doesn't have friends.' Patrick looked over me, eyes travelling the waves of my greasy, matted hair.

'I have friends,' I said.

The changeling boys laughed together, bright-eyed and inhuman.

'Can you remember the last time I taught you a lesson?' he said, pulling at my collar with his finger. There was a light scar left on my neck from a penknife scratch he'd left there a summer ago.

'Shut up,' I said.

'When we move on to big school, Abbie'll forget all about you. Her mam and mine reckon we'll be going to the same secondary school in September. Might even be in the same form group.'

I saw red. It came in clouds as I bit down on my tongue.

Grabbing Patrick's collar, I pushed him towards the

stone wall. Even though a whimper slithered from his mouth as his skull hit the stone, he put his fingers through my hair and tightened his fist. My head rang out.

The changeling boys gathered, pinning me back as I flailed. I clawed at them with my fingernails. Patrick pulled down my jaw with his fingers as wide as it would go. He leant right over and whispered something in my mouth.

'You want to be just like me,' he said. Then his jaw shuffled as he spat a puddle of saliva down my throat. I felt it, cold, running down my gullet and settling right at the bottom of my belly. It took its place with Abbie's strand of hair.

'No. I don't.' I wanted to kill him. My arms tensed. My knuckles whitened. As he laughed with his changelings, I bit down. The finger that held open my jaw crunched between my teeth. I imagined snapping them all clean off, but Patrick yelped out, pulling his hand away. I fell back into the bark pit, blood smearing my chin. His face was red as drool spooled from his mouth. 'Maybe I'm already like you,' I said.

'I'll make you miserable for this!' he cried, tears coming over the edge of his cheek. His hard shell dissipated. 'Even at the front of the bus, with the bus driver, I'll make you hate yourself.'

The boys scampered away, dragging Patrick towards the teacher. His cheeks were red as he pulled on the teacher's cuff. He held up his hand and fashioned tears in his eyes. I'd be in trouble for this.

Abbie took my hand.

'Abbie,' I said, tasting her name in my mouth one last time as it was spoken. 'I'm scared I will disappear.'

When I looked at Abbie, her eyes were large. She said nothing, but I knew one thing for certain. She was scared too.

I had been too loud.

Fifty-Nine

The world was still and quiet when I came home from school. Pulled by the breeze, the front door groaned open and shut as a gale teased it free from the latch. The taste of Patrick's blood in my mouth lingered, tangy like saltwater.

I gathered his taste in my mouth and spat it out at my feet. A small bead of spray hit the end of my shoe.

Hushed tones murmured beneath the wind. Waiting by the door, I crouched on the front step, untangling Mama's words from the quiet as she spoke. Peering through the glass, I noticed her fingers tightly wound around the ringlets of the phone cord. Her knuckles were white again, blood rushing to the highest peaks of her fingertips.

'I'm mortified. I can't put into words how horrified I feel about all this,' Mama said.

Head buried deep in her hands, Eden sat at the kitchen table. She took a deep breath. Craning, her neck arched. I followed the strained line of her trachea as it ribboned through her neck. Mama once told me there was a bone there called an atlas. Her favourite bone. The one she liked to lick once all the meat and cartilage and gristle was stripped off. She especially loved the way her tongue moved over its rounded shape. Eden rolled her head on her shoulders, relaxing as a breath came from her lips.

Through the gap in the front door, Eden spotted me. Her features were not soft the way I wanted them to be; they were hardened as stone, brow hanging heavy over her eyes. When she stood from her seat, the chair legs scraped hard against the floor. Jaw tensed, Eden came for me, pinching the cuff of my jumper with her fingers. She pulled me inside and pushed me onto the couch. 'Your poor mama. She's been on the phone with your school,' she said, cheeks burning red.

Hoping it would swallow me whole, I sank into the couch and put my eyes down. The fleck of spit I'd let perch at the edge of my shoe remained, glistening near the scuffs and scratches. The taste of Patrick had followed me in here. 'I—'

'Don't,' Eden hushed me. Mama wandered towards the hearth, phone pressed against her ear. 'Don't utter another word.'

I thought Mama and Eden would have been proud that I'd bitten Patrick's fingers, even if I had drawn attention to myself. I thought they'd have loved me for it. Held me for it. Seen me as animal – just like them. But when their eyes washed over me, there was no hint of love. No pride for my sharp teeth and all the good work they'd done.

The phone cord was pulled taut from its socket in the wall as Mama's fingers anxiously explored the rings and curves of the wire. She nodded a lot, listening intently to the person on the other end of the phone. I'd never seen her pretend to be so normal before. Not like this.

There was a low hum as someone spoke to Mama on the other end of the line. I wondered if it was Mr Hill, relishing the fact that his least favourite child had acted like an animal. Or maybe it was Roz. The nice stray from the school bathroom.

'Hmmm,' Mama uttered. 'I see.' She hated me.

Eden was wide-eyed, nervously forming patterns in the soot as her toes caressed the flagstone by the hearth. She came away from the fire and brushed soot over the gentle bend of Mama's toenail.

I shuffled, head sinking into my shoulders.

'I understand,' Mama said, but her voice was stiff.

Eden turned her head, watching over me. 'Don't you move,' she said. 'You stay right there.'

'She's going to be punished. I don't tolerate that sort of behaviour under my roof,' Mama said. 'I didn't raise her to be like this.'

I bit down on my tongue hard, hoping the sharp edges of my teeth would cut it open. Anything to overcome the taste of Patrick in my mouth. Even my own blood.

Eden's warm fingers brushed my chin, tilting it up. At first they were delicate, but the hard scrape of her nails pricked my skin. 'What were you thinking, doing something so reckless?'

I shrugged her off. I didn't want to feel her on my skin.

'Answer me,' Eden said, kneeling down. The puddle grey in her eyes wasn't like rain anymore. It pierced, like the sharpened end of a sewing needle.

'He deserved it,' I whispered. And he did. He was the itch I could never scratch.

'Look what you've done to Mama,' Eden whispered, coming to her feet. 'Selfish.' Her footsteps led her through the soot until she found herself close to Mama. Her hands tangled with Mama's, squeezing them tight. *We're going to be okay*, she mouthed. *Everything will be fine.*

'Thank you for calling,' Mama sighed, hanging up the phone. Grinding her teeth, she stared at the receiver. Beneath her skin, neatly guarded by her ribcage, her lungs swallowed air.

'He deserved it, Mama,' I said.

'Don't speak,' she said, holding on to Eden. Their fingers twined together, forming knots. 'You're not to move unless I say so. I don't want to see a finger out of place. Not a toe out of line. You're going to do exactly as I tell you to do. Nothing more. Nothing less.'

I nodded, fingers fidgeting with the cuffs of my school jumper. *I hate you*, I muttered under my breath.

Mama freed herself from Eden's grasp. She knelt close to me, fingernails combing over my knees and then burrowing down hard into my skin. 'You're being too loud,' Mama said. Her lips straightened into a firm line. I wondered if this was how she'd looked at Papa. Her eyes glazed over, pupils swallowed up by the green of her eyes. The dark part of her eye was a small pinprick. I wondered if she was bored of me. Bored of cleaning up after me. Mama leant forward, putting her lips on my ear. 'Maybe you were a mistake,' she whispered quietly. The words were secretive, a quiet breath for me to take in and swallow down into my body.

I kept my eyes low on the ground, focusing on the small fleck of spit still sitting on my shoe.

'I want you to know how much I really mean that,' she whispered.

Sixty

First light came with a chill, but Mama and Eden would sleep for hours more. They liked to wake when the hot sun made pools in their sheets. *I like to wake to a shine*, Eden once said on a bright morning. *A beautiful shine.*

When the beginnings of first light found me, I was outside in the mud. I dug until the beds of my fingernails were crammed with dirt. I'd been away from school for a week. Suspended. Eden told me that I was an animal and animals who bared their teeth and bit were put down.

But something was different now. I lived inside the walls of a new-found silence, like secrets were being kept. Doors were being closed. And Mama and Eden were not living around me anymore, they were lurking. I was going to disappear from this place. I felt it in the homestead's quiet.

I'd already dug up and patted down the other tombs by the verges. Hemlock had sprouted, keeping our secrets safe. The earth was moist, as wet as the mud by the banks of the beck – perfect for growing hemlock. I plucked a handful and stuffed it in my pocket.

Hidden beneath the newly grown flora, wrapped in a plastic bag, I found a toiletries pouch. Inside, there was a bottle of purple nail polish.

The nail polish looked the same as it had all that time ago on my fourth birthday. The glass was cool between my fingers as I slipped it into my pocket. I pulled the black vest top with spaghetti straps from a crinkled plastic bag. Beneath, there were a few pairs of underwear and a couple of scattered bones. The latter all clean and smooth from being stewed for days in stock. A femur. A sternum. A pelvis coiled by hungry shrub roots.

Mama must have taken the rest of the clothes for herself. When she saw them on the bodies of the strays, she imagined the tight cotton embracing her steadily beautiful and bloating belly. Pulling them off the carcasses, she would have tried them on and thought she looked pretty.

The next plastic bag I found had the remains of a suit kept inside. A bloody shirt and a tie that had hardened beneath the ground, cold and crusty. A pair of trousers. Scuffed dress shoes, too.

The skull belonging to the suited man was buried deep. Closer to the surface, a few bones remained. I think they were pieces from his hands and fingers. Holding the bones between my palms, I knew his hands would have been larger than mine. The bones rattled as I dropped them in a bag with his clothes, a sound like music. The last thing I took was the gamekeeper's boots.

They were buried in a shallow ditch. Eden wasn't very good at burying things. They came free from the loose soil as I tugged at the tops of them. I held the boots tight under my arms; they were heavy, waterlogged and a little worm was living inside the eyelets.

'I'm going to set you free,' I promised the strays.

The boots were quiet in my hands.

'More than just boots with a steel toecap. More than just a T-shirt. Why did you have to fall in love with my mama?'

Even though they were inanimate, I imagined they had the quiet, gruff voice of the gamekeeper. I waited for the boots to speak but they remained silent.

'It's the thing she's best at, making people love her. Fall in love with her. She turns them into something broken. Something that only wants and something that can't think. But she falls out of love so easily.'

I took everything I'd gathered from under the hedge and made sure the garden appeared untouched. I tousled the grass and the weeds over the garden ditches and carried the strays with me to the wood, dropping their treasures quietly in the long grass as I approached the treeline.

I was scared Abbie would forget all about me. That my belongings would end up in the ground with the strays, buried in plastic bags and kept compact by the mud. Beneath the crust of soil, my bones would rest. One day they'd be fossils. I would be moments and memories scattered through the minerals and roots.

When I reached the wood, I walked to the almond

stone and left the rest in a heap beneath its shadow. If I was going to disappear, this trail of long-forgotten trinkets would lead someone to our homestead. And maybe they could find me before it was too late.

*

I kept my eye close to the horizon. Our homestead slept between hills and the wood. Buried. I followed the trail of bones I'd left in the high oceans of grass, watching for the gamekeeper's waterlogged boots and the bottle of purple nail polish I'd dropped earlier. They were almost hidden. Only the most watchful stray would find them. Someone smart.

When I reached the gate, the house seemed to take a deep breath with me and hold it in. I imagined its cheeks turning pink, bloated and red.

The stones in the pebble-dash had started to crumble and fall away, and ivy had grown up the walls to clutch onto the guttering, but it couldn't quite reach. There was decay in our homestead, inside and out.

As I climbed the steps, the weight in my body grew larger. I shut the door behind me and wandered to the couch, wiping my hands on my shorts. My fingertips left behind brown rake-like lines on the denim. Though I expected the couch to groan as I sank into its cushions, it was quiet. I was less podgy than I used to be and lighter on my feet.

I curled up and closed my eyes. It was cold in here and there was a trail of soot from the hearth smeared across the wood towards the bedroom. I wondered if Mama and Eden had rolled around by the fire at some point, blackening their freckles. I pictured Eden's hand moving down Mama's back, leaving a jet-black charcoal line along her spine.

There was near silence, save for one sound. Whispers. Passed like secrets behind Mama's bedroom door. I slipped off the couch and wandered towards the room, kneeling down and peering through the keyhole.

Together, they lay in bed, swaddled by linens, bare skin soaking up the sunlight. Eden pulled the linens away. Her hands explored Mama's skin, bruising over every line of cellulite and every wormlike stretch mark on her belly. Mama's body stayed still on the bed. Her body parts were beautiful.

'I think it's the right thing to do,' Eden said, putting her hand on Mama's belly. 'We can keep her safe.'

'I've always wondered what it would be like,' Mama said. 'The homestead will be so quiet.'

Eden crouched over her, pressing her belly flat onto Mama's. I imagined how warm they must feel together, skin on skin. Hiding behind Eden's back, Mama smiled as their mouths overcame one another. Their cheeks blushed; the ghost of soot smeared over their bodies.

'We could have her in here,' Eden whispered, placing one hand on Mama's stomach and the other on her own. 'Carrying her until the end of our lives, letting her pass through us, like water through the ground. We have to take her in and keep her safe. She is a part of us and only truly a child when she is kept safe inside.'

Mama was silent, brow knotted. I held my breath, waiting for her to speak.

'It will keep her with us always,' Eden said. 'We can keep her safe. Don't you see how beautiful that is? We have to do this. Now. Today.' Eden stopped, pulling away from Mama and wrapping herself inside the sheet again. She kissed Mama's collarbones and whispered to them. 'I want to share everything with you, Ruth. And I want to protect Margot from everything. I want to keep her safe from a world that can't understand us.' Eden wanted to feel me by her flesh and organs. She wanted to keep me safe in a place I'd be quiet and do as I was told. A foetus in a belly couldn't be selfish. But a human child could be. To Eden, the potential of who I'd become was so much more beautiful than the way I spoke back. The way I longed to be around Abbie even though I was supposed to hate her. The way I had my own mind.

Mama was silent, considering Eden's words. Along with all my bad habits, all she wanted was for me to be quiet and disappear.

'All that hurt she's going to feel if we let her go on like this. And all that pain she'd go through. It can go away if you just let go,' Eden said. 'Stop worrying about hurting her. Hurt is inevitable. She would have felt it at her first heartbreak. Her first grief. Her first time. You can prevent it. *We* can prevent it from being so.'

But Mama wasn't worried about hurting me. 'It's inevitable,' Mama relented, sighing. 'She's a risk to us. Always getting noticed.'

My feet rooted into the ground, twisting down, down,

down into the floorboards, until they could feel the soil.

'Ugliness will find her and it will keep her. Spoil her,' Eden whispered. 'But we can stop that.'

I stumbled back. There was quiet, and the whispering ceased.

Mama and Eden's mattress groaned, springs taking a stretch as someone stood. When the door swung open, Eden, wrapped in a sheet, looked down upon me. Beneath the surface, I saw the monster. The ugliness made by her pain and grief. It was pushing out all the beauty she'd dressed herself up in over the months.

'Little One?' she said. Her footsteps were gentle across the floor as she came closer to me. 'I thought you were dreaming still. It's too early to be awake.'

Reaching out her hand, Eden came close. I kept my hands away from hers and lurched for the door. Eden was fast, riverlike, as her arms snaked around my shoulders and bound me still.

'Stay,' she whispered, shushing me. 'Stay and be quiet.'

I put my teeth on her arm and bit down. I broke her skin with the edges of my sharp teeth and sucked hard. Blood dribbled down my throat as I tried to tear at her flesh.

'You won't be like the others,' she said. 'You are not a stray. We will mourn you. We'll recount your memories as we place one piece of you inside us at a time. It will be a deep slumber. A good dream.' She didn't seem to mind that I'd bitten her. Her milky skin washed out and the white sheet she was wrapped in became broken by the long streak of blood blooming down it.

'I don't believe you,' I said, trying to shake her free.

Her hand came over my mouth as she shushed me. 'We love you, Margot. This is a kindness.' Eden dragged me towards their bedroom. My heels scraped against the floor as Mama watched absent-mindedly from the door. She moved aside when Eden brought me over the threshold. 'Lock the windows,' Eden said, and Mama moved to them, turning the key and keeping it in her fist. 'You're to stay in here. Just be patient.' Eden kissed my lips and pulled the door shut.

The last thing I heard was the lock crack into place.

Sixty-One

I'd done a good job of pulling weeds over the disturbed earth where I'd exhumed clothes and bones. So much so, Mama and Eden didn't quite realise they were standing upon an almost-empty graveyard.

Eden stood at the centre of the garden. It was as though she'd examined every blade of grass, memorising exactly where each sat in the verges and how it tousled and twined. Eden had Mama's church dress draped over her body, but it wasn't buttoned up properly. There were a few buttons fastened by her midriff but she wore it like a cloak. As she wiped her brow, a stray lock of hair fell over her face.

'Ruth, something is wrong,' she said, pushing the long grasses to the side with her feet. Though she wasn't quite sure what she was looking at, she had found her first empty grave. A pocket of empty soil where bones should have quietly slept.

From my perch at the window, I watched. Her eyes widened. Her feet moved through the underbrush, until she found herself at the back hedge. Eden dropped to her knees and dug into the verge with her fingernails. This shallow grave was empty too. The gamekeeper's boots were gone.

Eden moved near the hedges, hunching over and pulling at the weeds. With her fingers clawed, she dug up the empty bags of stray belongings we'd scattered through the earth over the years. Eden would soon know there wasn't much left. Her fingers traced dirt across her forehead as she wiped her brow. Stilling to a near pulse, Eden looked at the ground. It had finally clicked.

'Ruth!' she called again.

Mama wandered down the garden pathway.

'The bones,' Eden said. 'All the bones are gone.'

'They can't be gone,' Mama replied, turning her head.

Peering through the window, their stares pressed against my guilty face. I cowered behind the sill, cheeks and chest hot and bothered.

'I can't keep you safe anymore!' Eden shouted, but her words were murky, as though they'd been spoken through the water of a pond. 'Not if you try to harm us this way. Not if you try to take away my Ruth.'

She used the word *Ruth* as though she wasn't my mama. It was as though I'd not spent my life holding on to Mama's every sentence; being her whole world and her being mine.

Mama took Eden's hand. Eden's knuckles whitened as she tightened her fist and came through the grass towards the house, dragging Mama with her.

Seconds passed in silence before the door unlocked

and swung open. Eden's face was red, but she collected herself, dressing down her anger. Mama stood close behind, playing with Eden's hair.

'I've never seen you this angry before,' I said, holding my stare. Something of a smirk made its way across my lips. 'It's so easy to get to you.'

Eden took a breath, brushing off Mama and coming close to me. Close enough to touch. 'Where are the bones? Please. Where are the graves?' she asked. 'The bones. The clothes. The boots.'

I kept my mouth closed.

Eden's face hardened. Her breath fell over my face in hot flushes. 'Tell me, Margot.'

Sixty-Two

'Look at me, Margot,' Mama whispered, shuffling closer to me. Her fingers were muddy from hours spent pulling up shallow graves.

Inside the bedroom, mould had kissed the walls, breaking out into darkened pinpricks. Sharp black dots and grey smudges. When Mama got close, I turned my head, pressing my cheek against the wall. I breathed in the mould. I closed my eyes. Damp, like muddy puddles and brambles.

'Let me see you.' Her hands snared my face, holding me still. Pushing my cheekbones together, she watched my mouth pucker until she saw the glint of my teeth. 'When did you become like this? So harmful. So disobedient.'

I winced, jerking free. Edging back against the wall, I cornered myself with the mould. My heels scraped back the dust that had gathered over the years, kicking it up into the air.

'Eden has found some of the bones you left sprinkled

about the field.' Mama sighed, relaxing back near the foot of the bed. 'She's following that trail you left. She won't leave a stone unturned.' Her fingers traced the air, catching the specks of dust as they moved through the warm sunlight. 'And she'll comb the forest until she finds the very last femur.' Mama bit her lip anxiously and narrowed her eyes.

'You are always going to be lonely without me, Mama,' I whispered.

'You don't know anything about real life, Margot,' she said. 'Nothing. You've not lived yet. Not *really*.'

'I know you'll grow bored of her. The same way you've grown bored of me.'

'Is that what you think?' Mama asked, swallowing a desperate laugh. 'That I've grown *bored* of you? Margot, it's so much more than that. I'm not bored of you. I'm *sick* of you. Of all the stupid things you say. Of that disagreeable nature your papa gave you. Of all the things you've done to this body. *My* body.' She took the flesh of her belly between her fingers and squeezed tight. 'Do you think this is what I'm supposed to look like?' Mama's eyes welled up. She bit her lip. 'I could have been so much more than this.'

I took a deep breath. 'I hate you.'

Mama crawled forward and pressed her nose hard against my forehead. Taking a deep inhale, she closed her eyes. When the heavy breath escaped through her lips, it came warm upon my face. Grazing my temple with the point of a fingernail, her hands were gentle with me for the first time in so long. When she was this

256

close, I wanted to lap up the warm teardrops from her cheeks and taste the salt.

'I wonder, if we opened you up just here, would there even be a brain for me to eat?' Mama smiled. 'Or would you be completely empty inside.' Coming to her feet, Mama licked her lips. She meandered to the door, her footsteps slow and heavy. Beneath her weight, the floorboards complained, groaning. 'I've wondered for a long time what you'll taste like. The gamekeeper tasted like euphoria. Because that's what he gave me. But you, Margot? You'll taste of regret.'

The door shut behind her with a sharp slam.

Hidden away inside the top drawer, Mama kept dried-up hemlock. I imagined she lay bare and covered in the gentle petals while Eden drew pictures of her, but not like the pictures Mama had drawn of me. She would have drawn Mama to look beautiful.

When I pulled open the drawer, the hemlock was there. Enough to send a stray to sleep. I nibbled at a petal, letting the flavour settle on my tongue. I swallowed the bitterness and put the gathering of hemlock back in the drawer. I went to the wall again, tracing the freckle-like trail of mould with my fingertips. I opened my mouth and pressed my tongue to the edges of the wall, following the mould until my tongue was black.

I wanted my body to taste horrid. To spore like a busy night sky. Part of me even wished for my heart to stop before they had the chance to pick at my skin and leave me bare. As I took another lick of the black, I thought about my lungs stopping, heavy from being crusted over

257

by mould. Outside, Mama exhumed the almost-empty graves, searching to see just how much had disappeared from our shallow ditches in the mud. I couldn't help but smile as I watched.

Sixty-Three

My skin was greying. The blood in my body was hiding.

I woke up coughing, curled up on the floor in a mouldy corner of the room. In my sleep, I'd pulled a sheet down from the bed and snuggled up inside. It smelt like Mama.

When I looked out the window, Mama was sitting in the mud, head in her hands as she stared into an empty ditch. Eden fetched an old jumper from inside and put it over Mama's shoulders, kissing her forehead. Nearby, a small pile of bones and clothes had been gathered from Eden's search of the woodland. There were still body parts and trinkets left to uncover along the woodland pathways. Eden wouldn't stop until they were all buried in the cold ground again. A gale brushed past them both and tickled the bottoms of their dresses, kicking up the hems to cool off their thighs.

Mama looked up, catching me at the window. I searched her expression for something familiar, but I didn't recognise the woman standing in our garden. It's impossible to truly know someone who hides so much of themselves and consumes so much of others.

Over the years, I'd watched her pick up pieces of strays and wear them; weave them into her personality. Dresses. T-shirts. Nail polish. Jewellery. Bags. Shoes. Even lingerie. Everything and anything she could take to fill the hungry void. Now she was unravelling, because at the centre of it all there was nothing keeping her together.

I pressed my face to the window. It was cold against my cheeks. A lump formed in my throat as I thought about the bus driver absent-mindedly watching the roads and singing beneath his breath. And there, over the hedge, the school bus appeared, pulling up at the gate. My suspension was over. Smoke billowed out from the exhaust and drifted away with the Helm Wind.

Following my gaze, Mama peered over the hedge. When she saw the bus, she ran to the back gate and hurried down the path.

I tapped on the pane with my fingers. 'I'm here. Notice me,' I whispered, hoping the bus driver would look above his wheel and see my face at the window.

Through the glass, Eden raised her finger to her mouth. Coming closer, she stopped a short distance away and looked for Mama over the hedge. The ignition began again. When Mama came back to the garden, she and Eden stood close by the window, studying me. Eden's eyebrow cocked.

'What did you say to him?' I asked through the glass.

'He was terribly ugly,' Mama said. 'And he stank of smoke.'

'What did you say to him?' I asked again, tapping my fingers on the cold glass.

'Don't break the window,' Mama snapped. 'I told him you were sick. I told him you needed more time away from school.'

'But I'm not sick,' I said.

Eden took Mama's hand, leading her to the top of the garden. Together, wearing the old wellingtons and clothes of strays long gone, they escaped out the back gate and went out into the wilds together in pursuit of bones. There wasn't much left along my trails. Soon it would all be returned to the garden graves.

That day, I ate a whole stem of hemlock, picking at the petals and placing them on my tongue one at a time. My breathing sounded like wind scraping through the eaves of the house. There was a whistle.

I wheezed in and out as I curled up in the corner and told myself to fall asleep.

Sixty-Four

'There's not long left until school breaks up for summer. A week,' Eden said, fastening a cable bond around my ankle. It was tight, rubbing against my skin. Soon, small blisters would form over my heel. 'That will stay nice and tight,' she muttered while she concentrated. 'You'll feel happier out here with a bit of freedom.'

Because all strays had to be happy before they were taken into the dark. And that's what I was now. A stray.

Though it was a rare moment of freedom away from the bedroom, the bonds fastened around my ankle stopped me from straying too far. I curled up on the couch, keeping as far from Mama and Eden as I could. Together, they sat in the cinders by the hearth, tracing shapes in each other's skin.

'A week is fine,' Mama muttered to herself.

'A week is all we need,' Eden said, turning to me. 'You hear that?' She reached over to me, pressing a daub of soot into the arch of my foot. 'You're not going into school anymore. Isn't that what every child dreams of?'

Thinking of Abbie, I shook my head.

'I hated school,' Mama said. 'It was a wicked place. Full of wicked people.'

'I miss Abbie.' I held on to the image of the gap between her teeth, and her green ribbon too.

'She won't have spared you a second thought,' Eden said. 'Children only have room in their heads for one thought and feeling at a time.'

'Can you think or feel more than one thing at once?' I asked, pulling my foot away from her cindered fingers.

Eyes narrowed, Eden paused. There was only room for one thought at a time inside her head. That made me smile.

Collecting a blackness between the creases of her palm, she wiped her hand across the stone at the foot of the hearth. Once her palm was caked, she came close on her hands and knees and smeared her fingers over my cheek. 'If you're bad, we'll put you back in that cramped little room and you'll sit by yourself,' she said. 'But if you're good, all this will pass quickly. And you won't feel it.'

Her palm was warm on my cheek. I imagined the firelight. 'I'm cold,' I said. 'And hungry.'

'I can put the fire on,' Mama said, leaning down to fetch the matches.

'Let Margot light it,' Eden said, yanking the bond around my ankle. 'If she's out here with us, then she may as well be of use.'

I slid down from the sofa, crumpled up an old newspaper and pressed it between two half-scorched logs. Striking the match, I put it to the old paper and watched the flames grow, nibbling at the edges of slowly disappearing news stories. I added a few twigs and some coals to keep it going, placing one piece in at a time. 'I want heat,' I moaned, 'and something to eat.' For once, I felt like acting like a real child, one that would kick and scream if it didn't get its own way.

The first time I'd ever cried to Mama, I'd grazed my knee out on the road. I ran to her, blood curdling on the crest of my kneecap and dribbling down my shin. I cried harder and louder than I'd ever cry again. But she looked at me, large eyes unmoving, mouth in a straight line, apathetic. And with no warning, she opened her mouth and screamed. Her face was close to mine. I felt a wave of hot breath hit my cheek.

'Maybe we should give her something,' Mama whispered to Eden in a low hum. 'There's not a lot of meat on her bones. She's looking wiry.'

'I suppose we could treat her to something nice,' Eden said, measuring her options. 'Little One, will you make a cake with me? We can play with the flour.'

I shook my head. I was reminded of the first time we'd baked with flour together and she'd tapped it on the tip of my nose and brushed it across my chin.

'Come on, now,' she said. 'Don't be like that. It'll be fun. We'll keep those bonds around your little ankles and we'll go to the kitchen.'

I shook my head again, but she tugged at the bonds. I noticed a pink ring had appeared around my skin. The beginnings of a blister. Eden tied my bonds to the legs of the table. 'Keep an eye on her,' she called to Mama.

Mama came to the table and sat with me. She took

my hand and pulled me onto her lap, holding me tight. Her nose explored my scalp, taking in deep breaths of my scent. Her hands explored my ribs, seeing where I could be fattened up. 'You're all skin and bones, aren't you?' Mama said. 'We'll soon fix that, don't you worry.'

Though my stomach contracted, I did not want to eat. I didn't want the soft sponge of a warm homemade cake. Or the light whipped frosting that Eden would smear over the top of it.

I would keep my stomach empty and tasteless.

*

That night, Mama kept my shoulders pinned against the back of the chair. I curled my lips around my teeth and bit my tongue. I wouldn't eat the cake, but Eden's stare was heavy on me. Her brow knotted.

'I've put a lot of love into this,' she said, smearing icing across my mouth and pressing the sponge between my lips. 'You said you were hungry and now we're feeding you. So eat it.'

I pushed my chin to one side but Mama pulled down on my jaw.

The cake landed on my tongue. It was sweet and buttery and the icing melted down into the sponge. I wanted so badly to swallow it, but I let it ferment before spitting it out onto the table.

Eden looked down at the mess I'd made and then glared at me. 'You are going to eat that.'

Sixty-Five

To make me a happy stray, Mama and Eden told me stories, describing Abbie's features to me as I drifted into daytime slumber. The blonde hair. The gaps between her teeth. The green ribbon always on the verge of being pulled out by the wind. They told me about what waited for me on the other side and how it would feel to live inside both of their bellies at once.

'It will be warm. You will be in so many pieces, but you will be at peace inside us. You are a promise. You are a promise that we will both feel full and warm, always,' Mama whispered to me, but her words were drifting away. I knew the words had been stolen from Eden's mouth. They were simple, empty echoes. Hollow promises. I didn't feel full or warm. I felt alone and scattered.

Mama sat at the kitchen table, gazing at me as though I were a daydream. The *something* that would fill her void for good.

'Mama?' I asked, tugging at the bonds tied around my ankle. 'I want to go outside and feel the sunlight.'

Mama's gaze moved over my face. 'If you must,' she said, untying the bonds from the table leg, leading me towards the light. Dust fell through the air and caught the sunlight in glints. When Mama opened the door, the warmth hit me. The air was dry, filled with dirt being pulled up from the ground and swept about by the quiet summer breeze. Watching out over into the pastures, Mama's forehead glistened as we came to the grass and stopped by the gate. The treeline looked more distant than ever.

'You're looking a bit pale,' Mama said, brushing her hands through my hair and pulling me close into her tight embrace.

My knees were stiff as I took steps towards the gate, but Mama yanked back on the bonds. I stumbled to a stop.

'You're not to go near the road.'

'I just want to go to the beck,' I said. 'I want to lie in the water. Over the stones.'

Mama looked behind her. Eden was busy in the kitchen, flour everywhere again. 'Only for a moment,' Mama said, guiding me over the gate and walking me out across the road until we reached the banks.

I took off my socks and slipped down the mud, pressing my feet onto the cold, rounded stones sitting near the currents. The water moved quick, desperate to get away. Or desperate to pull me away with it.

'I can't go with you,' I whispered to the currents as I sat down and soaked. I lay my head down in the water and my hair bloomed like veins. 'If I tell you something, will you take it with you?'

The water didn't respond.

'I'm going to tell you anyway,' I said. 'Tell Abbie I am sorry. I'm sorry I ate her papa. I still feel her strand of hair at the bottom of my belly. It tickles my insides whenever I think about her.'

The currents bubbled on, carrying my words upstream, towards the estuaries. I dipped my head beneath the water and held my breath.

Sixty-Six

When they were together, the world felt slower. Time moved differently. It was damp, heavy, as though it was dragging behind the rest of the world. Soaking up the sunlight, Mama sat at the kitchen table next to me as Eden spun around in her church dress; she never did the buttons up properly. Missing splinters by a hair's breadth, her bare feet skimmed over the wood. When I listened hard, I heard the brush of her toes. It sounded like a quiet ocean tide pulling in and out. The music played low as Mama nursed a glass of wine and watched, lost in Eden.

Laughter and love came in abundance but it spoilt them. As Eden spun, her dress came up past her hips. She pulled down her hair and raised her arms up, desperate to feel her whole body move. Mama wanted to be close to her, skin on skin, but she couldn't bring herself to touch her. She was rooted to the chair.

There was something about the way Eden moved. It was like she moved in the same way the first humans did around their fires. I pictured her wrapped in thick fur, like the rabbit woman, dancing to the light of a fire in a cave somewhere cold and quiet.

Mama stood and reached out her arms to hold Eden. Her fingers were close enough to reach her mouth, but something stopped her in her tracks. Eden's arms dropped to her side. We all looked at the door.

Mama turned off the cassette player and we waited in the quiet.

A stray had knocked on our door.

Hungry, we watched the silhouette beyond the glass.

Sixty-Seven

There were two of them.

Both women. One was tall, wiry, and older than I'd ever seen a woman grow. Her hair was silver, falling off her shoulders in a long plait. The other was smaller, but fuller. She'd be tastier. Meatier.

Eden hurried to my feet, unfastening the bonds and sweeping them beneath a nearby counter where they would not be seen. Mama opened the door. Eden watched, doing up her buttons and pulling her hair back into a tight knot. I stood behind Mama, clutching onto the loops in her jeans.

'Sorry to bother you,' the silver-haired woman spoke. Her voice croaked. She'd chain-smoked and now was left with a voice like sandpaper. 'We're having some car trouble. Wondered if you could lend a hand swapping a tyre?'

I thought about the nails Mama had sprinkled on the roads a few miles away, somewhere people didn't drive often so as not to cause suspicion.

Mama stared at the strays, mouth watering. It had been a while since our last good meal but Eden and Mama had made a pact to fast. They were saving themselves for me.

Eden stepped forward, doing up the last of her buttons. 'We have some tools,' she said. 'I'll help get you on your way.' Around the strays she spoke differently. She spoke like a woman from this time and not another. Her otherworldliness slipped.

'Thank you,' the silver-haired woman said. 'I'm useless when it comes to this sort of stuff. And so is this one.' She gestured to the meatier one. 'We managed to roll our car to not too far from here.'

Eden disappeared into the back room and reappeared with Papa's old toolbox.

'Do you want to have a cup of tea while you wait?' Mama asked the younger one.

The younger woman, mouth kept shut, nodded and smiled.

Eden followed the silver-haired woman outside, beyond the gate and down the road. Almost out of view, hidden behind the deep overgrown hedges and trees, Eden and the woman settled by the car. I wondered, if I set off running, just how far my feet would take me before I got caught. Eden was quick on her feet. And Mama would never be far behind. As I watched out into the world, Mama kept a tight pinch on my shoulder and invited the meaty one inside.

The meaty one, with muscles on her arms, stood at the centre of the room as Mama closed the door, turned the lock and put the kettle on. The stray didn't want to settle here. She was flighty. While the kettle boiled, Mama stood behind me, wrapping her arms around my shoulders.

'You can sit at our table,' I said. I wondered how old she was. I imagined taking a knife to her skin the way axes bit at bark just so I could count the tree rings inside.

She had dark eyes, a deep green, and a rounded nose. 'Thanks,' she said, moving towards the table and taking a seat close to the door.

Hands pressing firm on my shoulders, Mama pushed me into a seat close by. I didn't take my eyes off the stray.

'Do you go to school?' I asked.

'I've just graduated university,' she said.

'What do you do?' Mama asked, bringing a warm cup of tea to the table and sitting with us.

'Medicine. I'm going to be a doctor,' she said quietly, as though measuring her words. Before Mama could speak, the meaty stray looked at me. 'What do you want to be when you grow up?'

My mouth opened as though an answer was ready to come out, but no words came. They stayed lodged in my throat. Mama watched me, raising her eyebrows. 'I don't know,' I said. 'I don't like school.'

'She's a bit slow, this one, but she has a good imagination in her,' Mama said, sipping her tea and pondering what my imagination would taste like on her lips. 'She'll find her use one day.' Mama scruffed up my scalp before leaning back into her chair and sipping her tea again.

The meaty stray watched me. I'd seen the look on her

face before. No, I hadn't seen it, but I'd felt it in my own muscles. She wanted to say something but instead decided to keep it to herself.

I looked down at the table and traced shapes in the wooden lines. My mouth watered. Soon Eden returned with the silver-haired woman. She thanked us for our hospitality, but the meaty stray kept her eyes only on me. She quietly watched over me as she finished the last of her tea and escaped our homestead – something no stray had ever done before. The green of her eyes caught the sun as she left.

'They were nice,' Eden said, watching as they disappeared towards the road. 'I wonder if they'll ever come back near here.'

'Maybe one day we can have a taste,' Mama said, smiling.

'I might even dream of them,' Eden said. 'The older one. She would taste beautiful and tender. So many memories.'

'The young one wasn't much to talk to, but at least she was meaty. Give it a few years and she'd be a perfect stray.'

Sixty-Eight

Mama sat in Eden's lap, resting her curved spine in the crook of her belly. Eden combed her fingers through Mama's hair as they curled together on the couch. 'How will we tell the world what has become of her?' Mama whispered to Eden.

They spoke as though I wasn't sitting beside them. Eden glanced at me. 'What do you want us to tell them?'

I wanted them to tell the truth. 'Tell them I disappeared.'

'Too simple,' Eden said, fingers toying with her bottom lip.

'Tell them I went to the woods one day, got lost too far beyond the almond stone and disappeared in the high ferns.'

Eden nodded. 'We can tell them you ran away from home,' she agreed. 'But you'll never really leave home. Not ever.'

All I wanted was to grow. But the truth was, I was growing up more than anyone else. I knew that had to be true because growing up hurt. My body was stretching. My teeth had fallen out and grown larger, more sharp, pushing through the holes in my gum. My hips were expanding. My waist was beginning to curve. Hair was pushing out through follicles in my legs, armpits and groin. I was a changeling, like the boys from school and the other children, constantly shifting while our parents wanted us, so badly, to stay frozen.

'Children run out into roads all the time,' Mama said. 'Maybe we could tell people you got hit by a car a few miles down. Leave some clothes. Some blood. A few bones. A bag. People will draw their own conclusions.'

Lost in thought, Eden nodded.

*

After the last of the sun had stretched over the west, Mama and Eden walked up the road for miles, searching for the perfect spot to leave a trail of my things. I don't know how far they travelled, but they were gone for hours.

Leaving my bonds in the living room, they locked me in the bedroom again. I sat on the floor, dragging my fingertip down the gaps between floorboards. Dust piled at my nail until a pinch caught at my skin. I thought it might have been a splinter, one I was ready to unearth, but it wasn't. There was blood at the end of my finger, red and bulbous. I put it in my mouth and tasted.

Then I saw it. A glint. A shine. Something silver in the light, hidden between the floorboards.

On my hands and knees, I came towards the strange object wedged in the wood. The wound was a pinprick left behind from a sharpened sewing needle. I tried to pry it out with my fingernail, but it slipped. As I pinched it up through the gap, I caught it through the first layer of skin on my thumb. Right between nail and skin. Dragging it back up through the floorboards, I dislodged the needle from my thumbprint. I let it roll into my palm.

The lock at the window was old, and I wondered if this was my way out.

Sixty-Nine

Mama and Eden still hadn't returned. It was getting dark out and the sky was marred with bruises of purple. In the garden, the bees were woozy from a long day of travelling the pollen from the clearing around the pastures. Inside, a bumblebee bumped its head against the glass, bouncing down the pane until it landed on the sill. Abbie once told me a teaspoon of water and sugar helped them get back in the air.

When I looked at my fingertips, they were bleeding from spending the hot summer afternoon picking at the lock of the window. I'd been fiddling, poking the sewing needle around in the lock, hoping to click it open. In the reflection of the window, my forehead glistened.

The bumblebee stumbled across the windowsill, but the heat was slowing it down. Outside the walls of this house, the world was heating up, getting too warm for all the creatures to keep their heads straight. But inside, by the bricks, it was cooler here. The draught whispered as it brushed across the floor.

I studied the sewing needle, picking it up again and holding it between my thumb and finger. It was rusted along its edge and slightly bent from trying to pry open the lock.

I wondered if Mama and Eden had chosen the spot yet. The place they were going to tell people I'd died. I imagined it to be a place where the tarmac had potholes; a place where the road was a little worn away and smelt like petrol. Maybe a crossroads. Eden would've known the spot as soon as she laid eyes on it. She was particular. Precise. Instinctive. She was a person who knew exactly what she wanted, and took it.

When she saw that spot of tarmac, miles away from our homestead, she'd have known in her bones it was the right place.

Next week, they'd put torn clothes at the edge of the road and leave a splash of my blood in a pothole. Maybe a small body part too. The world would go on believing what it wanted to believe – a quickly forgotten tragedy and an injured young changeling who, after being hit by a car, stumbled into the woods to die. Left unfound.

I kept an eye on the dying bumblebee as I fiddled with the lock. I curved the sewing needle and tilted it up as I held on to the handle.

Something clicked.

The window opened. Despite the oncoming darkness, the summer air was warm. The currents of the stream hurried away towards the rivers. All the birds sang as they tried to settle in their nests. Climbing up onto the sill, I brushed the bee aside gently and slipped out. My knees hit the ground with a scrape.

I could've saved the bee but my legs carried me away fast. When I found tarmac, I stopped, gazing at the length of road. My eyes moved across the pastures. I set my sights on the wood.

There'd be strays there. Maybe one that could take me away. I crossed the road, kicking up dust as I picked up speed. Running down the banks, I crossed the beck before reaching the pastures. Nettles stung my legs, but I didn't stop.

I was going to live.

*

It was cold beneath the stars. At school they'd said they were so hot they could kill you – take away your skin and muscle. Even your bones. Cook you. But, from the earth, I couldn't imagine those ice-cold stars being hot to touch.

I found shelter beneath the almond stone. Beyond, the woodland was wide. The trees seemed to go on forever, standing tall and strong. My stomach groaned, hungry for the next bite, but there were no brambles close by. Or berries to pluck from the branches.

My bare feet stung from the sharp cut of pebbles and twigs embedded in the shallow mud, but they could rest easy for the night. Mama wouldn't find me here, cosied into the dirt and leaves like a sleeping animal. That night I slept with a colony of woodlice. The birds were quiet in their nests as they dreamt with me. The sky was open. Cloudless. Each star was like a precious stone placed up high and out of reach.

Tomorrow, I would find Abbie or the bus driver.

Seventy

I only remembered the fringes of my dream. The hazy, watercolour edges that bled into real life. Abbie and her green ribbon. I'd pulled it from her hair and twined it between my fingers, watching it twist and flap in the breeze. Her green ribbon was beautiful, even as it spindled away from my fingers and disappeared into the darkest black of the woodland.

I didn't know what time it was when I woke, but it was light. Curled up beneath the shadow of the almond stone, dried-up leaves and bracken bonded to my skin. When I peeled away the leaves, branchlike veins were left imprinted in my skin, like the scars left behind from a deep sleep against a crumpled bedsheet. Twigs knotted in my hair and mud smeared across my forehead. I was a piece of the forest. A small flake of skin upon its back.

One at a time, I untangled the twigs from my hair and pulled the leaves away from my skin, rubbing my arms to wipe away the new veiny imprints. There were new scrapes on my knees from the thorning bushes and the stones half buried in the ground, but Abbie's house wasn't far. A few hours on foot. It was right by school. Every night, after the last bell rang, I'd watched Abbie pass through the school gate and tumble into her mam's arms. And together they walked the curved country road towards their little cottage.

I tried to picture it in my head. The tired sandstone bricks. The broken window by the front door that the gamekeeper had never found time to fix because he'd spent every spare afternoon in the dust with Mama's body. Writhing. Their home was scruffy-looking since we'd eaten up the man of the house.

Even the rose bushes had wilted.

I couldn't wait to feel Abbie's green ribbon between my fingers again, soft as I'd wrap it around my knuckles. Maybe Abbie's mama would give me a green ribbon of my own and fasten it tight in my hair. So tight it could never be pulled away by the breeze or the greedy fingers of a schoolboy. I'd become neat and normal. And I'd never think about eating strays again. Ever. Not a single tender rump or velvety kidney. Instead, we'd have shepherd's pie and Yorkshire puddings. Thick and salty gravy that drooled over our crispy roast potatoes. Fish finger sandwiches and bowls of cereal. Picnics. Stray food.

As I moved beyond the almond stone, I counted my steps. I was only a few hours away from that pretty green ribbon. Grey clouds came overhead and rain fell from the sky. I opened my mouth, stuck out my tongue and lapped up the raindrops.

'Margot!' Between the trees, I saw her. Mama. Her eyes were large, filling with tears as she tilted her head. 'Little One?' Mama shrieked, but weeping overcame her words as she stumbled through the leaves.

I took off into the shadows but Mama pushed on through the ferns. Her boots kept her soles safe from the ground, but mine were pinched and cut by the tough stones and roots.

'Come back!' she shouted, words echoing through the trees.

'I'm not one of them,' I called, out of breath. 'I'm not one of your strays.'

The wood was wide. Stumbling over fallen logs and surfaced tree roots, I ran. My chest was knotted tight. The air wouldn't come to my lungs. My calves trembled, tense and tired. My kneecaps knocked together as I lurched between the winding tree trunks and the tip of my toe caught on the crag of a stone. Hitting the ground with a hard slam, my head rang out. Fumbling to my feet, I squinted, but the world was hazy. New scrapes formed on the heels of my palms and across my knees. Tingles came, sharp and pointed where my skin had been shredded.

A smear of blood scurried down my calf, escaping from a cut on my knee. Mouthlike, a gash had been sliced into my skin. I limped between the trees, reaching out to stay upright, but the bark was serrated against the newly formed scrapes. My skin burnt hot, my cheeks searing.

Mama's arms came around me as she pulled me close.

'How could you do this to us?' she asked, words echoing. She fell to her knees, binding me to her body. The sounds waned in my ears as I searched for the quiet of the wood.

'I'm not a stray. And you cannot make me one,' I spat, but the world was still spinning.

'You left the bones out here in the woods to be found. And then you ran from us,' she said.

When her cheek pressed hard against mine, I felt the warmth of her tears. But these were not tears for me. I could taste that in the tart salty plume on my tongue. These were selfish tears. All for her.

'I don't want to be in your belly,' I said. 'I want to be far away from you.'

Eden emerged from the trees and came to Mama's side.

'This won't do,' she said. 'Did you not think we'd find you, Little One? I combed these woods. I know your trails.' Eden pulled Mama into a tight embrace. Sandwiched between two firm ribcages, their bones trapped me in. I was crushed between them as Eden embraced Mama and kissed her mouth. 'Dry your tears. There's no more time to waste.'

Seventy-One

Mama and Eden were talking, but I wasn't listening. I was watching over the dead bumblebee on the bedroom windowsill. Maybe it wouldn't be crusty and dead if I'd stopped to feed it the sugar water it needed to leave this place. Or maybe it would have keeled over anyway, sticky and hot, coated in sugar. Maybe it was meant to be here forever. Maybe it was inevitable.

Mama and Eden were sitting close, fingers playing with the edges of my blanket. Together, they were still, keeping their whispers hushed. Mama bit down on her bottom lip, consoling herself. She was ugly when she wept. Swollen and red, cheeks and nose wetted. Eden glanced at me.

'You won't have long left. A week at most,' Mama said, pulling at my ankle and fastening the bonds around it.

'We can start putting things into motion in the coming days,' Eden said.

'You weren't supposed to be a mama,' I said, cutting

them off. 'Neither of you were.' I caught Mama's stare and I held it. 'You are badness.'

'After everything I've done for you,' Mama said, gritting her teeth. 'After everything I've sacrificed. Every meal I've put on the table. Every piece of clothing I've put on your back.'

'She's just afraid,' Eden said. 'And she needn't be. There's nothing to fear.'

'I didn't want to carry a child!' Mama shouted. 'I never wanted to be a mama. I just wanted to be a person. None of this was supposed to happen.'

I kept breathing. In and out. One breath at a time.

'It's okay,' Eden said, hushing Mama. Her hand stroked the bumps of Mama's spine. 'You don't mean that. I know you don't. Things will be different with me.'

'I do mean it,' Mama said.

'Being a mama is what we're supposed to be.' Eden held Mama's belly as she dried her tears. 'I'm going to blanket her in pastry. I'm going to keep her warm in the oven until she's cooked through nice and good. Then I'm going to put her in a baking tray with some potatoes. And she will be the most beautiful thing you've ever eaten in your life.'

'No. I won't,' I said. 'I'll make sure to be tough and gamey. I'll have big chunks of fat. I will be impossible to swallow. You'll have to spit me right back out.'

Eden smiled, brushing my hairline with her fingernails, following the ridge of my scalp. 'You'll taste exactly the way we want you to.'

'I don't want to be a mother,' Mama said. That word,

mother, sounded alien on her lips. 'You make me hate myself,' she said, glowering at me.

'You don't mean that,' Eden said again.

'You make me hate myself too,' I spat. 'You make me want to disappear.'

Slamming the door behind her, Mama disappeared into the living room. She left us alone in the bedroom, my ankle bonds fastened to the bed. Eden sighed, putting her head in her hands. 'You'll apologise to her,' she said. 'That was very rude.'

'I'm never going to tell her I'm sorry.' I folded my arms and burrowed into my little corner.

'Is that really the last thing you want your mama to hear you say?'

Yes. It is. I stayed quiet and still.

'I'm going to lock you in here. Then, once I've done that, you see that window?' she asked, pointing towards it. 'I'm going to bar it up with wood so you can't even see sunlight. When you're *really* sorry, I'll take down a few planks so you can see the beck. And the wood. But you need to learn to behave yourself.' Eden fastened together my hands and checked the bonds around my ankles to make sure they were nice and tight. The blisters stung.

'I'll never be sorry,' I said. 'Not ever. I will feel this way until the end.'

Eden smiled warmly, taking a deep breath of calm. She gazed at me like I was a memory she sorely missed. Then, more collected than she'd ever been before, she closed the bedroom door behind her.

Seventy-Two

I sat by the window, pressing my skin to the cold tiles on the bathroom floor. Close by, Mama hunched in the corner. The incessant etching of her fireside charcoal scratched against the paper Eden had made her. Mama's eyes moved down my spine, collecting every bump and curve as they rounded down to my coccyx. Mama's glances traced the back of my ribs and she licked her lips. She was calm today.

'Sit up straight,' she said. 'I don't want to remember you with a bend in your spine. Back up, straight and beautiful. I want to remember you the way I remember myself as a girl.' I saw her reflection in the window. She was focused and determined. Flecks of black mould had eaten away at the edges of the glass, eating up Mama's reflection. And mine too.

Mama looked like a changeling now too. Love had changed her. She wasn't frightening anymore, the way she used to be. Instead, I saw something as fragile as glass. Always on the edge of breaking.

288

With this new-found love, it made me wonder about
the love she'd shared with Papa. The love she'd forced
herself to feel. I'd looked through photographs for too
long, placing smiles over frowns and closeness over
distance. Presence over absence. What remained now,
when I thought of Mama and Papa, was a union of two
lonely people. They were the remains of a fire, charred
and burnt and broken.

Mama's charcoal scratched against the paper some
more.

'Can I relax yet?' I asked.

'I'll have to start again if you move,' Mama said, eyes
darting over the top of her page. She was urgent today.
In a rush to get it all done and dusted.

'Tell me about love,' I said, brushing the mould on the
window with my fingers and then sucking on them. I
pretended it was bitter brambles from the wood. Sweet.
Ripe. Something to walk me to the edgelands – a place
I could finally sleep. 'Real love.'

'What of it?' Mama asked, looking at me in earnest
over her sketch paper.

'What do you think it is?' The trees outside were still,
pine needles clutching onto their branches.

'When I think of the word *love*, I think of the first
time I knew I looked beautiful.' Mama's shoulders dropped beneath a deep breath and she found a nostalgic smile
from her memories. 'I was eleven. People started looking
at me differently. I knew then that I was beautiful, even
in my strange sort of way. Even with my teeth all jumbled
up in my jaw. Their attention felt like a promise that I'd

be loved and looked after for the rest of my life. A human sort of love.'

But that didn't sound like love to me. 'Are there different sorts of love?' I asked, thinking of Abbie's nimble fingers trailing along the creases in my palm. I entwined my fingers, pretending she was close.

'Sometimes I think it's all the same thing.' Mama paused, her face softening. She was thinking of Eden. 'I think our brains will love in whatever capacity they can.'

'I don't think you love me,' I said.

Mama was quiet, measuring her words. 'Sometimes I feel connected to you,' she said. 'Drawn to you. Like there is a thread between you and me that can never break or be severed. I think that's something like love, don't you?' Mama paused again, resting her drawing on her lap. 'I think.'

'I don't think I love you either,' I admitted.

Mama dropped the charcoal on the tiles by her feet. Her face stilled, but with that strange smile that lingered on the edge of her mouth. 'Why do you say that?'

'Because I dream of hurting you and I like the way it feels.' I looked down at my toes, wiggling them to revive them from the cold. 'And I know you feel the same way about me.'

Mama picked up her charcoal again and scratched the pages. Between the brushes of her sketches, the silence bled. Only when she was finished with her picture did she speak again. 'So, maybe I don't love you. Does that really make me a terrible mother? Lots of mothers don't love their daughters.'

I waited for her to glance at me over her sketches, but she kept her eyes down.

'Get yourself in the bath.' Mama spoke as though the words we had shared were not an open wound, still bleeding.

One toe at a time, I climbed in the tub and embraced the heat. The water was still searing hot and cloudy from a modest spill of bubble bath, but there were no bubbles and the water did not sparkle. The faint scent of soap flooded the decay. While I sank into the water, I hoped for my fingers to prune, so my skin could wrinkle and float away, bloated and broken. I wanted to taste cold and flimsy in her mouth like the soggy pasta shells she'd cooked me so many times before. I closed my eyes and wished for the mildew and mould to entomb me. I took a deep breath from the cold air.

'Do you think I'm ugly?' I asked, looking at my fingers and pretending they were webbed beneath the water.

'What does that matter?' Mama asked as she scribbled, adding line after line of charcoal to her already tortured sketch.

'When you draw me, I look ugly.' My chin settled beneath the water's lip and I watched Mama in the corner of the room, still drawing, cutting harsh lines into the page.

'I draw you as you are,' Mama said. 'How I see you.'

When I looked at my reflection in the windowpane by the bath, I saw something ugly and pale too. My skin was pasty and bruised, and I was getting skinny in all the wrong places, malformed where flesh stretched out and trailed newly forged stretch marks. My hips were wider too, not by much, but enough for my clothes to be a little bit too tight. I looked out of proportion. Inhuman.

I was an awful mix of Mama, Papa, and now Eden too. When I stared a little too hard at the windowpane, my eyes looked like Eden's. A new fleck of gold had appeared in my left eye. I wondered if perhaps a piece of her had always been inside me, just waiting to be brought out.

Eden was a woman who seemed ancient, but her skin was young, tight and freckled where the sun had touched it. But I wouldn't grow to be beautiful like Eden. And I wouldn't grow to be ancient. I was going to be an ugly little girl for the rest of my life.

I didn't see *my* eyes anymore. They were fragments of strays who'd come before. I wondered if this was what being a real human was: accepting you were pieces of other people too. The people you loved and the people you hurt.

Seventy-Three

I swallowed my hunger. I would not eat their food. The last meal Mama and Eden made me was a warm rabbit pie. It sat in the middle of a clean plate. Green beans and boiled potatoes were tucked in close to the pastry.

Eden pushed my chair in nice and tight so I was crushed against the table. I looked at my portion, hungering to feel the crunch of the pastry between my teeth as Mama and Eden took their seats beside me. My mouth was dry, but saliva filled the dip beneath my tongue. I wanted my body to do as it was told. For my belly to remain empty.

Watching them between the flickering candles, my fingertips grazed the sharpened edges of my knife and fork. Eden gazed at the shimmer of the china in the candlelight, biting her lip. The bags beneath our eyes looked longer in these shadows. The shapes of our skulls were prominent where the light touched our skin. Our temples dipped by our eyes and our skin hung from our cheeks. Mama opened a bottle of red wine and filled the glasses.

My lips stayed closed, but my mouth watered still. My stomach twisted in knots, groaning as the rich scent of gravy made its way into my nostrils. Meaty but sweet, with onions soaked through. The scent of rosemary and sage was strong on the air. My fingers found themselves teasing the edges of my fork. I pressed the prongs deep into the pastry. They sank down with a crunch before hitting the china. The pastry flaked, buttery and golden brown.

'We're saving ourselves,' Mama said, resting her chin in her palm. 'Go ahead. Eat up. Lick the plate clean.'

'Every potato was plucked from the ground with our bare hands and the green beans were taken from the bush,' Eden said, nursing her glass. She had so much pride in her work. There was still dirt in the creases of her palm from the harvest. As I took my first bite, the rabbit lay on my tongue. It was ready to be swallowed, and yet I couldn't bring myself to enjoy it. The spores at the back of my throat were getting larger, closing up my gullet. The hemlock I'd been nibbling squeezed my lungs tight. I imagined Mama's hand around the tissue of my lungs, grasping as her nails lay on the brink of puncturing them.

There wasn't enough air in the room to take in.

'The rabbit,' Eden said. 'We found it caught in your trap.'

I chewed down. The meat came apart between my teeth.

'That trap will be good and strong for years to come,' she said. 'And every time we eat from it, we'll think of you.' She took a pregnant pause, reaching her hand, pressing it on my thigh and squeezing tight. 'Poor little thing struggled so much. The fishing twine almost cut away its limbs and floppy ears,' Eden said, but her words faltered into a warm laugh.

I ate the potatoes one at a time, taking them between my fingers and slipping them in my mouth. They were like clouds, fluffy and buttery and perfectly seasoned.

'Slow down. You don't want to give yourself indigestion,' Mama said, scolding me.

'It's okay, Ruth. Let her be. She has a big day tomorrow.'

Mama slapped her lips closed and took another sip of wine. 'I'm hungry too,' she said, bitterness overcoming her tone. 'I want to eat well tomorrow. Her meat will be twisted and gamey if she eats like this. She'll spoil herself.'

Eden shot her a glance. One that silenced her.

'Because you've been so good,' Eden said, turning her stare to me, 'we wanted to give you something special. Something to make you feel a little bit warmer on your last night.' Eden pulled an envelope from her pocket and dropped it on the table. 'It came through the letterbox,' she said.

I licked my fingers clean and took the envelope, pulling out the card inside. *Get well soon*, it said in cursive pink writing. There was a watercolour of a poorly teddy bear wrapped up in a blanket on the front. The handwriting inside was primitive, letters scrawled with an almost-empty biro. Time had been taken to put the words down on the card.

Youngen,
Get well soon.
From Steve, the bus driver

I put my nose to the centre of the card and took a deep breath. It carried the faint scent of smoke. Familiar and warm, it brought a smile to my mouth.

'Who's it from?' Mama asked, straightening her back.

'The bus driver,' I said. 'Steve.' As I spoke his name, I realised I'd never known it before now.

'He must have dropped it off on the last school run,' Eden said, flashing a look of concern towards Mama. 'How nice.' But she didn't really think it was nice. She wanted him far away. She wanted me unnoticed.

I'd broken Mama's biggest rule. *Don't put up your hand to answer questions, and if you are called upon, say you don't know the answer. Always hand in your homework on time. Draw. No. Attention.*

I kept the card on my lap, holding his words.

Eden smiled when I picked up the plate. I pressed my tongue to the bottom and rolled it all the way to the top. I tasted the rabbit and its final moments. I tasted its grief. And then I swallowed. When the plate was empty, Eden's smile was wide.

*

After the meal was done, my bonds kept me tied close to the chair. Mama and Eden had escaped to share their kisses. Away in the bedroom, I knew they were rolling around in their bedding, cosy and soft. The sheets crinkled as their bodies entwined like tree roots. The heat from the fire touched my shoulders as it danced in the hearth, and behind me, close enough to reach, the pot of stock I would soon stew in simmered on a low heat.

Stumbling towards the large cooking pot on the stove, my ankles stung as the bonds pulled on me. I watched the closed bedroom door. My footsteps murmured over the floorboards. From my pocket, I clutched the handfuls of dried-up hemlock petals I'd found over the weeks and folded them into the stock with the wooden spoon. The bones from the last stray soaked inside, eating up the poison I fed them. As I stirred, I realised the bones were from the injured stray I'd brought home with me from the wood that day. The stray with the hazelnut eyes.

I regretted bringing her to this coffin.

Carefully, I watched over my shoulder. My free hand crept into my pocket again and dropped another handful into the simmering stock.

Once soaked, the petals sank to the bottom of the pot, burying themselves in the remains. With more hemlock than we'd ever given a single stray, I would walk Mama and Eden into the arms of their deepest slumber.

*

When the sky was black, Mama and Eden led me to the bedroom, tied my bonds to the legs of the bed and wrapped me in a thick blanket so I'd stay nice and warm through the dark. For the last time, they kissed my forehead goodnight and turned out the light.

Mama and Eden were still up in the living room. The light beneath the door faltered with their shadows as the soft ebb of music played. Rolling away from the blankets, I went to the wall. It was uneven and cold as I pulled my fingers across its surface. I wanted to remember this wall. I wanted to remember the way it felt and all the nights I'd spent counting sheep while looking at it. I closed my eyes and from the skirting board to the window I lapped up the mould. Spoiling my insides, I tasted every spore of black that freckled this bedroom.

When Mama and Eden consumed me in morsels, they would sleep too. The world would forget us all. Tomorrow was the end.

Seventy-Four

'Mama?'

'Quiet,' she whispered as she pulled the bonds around my ankle towards the kitchen. She clutched her forehead and put the kettle on the stove as I stumbled behind her – an animal bound to its leash. 'Just be quiet,' she said; her words came out as a sigh. Mama absent-mindedly stirred the stock. It wasn't on the heat anymore. It had been left to cool off overnight. The wooden spoon dragged a thick lip in circles. 'The world is echoing this morning.'

A spider crawled out from a crack between tiles and settled on the counter. It was silent in the presence of us giants. Mama glared at the creature. Reaching for an overturned wine glass, she trapped the spider. A proud smile grew across her face. 'I got you,' she whispered to it, leaning down to look into its eyes. The spider wriggled beneath the glass, trying to escape. Mama leant closer, studying the little beast. She reached for my wrist and pulled me closer.

'Isn't it beautiful?' she asked as the spider's desperate

legs quickly fumbled for escape. 'It will never get out of there,' Mama said, her voice hoarse and her mouth watering. 'Not unless I set it free.'

I was still. Mama's hot breath flushed over my cheek. The spider was losing its will to fight as it settled beneath the glass.

Mama pulled me close, putting her nose to my scalp and holding my scent. 'Eden is everything I've been looking for, Little One.' She glanced over her shoulder. Eden was still dreaming on the couch. She shifted beneath her blanket. There was a line of soot across her cheek and stray hairs fell over her face. To look at her, peaceful and dreaming, you'd not know what sort of creature she truly was.

'I know you think I'm a monster, but we all have a bit of dark inside. And light too,' Mama whispered, combing her fingers through my hair.

'Is that why you're doing this?' I asked.

Mama shook her head.

'I thought families were supposed to keep each other safe,' I said, leaning my head on her shoulder, playing with her hair.

Mama watched over Eden. 'They are,' she said. Her lips trembled, but she tightened them into a firm line. Her eyes watered. 'I tried so hard to love you. To feel love. *Real love*. But I couldn't do it. It just didn't come out of me.' Mama closed her eyes. 'You were supposed to be a promise of happiness, but you've eaten me alive. You will be happier this way,' she said. 'And so will I.' Mama squeezed my hand.

300

I wondered why we couldn't fit together like other mamas and their kits. I wondered if we were born with something broken inside us. Maybe it was in the deepest marrow of our bones, some place we couldn't see or touch. Maybe that's why we couldn't love each other the way we were supposed to.

*

I had only hours left.

The water in the bath was searing. It left a trail of red over my shoulders. A rush of blood pushed through my veins as Mama scrubbed my back with an old sponge. I felt red scratches form from the rough side of the sponge. Every tiny sting as it left small cuts on my skin.

When Mama wasn't looking, I put my tongue over the black mould and took it in.

'We need to get you nice and clean,' Mama said, lifting my arm and scrubbing my pits. She took her razor blade and sliced away the small hairs pushing out from my pores.

'You didn't bathe any of the other strays. Or shave them,' I said, counting each drop of water still on my shoulder. 'Eden has changed you. Your brain has broken, Mama.'

'It's not broken.' Mama stopped to take a breath. An impatient one. 'She's shown me a new way to live. I can be myself now.'

'Do you think I'll be inside of you forever? The way Eden said I would be?'

301

Mama shook her head. 'No,' she whispered, brushing clumps of wet hair back over my head and pressing her forehead against mine. I wondered if that meant Abbie wasn't inside me anymore. Or the gamekeeper. 'I think you will pass. And one day you'll be gone completely. No one will remember you. Or me. Or us.' Mama pulled away and carried on scrubbing. 'I wish you knew how hard it is to be a mama. It's the hardest thing in the whole world. It's a promise you make to be perfect and make no mistakes. And to put yourself second until you die. It mutates into this horrible burden. A weight you have to carry forever.'

'What are we talking about?' Eden asked, slipping in and closing the door behind her. She wore a nightgown, but it was far too big for her. Her collarbones stuck out, catching the flickering light of the bulb above.

'Under you go,' Mama said, pushing my head beneath the water and running her hands through my hair to get the suds out.

From under the surface, I listened in on Eden and Mama. Their words drifted, misshapen as they left the mouth of their speaker and found me in the water.

Eden's head came over the bath. Her features shifted and shimmered, rippling like a monster on the other side of the mirror. As I held my breath and studied her, I wondered if this was what she'd look like from the cooking pot on the stove.

I came up for air. My lungs ached, ready to give out.

'Not long now,' Eden said, kneeling down and holding my face between her hands.

In her own twisted way, Eden loved me. When she looked at me, her eyes were large, pupils growing larger as her gaze moved across my face.

Maybe *love* wasn't the right word.

Eden wanted me. She wanted me so much she would eat me up.

'Will I grow inside you?' I asked her, pulling at her hand and holding her fingers between mine. Her skin was dry. Coarse.

Eden pulled on my hands and kissed my palms. 'No, Little One. You will stay as you are. You will be kept warm and loved inside our bellies. Sleeping forever. When we dance, you will dance too. And when we feast, you will be full.'

Watching Mama, I noticed a knot appear on her brow. She focused in on each of Eden's freckles, soaking up the details and memorising them. Though she loved Eden dearly, more than anything, perhaps Mama wanted different things to Eden. She didn't want me inside her forever. She just wanted me gone.

Seventy-Five

Mama and Papa's old bedroom door had been left open. Inside, Eden crouched on her hands and knees, laying out a black plastic tarp. Her hair was pulled back with an old rag, braids tangled as she flattened the tarp across the wooden boards. It reached from corner to corner.

Today was the first day Eden looked unremarkable. Not beautiful like I'd thought of her so many times, but plain. The bags beneath her eyes were darker than before and her skin somehow paler. Her stomach grumbled as she nailed down the corners of the tarp.

Mama sat with me on the couch, brushing my hair and neatly folding it into plaits. Together, we watched Eden spread our canvas case of tools over the surface of the kitchen table. Inside, blades were snug in their pockets. There was a saw for stubborn tendons and bones that wouldn't snap the way we wanted them to. Eden took a kitchen rag and polished the blades until they shone. Once she was finished, she rolled up the case and put it beneath her arm before striding back into the strays' room.

Mama watched her, anxiously tugging a little too tight on my plaits.

'Ruth, could you help me with the hook?' Eden shouted.

'Coming,' Mama said, passing me the end of my braid to finish.

I curled the hair, folding one section over the next but Mama's perfect plaits were eaten up by mine. Now they were messy and uneven.

Through the open door, I watched them. Mama and Eden wiped down a large chain with a hook on the end. It clanked and scraped as they passed it through a cast-iron screw eye bolted above them. They fastened it good and tight, and when they were finished, the chain I would hang from just hours from now shifted back and forth, settling as gravity took hold.

Quiet and still, it was waiting for me.

Eden came to me, wiping her brow with her arm. 'Why don't you go and set the table?' she said, pulling a smile to her face. 'Make yourself useful.'

As I put a tie around the last plait, I nodded and hopped off the couch. The bonds dragged behind me, pulling at my ankle and scraping against the wooden floor. Eden followed me to the kitchen and watched over my shoulder as I reached for the plates in the cupboard.

'Just two,' she said, taking the top plate off the pile and putting it back in the cupboard. A forgiving kiss found its way onto my cheek.

I looked down at the shimmer of the plates as Eden's hand coved around the small of my back and nudged me towards the kitchen table. It was strange to think I'd soon be sitting on these plates in pieces. Snuggled in next to some potatoes and carrots.

'I think I want to sit here,' Eden said, brushing the chair next to the head of the table with her hand. Her words were focused and thoughtful. 'Don't you think Mama should sit at the head of the table tonight?'

'I normally sit there,' I said, ignoring her and glaring at the chair Eden would soon occupy.

'I'll keep it warm for you,' she said, moving towards me and placing her hand on my cheek. 'Come, now. Learn to share.'

I dropped the plates down on the table, secretly hoping they would shatter. Eden glared at me as they clattered.

'Do you want to go get the nice glasses and the cutlery?'

'No, I don't,' I said, folding my arms and stamping my foot on the floor. I was a child, but I could be stern like the elders.

'Do as you're told and don't be disrespectful.' Eden's face straightened and her foot tapped the floorboards impatiently.

'This isn't what I want,' I said.

'You don't know what you want,' she whispered, coming closer and kneeling. Her hand squeezed my arm a little too tight.

I held her stare, but her eyes were too cold to linger on. I shuffled back to the kitchen cupboards. When I looked over my shoulder, Eden was putting the plates onto the place mats, straightening them and brushing the tabletop with her fingertips to rid the world of dust. I came back to her side and set out the cutlery, keeping it close to the edges of the plates.

'Lovely,' Eden said, gleaming as she fussed over the table settings. 'Ruth, come look.'

Mama shuffled out from the strays' room and came to Eden's side.

'Hasn't our Little One done such a good job?' Eden mused, taking Mama's hand.

Mama forced a smile, straightening the knife closest to her. 'I suppose.'

'You're going to sit here,' Eden said, pulling Mama to the head of the table and placing her hands over the back of the chair. 'And I'll sit here, right next to you.' Eden stood behind her chair and watched Mama. 'It'll be perfect.'

'Have you decided how you're cooking her?' Mama asked, turning to Eden and playing with her fingers.

'I've got puff pastry dough in the fridge. I want it to rise big and soft so Little One can be nice and buttery.'

'Like a pie?' I asked.

'A beautiful pie. With a creamy sauce made from the stock. It's been simmering overnight – left over from the last stray.'

'I don't know if I'm in the mood for pie,' Mama said, pushing a knife askew.

'This will be the nicest pie you've ever eaten. It won't be heavy. It won't weigh down your stomach. It will be light, fluffy and creamy. The meat will be tender. It'll melt on your tongue,' Eden said. While Mama's eyes were cutting across Eden's face, Eden straightened the knife.

Mama nodded. 'I love you,' she said. 'I *really* love you. And I don't need anything else except this.' Mama took Eden's hand.

'I love you too.' Eden pulled Mama's cheek close and left an earnest kiss behind.

While they embraced, I returned to the quiet of the bedroom, dragging my bonds behind me. There, I fed upon the hemlock until I was breathless and tired. My lungs felt tight. I wanted to sleep.

Seventy-Six

The room was warm, sun swimming on the bedroom floor as I lay still in the shadows. The places the rays of sun couldn't reach. A gale whistled outside, pulling at the tree branches and tangling their leaves.

Mama and Eden got to work on me straight away. There was no hesitation. I was stripped of my clothes and bound to the floor. The bonds scratched against my wrists and ankles. Mama put a wooden spoon between my teeth to stop me from screaming. My jaw tensed around the handle. For the first time, I felt the roots of my canines cut through my gums as I bit down on the spoon. I could taste the blood in my mouth.

The world was already ebbing in and out. I wondered if the hemlock would beat Mama and Eden to the punch, taking me by the hand and guiding me towards the dark.

I closed my eyes and I listened.

It was hazy when I heard Eden's voice.

'It'll be over quick,' Eden said, her voice hot on my

cheeks as she wiped my hair away from my face. 'I promise.' I felt a kiss land on my forehead.

When I opened my eyes, I saw the glint of her knife. A smile found Mama's lips. She looked happy.

The world was hot and bothered. Redness webbed across the room.

My organs throbbed. The pain was sharp but, as the world faded from reach, it all became dull. And soon the redness faded to grey.

There were no final thoughts in my head. I was only afraid of the darkness I felt coming around me. At some point I fell asleep, and the pulse I'd felt all my life finally stopped beating.

Seventy-Seven

It felt like waking from a long sleep.

Everything was slow. My arms were like cobwebs. I told my fingers to wiggle but seconds came and went before my knuckles moved the way I'd asked them to.

Below my feet, I felt the floor. A glint of sunlight hit the plastic.

Then I heard it crinkle.

There were pools of blood at my feet. The smell of metal came next and the faint clanking of chains brushing one another.

The world returned to me in pieces.

In sounds.

Smells.

Sensations.

I was an echo. Or a ripple.

A warm waft passed over me – the scent of meat. The radio stumbled over music. And a cold draught came from the cracks in the window. The door was closed and the plastic tarp, while still nailed to the four corners of the room, had torn in the middle. The blade had cut through.

There was a copper basin filled with blood. Knotted hair floated inside, plaited, spinning slowly, keeping to the surface where the light could feel its strands. My blood looked darker in the basin. Black as night.

My lungs ached. I wondered if the hemlock had stayed with me in death. It was hard to breathe.

The pale canvas bag, once home to our blades, was red and empty. I searched the floor for shimmers of silver and steel but there was nothing. The pieces of the world felt scattered and out of reach.

Above, the chain still hung from its cast-iron hook. It was pulled taut by something weighing it down. My eyes travelled down the chain, following the metal links all the way to the end. What remained of my body swayed from left to right. The chains groaned each time the weight of my carcass pulled them back and forth.

At my feet, bloody footprints glinted beneath the light. I followed them around the room. Some of them were precise and whole. Some were dragged, leaving a smeared trail of redness in their wake.

At the end of the chain, two bare feet were twined together. Painted toenails. Purple nail polish.

Smoke came in waves. Then the sharp scent of iron. Then the sound of a cassette in its player, twisting up a tape to crush out a crackling tune. Bloody fingerprints smeared over the player. Red, sticky smudges were thick over the buttons. *Love, after all these years, has finally found us. No more lonely days for you and I. Amour. Amour Amour.*

Mama lay against the wall by a bucket of organs. Intestines. Lungs. Kidneys.

There was a bucket by Eden too. In it, ribs and steaks for meals to come. Her fingers stroked precious circles into the meat.

Mama and Eden sang the song's words between puffs of smoke, whispering the lyrics aloud to one another and sneaking in kisses between verses.

I followed their legs to their bloody groins and bellies. And to their faces. They were drenched in viscera. Their dresses soaked in ruin, consumed by human matter. Mascara ran down their cheeks and red lipstick smudged around their mouths as they shared the last of a cigarette between their lips. They tried to catch their breath among the euphoria.

I knelt at Mama's feet and watched her face shift, her mouth changing, still deciding whether to land on grief or desire – but I supposed she had always lived caught between those two worlds.

Eden smiled to her. 'I love you,' she said.

Together, they were breathless.

Eden, soaked in blood, came to her feet. Her dress stuck to her limbs, clinging to her skin. 'Let's put her in the freezer,' she said. 'So she doesn't go bad.'

Mama nodded, taking one last drag of the cigarette and putting it out on the wall.

Eden held out her hand and Mama took it. Rising to

her feet, Mama stole an embrace. Their clothes squelched together as their skin met, and when they parted they took their buckets in hand. Behind them, bloody footprints left a trail.

I fumbled for the front door, moving slow and heavy. The world outside looked warm, but when I tried to push the handle, the door stayed closed. It was like stone, too stubborn to move for me as it had done so many times before. I put my hands to the window and the glass scorched my palms, burning them up and leaving a trail of quickly disappearing red blisters on my palm.

'You don't have to keep me here,' I whispered to the walls.

When I looked out, the sun was hot on the grass. The woodland beyond shared its whispers and the beck babbled, but the touch of sunlight was absent on my skin. I was still trapped.

Seventy-Eight

Standing before the mirror on the wall, Mama combed her hair with an old hairbrush from the deep trenches of her girlhood. It was opulent, golden around its edges, and had always been kept out of reach of my curious fingers. From the top of her scalp down through the knots and to her tips, she combed away her imperfections. She wanted to be beautiful again.

Once she was done, Mama pressed the red lipstick over her bottom lip and pulled it across to the edge of her mouth. She rubbed her lips together, spreading the colour over the plump curves.

'This is the woman I was supposed to be.' Unheard by Eden, the confession hung in the air.

Nursing herbs in her arms, Eden meandered inside from the warm summer air.

'Let me help,' Mama said, nipping the long stems from Eden's arms.

'You look beautiful,' Eden said.

'So do you,' Mama said, a smile forming. 'This, just

you and me – it feels right for the first time in my life.'
Mama took a breath. 'I've spent thousands of days
hiding. Changing myself.'

Eden pulled Mama into her arms, gently tugging her
to and fro. 'This is what love is supposed to feel like.
We can just start again together,' Eden said, brushing
Mama's belly with her hand. 'The way we were supposed
to.'

Eden kissed Mama's mouth, making sure to leave a red
smudge of lipstick behind in just the right place. When
she was done, she took to the chopping board to slice open
my kidneys. Then my lungs. And legs. It was only now,
watching the meat, that I realised how small my fingers
and toes really were. How much they had yet to grow.

Mama chopped up onions, carrots and potatoes, peering over her shoulder at Eden. Her gaze was gentle. The
stock boiled on the stove.

Later that day, as the sun hesitated at the bottom of
the sky, they baked me in a pie. They made sure to cradle
me in a blanket of golden pastry. A buttery crust bound
the meat and stock and cream together. I knelt by the
oven, watching through the glass as the pastry rose. My
mouth watered.

*

It was dark outside when Mama and Eden came to the
table. Their glasses were filled with wine, neatly placed
above their plates near the candlelight. At the centre, in
a baking tray, the pie was ready to carve into.

'You've changed everything for me, Eden.' Mama gazed at her, pressing her fingers to Eden's chin and pulling her close into a soft kiss. 'It's just us now.'

Eden took the serving knife and laid a handsome portion of pie onto each plate. Vegetables were snug at the side of the pastry. Mama watched her plate fill, licking her lips and taking a deep breath of the scent that came with it.

'I've never been so hungry,' Mama said. She looked like a girl again, aglow in the candlelight. Velvet skin and glassy eyes.

'Are you ready?' Eden asked, staring at Mama. Her eyes glimmered in the flicker of candles.

Mama, with her knife and fork in hand, ready to consume the meal before her, hesitated at her plate. Her brow knotted as she looked upon the tall peaks of puff pastry.

'This will be unlike anything you've ever done,' Eden said. 'Unlike anything you'll ever do again.' She smiled softly.

Mama's face hardened as she leant back from her meal. Her cutlery relaxed between her fingers. She wanted to feast but wasn't ready to have a bairn inside her once again. Not in the way Eden had so ardently promised her. She didn't want to be a mama, but she wanted Eden. Her fist tightened around her fork, steadfast and determined.

Eden took her first bite. As her eyes closed, a moan slipped out. 'Beautiful . . .' she said. 'The meat . . .' Eden couldn't get her sentences out in one go. 'It's so tender.'

She swallowed and took a deep breath. 'Eat, Ruth. You'll never taste anything like this again.'

Mama stared at her meal and pressed her fork into the pastry. It crackled as it ruptured apart in flakes. When she brought her fork to her mouth, a creamy piece of meat waited for her at the end. She opened her mouth and dropped it on her tongue. Chewing slowly, Mama closed her eyes. 'Eden . . .' she said.

As they feasted, I made a wish for the black mould to spore throughout their blood. And for the hemlock to squeeze their lungs tight behind their ribcages.

'Being a mama is a promise to try your best,' I whispered into her ear. 'But you didn't try.'

Mama flinched as she chewed on the food.

Soon the plates were bare, and Eden and Mama were languid together, out of breath, cheeks burning red. The meal was done.

'We're going to live here forever,' Eden said. 'Together.'

'Maybe, one day, you could show me the world,' Mama whispered, shuffling her chair closer to Eden's. I took my seat at the end of the table and watched them closely as they mused together about their future. They sipped on their wine until the bottle was empty and the candles were low on the table.

They mistook the hemlock for euphoria as their fingers toyed with one another. Their mouths gasped for air. Knuckles grazing, they slumped into their chairs, gazing in wonder at the oncoming dark. Eden's eyes widened as the hemlock took its hold and her chest flushed as the blood rushed to the surface. Mama let out a last breath. One at a time, their heads rolled back.

Empty glasses waited on the table. Plates, licked clean, lay empty. Cutlery was clumsily scattered over the tabletop and, sitting in their chairs, Mama and Eden drifted from one another as their hands parted. Their fingers unlinked. From this slumber they would never wake. I made sure of that.

Seventy-Nine

Mama and Eden had been sitting at the table for days now. Their beauty faded. Bruised and blackened, their skin lost its colour and their cheeks hollowed deep into their skulls. Their eyes clouded, jellied and sunken. And, over time, their limbs stiffened as they bloated at the dinner table. They decayed as maggots and moths feasted on their clothes. Their beautiful church dresses were in ruin.

Insects made their way inside to pick at their bodies. The remnants of the meal deflated as flies came from near and far to feast. They gave birth to their larvae inside the folds and layers of the puff pastry and skin.

Mama and Eden's fingers were parted, but almost close enough to touch. There was very little left of them I recognised. Seeing them like this felt right. Who they were on the inside had finally made its way to the outside.

Mama's body was still as she cosied into her seat. Reaching my hand towards her hair, I stopped. Twisted up and knotted, her curls twined. I only let myself count the blonde strands escaping out from her scalp, but I didn't let myself touch her. A fly crawled out where the plump of her lip used to be and buzzed away from her mouth, disappearing into the kitchen. The flies liked it there. A few clusters of dried-up fly corpses lay by the remains of the hemlock-soaked stock, their legs brittle and caved inward towards their bellies.

Eden was quiet, head draped over the back of her chair. The curve of her neck looked like Alpine mountain peaks. Eden's gums had started coming away from her teeth. Each tooth, resting behind those blackened lips, yellowed. It felt forbidden to touch her.

Together, they were quiet, skulls listing towards one another. Even in death, they craved touch.

Eighty

The days were long and slow. I wasn't sure how much time had passed when I heard the knock on the door.

A wiry silhouette pressed his face against the window. The figure knocked again as he peered inside. Eyes darting across the room, he stilled at the sight of the table. Eden and Mama slept in their chairs, bellies full from their feast.

The man used his elbow to break the glass and open the door from the inside. The door crept open and the figure's vacant eyes hardened as he covered his nose with his sleeve. Their quiet disturbed, flies hurried out from their crannies. Watching over the table as Mama and Eden festered together, the man didn't stir. His shoulders rose and fell.

I imagined his lungs blowing up big, but there was not enough air in this room for him to breathe in.

'Youngen?' he called to me, breaking the silence, but his voice faltered as he said the word.

He knew I would not answer.

The man's name was on the tip of my tongue, but it was too far out of reach to remember.

'Youngen?' he called again, running to the first door he could find. He rattled the handle until it came free. I followed the man into the bedroom, watching him drop to his knees to check under the bed.

'I'm here,' I said, feeling a calmness as I watched over him. I knelt down, looking for the glint of light his eyes kept in their darkness. Beneath the bed, he found the bonds that had kept me inside the homestead. There were hemlock petals sprinkled over the floorboards and boarded-up windows. I looked into his eyes and I held on to their colour. I wanted to remember them forever. Large and brown. Kind. His pupils dilated as he moved on.

The next room was the one housing the swinging chains and hook. He spluttered something up and then swallowed it back down into his belly. My blood had dried up on the tarp, but there was a full bucket of it in the corner. Thick and jellied.

The man was still and quiet, jaw falling. He steadied himself against the wall. His fingers couldn't quite hold on, and where they drifted over the plaster he found a small mark where Mama had put out her cigarette. Finally, he confronted the chain hanging from the ceiling. And the large hook fastened to its end.

Speaking my name, the kind man wept.

*

The house had been swept from top to bottom by people in bright jackets, but the haze had died down now. From the window, I watched the man sitting out near the front step. Wrapped up tight in a silver blanket, he stared at the ground. I wondered if he was counting blades of grass. Though I lingered by the door, watching his mouth and waiting for it to move, he hadn't spoken a word.

This man, familiar and warm, had spent most of the afternoon covering his face with his hands, but when he lifted his chin I caught a glimpse of his eyes. They were bloodshot but hardened.

Coming to his feet, the man wiped his eyes. His silver blanket fell from his shoulders as he brushed down his jeans and glanced over his shoulder for the last time. He took a deep breath, paced down the steps and passed through the gate. He didn't look back. Not once.

Soon he was gone, off in his minibus, until there was nothing but a dot passing between the distant trees.

Eighty-One

The homestead was quiet now.

When I felt lonely, I sat in the bathtub. The curves of the bath were crusted in limescale but no water came from the taps. Black mould spored in abundance around me, reaching across the walls to live in the grout.

My fingers danced in circles around the drain. I watched the plughole. It was browned and rusted around its edges, like a bruise. Dark down in the deep of the pipes. There were no severed fingers in this bathroom anymore. Nor bodies or bones. But the memory of body parts lingered. The scent stayed tucked inside my nostrils. Stray thighs. Rumps. Ribs. Meat and blood.

Just like the rabbit woman, somehow I knew I'd linger long after the homestead was lost and I'd become secrets and stories told around fires. I wasn't sure how much time was passing, but I felt ancient, like a long-forgotten standing stone or a language no longer spoken. As old as hills, as old as water, and as old as the beginning itself. Soon enough, the landscape would shift, the beck becoming a stream and the stream becoming a river. Then, one day, hot and bothered, this earth would become an ocean and forget all about us.

Slumbering, keeping out of trouble, the monsters were fated to dream. Because I made it so, this ground was safe for the strangers to tread.

Acknowledgements

I'm grateful for all the remarkable and hardworking people at W&N, Harper and Curtis Brown who've helped shape this book and bring it to shelves. I owe an enormous debt of gratitude to my UK editor, Alexa von Hirschberg (and Georgia Goodall/Silvia Crompton), and to my US editors, Noah Eaker and Edie Astley, for everything. To my agent Cathryn Summerhayes (and to Sarah Fuentes/Rebecca Gradinger in the US), I'm so grateful for your unending support and passion for this story.

A special thank you to my mentor, Kirsty Logan, who has been an endless source of support and inspiration. Without the generosity of Kirsty, Jack Hadley and the extended team at Curtis Brown Creative, I don't think I'd be writing these acknowledgements. I've been very lucky to meet an amazing village of authors along the way, who've each uplifted and supported me: Caroline Deacon, Charlotte Paradise, Jen Delaney, Vikki Patis,

Lauren Wilson, Louis Glazzard, Molly Aitken and Tony Williams.

With every fibre of my body, thank you to my friends and peers: Alice Clarke, Caitlin Bramwell, Caoimhín De Paor, Dan Shaw, Jack Keating, Josie Deacon, Kristel Buckley, Lizzie Gilholme, Luella Williamson, Maria Caruana Galizia, Rory Power-Gibb and Russell Edge. Thank you to my team at Inpress Books: Sophie, Jane, Ceris, Kate, Meg, Alice, Rebecca and Emily. Thank you to Jake and Figgy, and last, to Jane Kirk, for giving me the book that changed my life – I really wish you could have been here to see this happen. I know you would have been proud of me.

About the Author

Lucy Rose's fiction and non-fiction have been published by Dread Central, *Mslexia* and more, and her films have visited BAFTA- and Oscar-qualifying film festivals internationally. Lucy's debut novel, *The Lamb*, is being published by Weidenfeld & Nicolson in the UK and HarperCollins in the US. Lucy lives on the northeast coast of England with her black cat, Figgy, and is currently working on her next story.